Always Sunny

Isabel Jolie

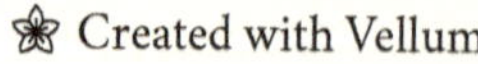 Created with Vellum

Chapter One

Ian

"I'm here. Let me in."

I could pull a pillow over my head to drown out the noise but don't particularly feel like making the effort.

The banging gets louder. *Fuck, is he kicking the door?*

Damnit. He's going to piss off my neighbors. Whoever is working the shift downstairs and let him up without ringing is getting a shit Christmas tip.

Bang. Bang. Bang.

With a resigned exhale, my feet thud down the hall. The door opens, and Harrison's fist plunges through air. His nose crinkles and his head jerks back.

"Dude, when did you last shower?" His brow furrows with his critical assessment. It's the look he gives every patient needing a diagnosis. He steps past me and down the hallway. "Man. This place is a shit hole. Did you fire your cleaning service?"

Harrison is a Type A clean freak. A stack of three pizza boxes rests on the kitchen counter, empty beer bottles are neatly lined up beside it, and there's an array of take-out bags. The coffee table is cluttered, but I didn't expect company. I don't want company.

"Cleaning service comes Tuesday." Tuesday, because there was a time when I had a house guest Saturday through Monday. I need to remember to reschedule them for Friday so my apartment bears the distinct aroma of cleaning detergent on the weekend.

"How many days have you been wallowing in your own filth?"

The answer doesn't matter, so I don't respond. I needed a few days off. I got a nasty cold, and no one wants a surgeon slicing into them while coughing uncontrollably.

"All right. I'm getting a trash bag. You are getting a shower."

Harrison is a good friend, something I remind myself to avoid throwing a fist into his well-moisturized jaw. I glance down the hall, and my stomach freefalls. The guest room door is ajar. How?

"This is all over that girl, Sunny." Harrison hunts beneath my sink, presumably searching for garbage bags. "I warned you."

I cross my arms and lean against the wall, centering my gaze on Harrison, my vision perimeter gray and dark, matching my mental state.

"Get your shower. You called in sick all week."

"I've been sick."

"The steam will do you good. You've spent long enough mourning this girl."

"She's not dead."

"She is to you." His counter slices with greater precision than a scalpel. *Truth.* "Come on. Hop to it." He stands in front of me, an arm's length away, and places his hand on my shoulder. "You are a surgeon. Women love to fuck surgeons. But not when they're ripe. Go. Shower. Then we're going out, and you are putting all the bullshit behind you. I've been where you are, and trust me, this is what you've got to do. Move forward, my friend."

He forcibly turns my shoulders and pushes me down the hallway, past the vacant guest room.

"I'm not going to Jack's."

"Well, that goes without saying." He turns his attention to my kitchen counter, and the bottles crash against each other as he unceremoniously drops them one by one. "No need to revisit the place of the crime."

He acts like it's obvious we won't go there. Meanwhile, it's been our standard on weekends since year two of residency. Sunny got her gigs there because we were the regulars who got to know the owner. Now we'll need a new place to blow off steam.

My thumbnail scratches my itchy eyebrow as I consider all of this. "What crime?"

"She destroyed you. And I don't let that happen to my friends. She's officially dead to me. And yeah, I gave you a week to mourn. We're going out tonight, tomorrow we'll hit the court or the trail… your pick, and Monday, you are back in the OR."

Harrison always has a plan. I have no idea what he's talking about when he says he's been where I am. I've never known him to care about any woman, much less date. He's probably just spewing bullshit to get me moving.

I follow through on autopilot. Shower, dress. I don't bother with shaving. Numbness permeates my ribcage and my thought processes. At least the week's facial growth is visual proof some part of me thrives.

"That's what you're wearing?"

I look down at my outfit. My black jeans are snug, maybe too snug, and my tight-fitting button down is untucked. The custom shirt should be tucked in with a belt, but I really don't give a damn.

Harrison heads past me into my bedroom, and I dutifully follow. He picks out a blazer and a lightweight black crewneck. Everything he picks is black or some shade of black, which matches my mood. He picks out low black boots with a European cut. That means we're not going anywhere that plays country music, and that works for me. Probably nowhere with a sexy blonde acoustic guitar playing singer, another bonus.

Outside my apartment building, Harrison holds the back door to a rideshare sedan open. I raise one mildly curious eyebrow.

"We're drinking." His answer to the unspoken question has me looking at his outfit again. He's not wearing jeans. *Fuck.*

"Are we going to your club?"

"I'm a lifetime member now."

That's a million dollars incinerated. "Are you out of your mind?"

"What? I plan on getting my money's worth. Starting with lifting your spirits tonight."

I sink back against the leather seat as Harrison passes an address to the driver. He means well. And he's right. I've got to get my head back on. This cold can't last forever.

The club Harrison loves so much is about as high-end and exclusive as it gets in the States. They have locations in San Francisco, LA, New York, and Miami. The partners at Harrison's private surgical practice offered to sponsor us for an event two years ago when they were evaluating if Harrison would be a fit for their practice. The ticket had cost around a grand, and I'd balked but paid when Harrison threatened to buy my way.

I haven't been back, but Harrison loves this place. He's out of his mind to spend a million on membership. As a plastic surgeon, he'll rake it in, but to me, it's a better use of funds to invest in medical advancements. Every time I cash in on an investment, I seek out my next investment. That's how we improve healthcare.

The black tiled entrance glitters under the streetlights. Four black letters discreetly hang beside the door. Only the discerning eye would pick them out. TMPL

Harrison checks in with the bouncer, flashing an ID. He taps my shoulder, and the bouncer requests my license. With the eagerness of a sulky teen preparing to mow the lawn, I pull out my wallet and hand over the required identification.

"Your phone?" he demands.

"Didn't bring it." He raises one dark eyebrow, and the forehead wrinkles nearly blend into his shaved scalp.

"It was dead." It was vibrating too often, and for the first time in my medical career, given I was contagious, I didn't need to hear from the hospital. I shove my hands in my pockets and stare down the bouncer. If he doesn't let me in, I truly do not give a damn. It's the theme of the hour.

Harrison speaks to the beefy man, and I turn my attention to the street. If I remember correctly, this place doesn't open until ten, and it's barely after nine. It's going to be dead inside. Which is fine by me. If the man lets me in, I'll find a seat at the bar and get obliterated. If he doesn't let us in, I'll walk across the street to the dive bar and get obliterated. Either way, it's a win-win. The thought has me cringing as the sentiment hits a little too close to home.

Harrison approaches. He bows his head and in a low discreet voice asks, "You don't happen to have test results on you, do you?"

Are you for real?

The last time I came here, I did have my monthly test results on me, because we'd been forewarned, but that was a lifetime ago.

"Don't worry about it. Andrea's working tonight."

I'm not sure what that means, but I don't care. Harrison talks under his breath to the bouncer like they're tight friends.

The dive bar across the street calls my name. But, as luck would have it, the bouncer waves us into TMPL. Joy and gratitude combust. And yes, the sarcasm is full-blown.

Another bouncer frisks me in the hallway, and smoky glass doors open, revealing a bar. This place has many rooms and venues. They used to be closed on Saturday night, so maybe only the bar is open. That's all I need, so that works.

Black leather wraps around the edge of the smoky glass bar. Dim lights give the place a sultry vibe. The bartender behind the counter is a woman with fantastic tits. Her sheer fitted black t-shirt ends an inch or two above her belly button, which sports a diamond solitaire.

"What can I get you?"

"Bourbon. On the rocks."

"He'll take the best bourbon you have, and I'll take the same. What's your name?" Harrison leans over the bar, smiling at her like she's a menu item he's considering devouring.

"Lola. What's yours?"

"Harrison. It's nice to meet you, Lola."

She asks him for his member number and they chit chat. This was a horrible idea. I don't have any business being here. I. Am. Sick.

Lola slides the glass to me while laughing at something Harrison says. I knock back the entire glass in one swallow. It burns going down my esophagus. It's a welcome burn. The discomfort reminds me I am alive, no matter how dead I feel.

"Another one," I say, clinking the glass against the glass countertop.

Lola looks to Harrison, and I swivel my barstool away from the two of them. She'll either serve me, or I'll go across the street.

Long fingers with fire engine red nails clasp my thigh. I brush the hand off my leg and glance back to the bar. *Where is my drink?*

"Ian, you don't remember me?"

I lift my gaze and take in the brunette before me. Dark eyes, long, thick lashes, sensuous red lips. Her silky black hair is looped into a low side bun with a gaping hole for someone to fist.

Memories surface. I fucked her. Harrison and I fucked her at the same time in one of the back rooms in this massive place. She's a member here, too. It was the first and only time I've ever shared a woman. The heavy bass vibrated through the walls and floor and lights flickered as we explored her orifices in highly erotic ways.

"Andrea. How could I forget?" I attempt a smile, but fuck if I succeed. Those long fingers return to my forearm, and her expression shifts into one of concern.

"Baby, you look so sad. What can I do for you?"

Lola slides another glass my way. I knock it back in one long swallow. I wipe my lips with the cocktail napkin Lola thoughtfully set out. Pressure on my wrist and a potent floral scent remind me Andrea is still there and she awaits an answer.

"Can you help me forget?" I ask.

"And what, exactly, are we forgetting?" Her breath warms my ear, and those fingers stroke my thigh.

"The sun." Her breast presses against my bicep.

I drop my head and have the strangest desire to lean against Andrea and just ask her to hold me. How the fuck did I get here? How did I get to this place?

"The sun?" she questions. I probably don't make sense. It's a long story. One Andrea probably doesn't want to hear.

"Or maybe the rain."

Chapter Two

Sandra

The Christmas Before Last Christmas

"Merry Christmas, Dad." I set the mix of red and white carnations against the gravestone. "I've got to get back to the house. Having Christmas breakfast with the Dukes this morning. You'll be happy to know Patty and Sam Senior are doing good. I don't get to see them as much since they've retired to San Pedro Island, but they still look after me. You always said they were good people, and you were right."

A breeze spreads across the cemetery. Territorial blue jays squawk in a nearby tree. The bare limbs of the trees are the only nod to winter on this sixty-one-degree day with blue skies and scattered, wispy clouds.

"I'm wearing the white snowflake sweater you gave me." The too-warm-for-Texas sweater is my Christmas staple.

The pads of my fingers dip into the uneven divots on the arch of the chilly granite. Dad designed this gravestone nearly forty years ago. All I had to do was have them add the date of his birth and death next to my mom's engraving.

The tires of an old Buick scrape against the curb, and I wave.

Mrs. Mitchell gets out of her car and ambles to her trunk. She lifts a red and white wreath out of the car.

"Merry Christmas," I call out to her.

"Merry Christmas, Sandra," she calls back. Her trunk slams closed with a bang that travels across the sloping cemetery, and she trudges up the hill to her family plot.

"Well, Dad, I guess I'll get out of here. Gotta check on that casserole."

My eyes tear up like they always do when I choke on the words that I miss him. But I don't need to say them. Somewhere out there, Dad knows. Another way of looking at it, he's finally spending Christmas with Mom.

Back at the house, Polly hangs her dappled gray head over the fence and nickers softly.

"Hey, girl, you ready for breakfast?"

She slings her head up and down in answer. Dad would say the flies drive her crazy, but I prefer to think she understands English.

"I'll give you a good brushing later on today, after I take off this white sweater." My palm flattens against her neck, and a light cloud of dust floats into the air. Polly's ears prick forward, her neck protruding into the small tack room as I break apart carrots and dump them into her morning oats. "A little Christmas treat for you."

The soft skin along her nostrils vibrates as she lets out her noise of appreciation, a light whinny. After hanging her bucket in her stall and giving her one more pat, I gather all my contributions for breakfast and get in my car.

It feels lazy to drive to the Dukes', but with the presents and food, I suppose it's not. Dad and I used to join the Dukes for Christmas every year. Even after Sam, their oldest son, and I broke up, we'd join them. But then Sam met his wife, and I didn't want to make her feel uncomfortable, and besides, family traditions evolve. Dad and I were good at doing our own thing.

But this year, everything's out of whack. Dad's no longer here. Sam's kids are sick, so they canceled their travel plans. Oliver, their second son, flew to Jackson to go skiing with some friends. Patty didn't say what her youngest son, Ian, would be doing, but he's missed Christmas several years in a row. It wouldn't surprise me if he needs to stay in Houston and work this year too.

When Patty called and asked me to come for breakfast, I figured she and Sam Senior would welcome the company, given they're used to a gaggle of family around them on the holiday. But as I park the car in front of the old ranch house, a wave of unexpected memories floods me. Little flashes, like mental photographs, flip in sequence.

Sam, Oliver, Ian, and me sitting on the front steps, posing for a photo on Christmas morning. We did it for years. Dad and me walking around the house, skipping the front door and going to the back, to join the Dukes for dinner. Me out here in this gravel checking out Sam's new pickup truck. Then a couple of years later, doing the same thing with Oliver, then even later, with Ian's Prius. He didn't want a pickup truck.

I shake my head, trying to shake all those bittersweet memories. There's no need for flashback sequences. I visit Oliver all the time. Back then we called him Ollie. He still lives in the ranch house, which is walking distance from the house that's now mine. It must be Christmas dredging up memories.

I gather the bag of presents, a cooler of baked goods, and my casserole, step up to the front door, and press the small circle doorbell. In the foyer, the Christmas tree lights flicker. It's a smaller tree than the Dukes used to get, back when they bought real trees. A few years ago, Patty and Sam transitioned to a fake Christmas tree. Through the narrow windowpane and down the hall, I can see the corner of Sam Senior's newspaper. I knock louder in case they can't hear me.

I step back and wait. I rock back on my heels, as uncertainty about whether I should ring the doorbell twice rocks through me. Doing so would be rude, but Sam Senior isn't moving.

The door swings open, and my breath gets knocked right out of me.

"Sunny." Ian beams, and before I can get a word out in greeting, he's bending down and pulling me in for a hug. It's been years since I've seen Ian, and he's different. His dark, shaggy hair frames familiar warm brown eyes and a full trimmed beard. His slim build strikes me as somehow taller with broader shoulders. Nothing about Ian says little brother anymore. I suppose it hasn't in years, but this is unexpected.

All the Duke sons grew into good looking men. Sam got the darkest head of hair, and as the oldest, for years he'd been the tallest. Oliver takes after his mom and has sandy brown hair, and he ended up maybe an inch shorter than Sam. As a rancher, Oliver spends his days outdoors, and the guy almost always has a suntan. Growing up, Ian was the wiry, indoor kid. The momma's boy. The one who pretty much refused to go to the slaughterhouse but would collect old deer and cow skulls from the woods.

Ian filled out years ago, but the beard is new. His loose, unruly cut is longer in the front, and nearly touches his dark eyebrows. The chocolate brown shade lies somewhere between Oliver's sandy brown and Sam's nearly black. The Merry Christmas t-shirt he's wearing has a snug fit and hugs his broad shoulders and biceps in a way that leaves little doubt Ian finds time to do more than just work these days. The long sleeve tee dips down over red and green flannel pants. Patty Duke always buys matching holiday pajamas for her boys, but I don't think she meant to buy an outfit this year that deserves prime placement on a holiday calendar.

"What all have you got here?" Ian busies himself lifting the package and cooler from my arms.

"Sandra, I told you that you didn't need to bring anything," Patty calls from the kitchen.

I smile at Ian, and he gestures for me to lead the way.

"I just brought a few things." There's no way I'd show empty-handed.

"How long has it been since you spent Christmas with us?" Patty rounds the corner, one hand on her waist apron with red fringe and peppermint candy designs all over the front.

"It's been a while." I don't want to put in the mental effort to answer that question. "How can I help you? It smells great."

Ian sets my cooler on the counter, fills his coffee mug, and joins his dad at the breakfast table. Patty and I join forces, setting out the table with all the food. In retrospect, I probably shouldn't have brought anything, because we have enough food for twelve.

After Mr. Duke's quick blessing, we pass dishes around and fill up our plates.

"So, Ian, your mom said you finished residency and you're a full-fledged surgeon now."

Ian is about eight years younger than me. But I kept up with his accomplishments through Patty and occasionally Oliver. He doesn't do social media, but he and I text every now and then. I got to know him better after Sam and Oliver went off to college and he was the only one down the road at the ranch house. Like Oliver, I attended UT Austin, but I didn't live on campus. I lived at home in Whispering Creek with my dad to save money.

"Orthopedic surgeon," Patty clarifies, dripping with pride.

Ian spreads butter across his toast, somewhat oblivious to his mother's fawning, but I suppose he's probably grown accustomed to it.

"Do you have a private practice?"

"I joined a private practice, but I still work out of Houston Grace."

"What made you choose orthopedics?"

Patty and Ian glance at each other, and for a second I expect her to answer.

Patty Duke was a nurse before she had her boys. When Ian was a kid, Sam Senior would privately complain he was a momma's boy, but as Ian got older, the grumblings transitioned to pride when he'd mention Ian was following in his mom's footsteps.

"In orthopedics, there's a problem, and you can solve it. Almost all your patients live. Ideally, you give your patients a better life. That's not true for every discipline." Patty reaches over and pats his forearm. "I love the precision of orthopedics. I'm exploring options for a spinal surgical fellowship to specialize in spinal surgery, but there's a degree of uncertainty to the discipline that I don't love."

God, all the Dukes boys have always been so smart. Butter leaks out of the biscuit I'm holding, so I rush it to my mouth, taking a big bite so the golden melted deliciousness doesn't drip.

"What are you doing these days? Still got the salon?" Ian asks.

My mouth is full as full can be, so I press my fingers over my lips to cover my chewing.

"Sandra has two locations," Patty answers for me. "One right here in Hill County on Main Street. Same place as always."

"Where your aunt had the salon?" Ian asks.

I nod and sip some orange juice to help wash down the biscuit.

"And her other location is in Austin. It's super fancy." Patty's wiggling fingers and dramatic eyes describing my salon brings out my giggles.

"It's not that fancy," I say before Ian goes off getting the wrong idea.

Patty cocks her head and in a parental tone I know well, she goes, "Now, Sandra."

"Okay. It's… nice," I admit. "It's a high-end spa. It's actually quite different from the location here. The space in Whispering Creek is primarily hair and nails, although we do facials there two days a week. The location in Austin is a health and wellness center.

You know, in addition to a full-service spa, we also have a yoga studio, Reiki, acupuncture. It's a much more comprehensive—"

A loud ringing fills the room. Sam Senior half gets up out of his chair and fumbles around, searching for his phone. He finds it, squints, presses it, and then holds it up to his ear.

"Sam. Merry Christmas." Sam Senior smiles and motions to Patty.

I push my chair away from the table and begin gathering dishes.

"Yes, sure. We can jump on the Zoom. Do you think Ollie's up? Okay. Yeah. Patty… can you call Ollie? He didn't answer for Sam."

"Oh, Sandra, don't worry about those dishes, dear," Patty says to me.

I disregard her and busy myself. I don't need to be a part of the family video session, and being useful gives me a purpose. Ian gets up and joins me, and we fall into a rhythm of him bringing plates to the counter while I scrape, rinse, and set them in the dishwasher just like Patty likes.

Patty and Sam Senior fuss over a laptop on the kitchen table.

"Dad," Ian says, "if your face needs to be that close to the screen, you should increase the font size."

"Don't give me trouble," he mumbles.

Ian and I exchange an amused glance.

Voices emanate from the computer, and I gently nudge Ian and motion for him to join his family. He wrinkles his nose and gives a quick shake of his head.

"Where's Ian?" someone calls out. I'm pretty sure it's Oliver.

Sam's kids yell through the computer, shouting out gleefully about their windfall from Santa, which is my cue to leave them to their family Christmas morning. I dry my hands on a towel and slip down the hall to the bedrooms. Once they're done, I'll return and help finish up with the kitchen.

The bedroom doors are all ajar. Oliver's bedroom is first in the series of doors, but he still lives here, and it feels a little too personal to escape into. The second room is Ian's, which has been converted into a guest room. I've actually crashed in this room a few times over recent years when we've hung out at the ranch house with friends and sleeping here won out over walking a mile down the road to my house. Oliver and I share a few friends in common, and we don't do it as much as we used to, but we'll all come over here every now and then to hang out.

There's an acoustic guitar in the corner, and I pick it up and sit on the edge of the bed. The strings bite into the pad of my thumb as I strum. The Gibson is severely out of tune, so I set about tuning it. Once it's more or less good to go, my fingers strum a favorite section from *Complicated* by Avril Lavigne.

I sense a presence in the doorway, and I still, glancing over my shoulder. Ian leans against the frame. A chunk of out-of-place hair dips down between his dark, thick eyebrows, and he grins with a smile that's reminiscent of the teen boy I used to strum guitars with in this very room.

"You keep your Gibson here?" I ask, surprised mostly because he rarely comes home.

"Didn't have too much time to mess with it in med school." He shrugs and steps forward. The mattress dips when he sits close. "I'm not sure I remember how to play."

"I bet you do. It's muscle memory." Voices drift down the hall, but the distance blurs the sharpness of their speech into indiscernible tones. "You're not a resident now, right? You should bring it back with you."

"Only if you promise to visit." He's probably completely unaware of how sexy his grin is, or the effect it has on women. "I could use some lessons."

The eyebrow wiggle is full of innuendo, and yeah, I can't help my grin and the heat surfacing all over my skin, but this is Ian. A shameless flirt. Too young, and my ex's brother. Good things to remember.

I turn my attention back to the lady in my hands. For me,

playing the guitar soothes. It's meditative and feels so much healthier than watching TV or, god forbid, scrolling through social media and witnessing all the better lives out there. I dip my head and strum.

"Do you still have a horse?"

My fingers still and flatten against the strings. "Yeah." I give him a big smile. "Believe it or not, I've still got Polly."

Ian's mouth gapes open in shock, and I laugh.

"No way. That horse has to be…"

"Thirty-nine," I fill in for him. "She and I are the same age. She'll be forty next month. She's a Capricorn, like you."

"I didn't know horses lived that long."

"Well, she's lost most of her vision, and I don't ride her anymore. Her vet bills are getting…" I scrunch my lips and widen my eyes.

"High?" he supplies.

"Steep. If Dad were alive, he'd probably be talking about putting her down, but there's no way. I'll go broke before I do that. Unless she gets to where she's in pain, then I'll do whatever I can for her. But she's got a nice life. She knows her paddock, and she whinnies for me every evening. An apple or a carrot makes her day."

I return my attention to the strings, thinking about the mix of carrots and oats I served Polly this morning. I should've probably added some maple syrup for a special treat.

"What're you doing for New Year's?"

The heat rising along my neck reaches an unbearable level, and I set the guitar down. I lift the sweater over my head and place it behind me on the bed. My hands are clammy.

"Sorry. I was baking in that sweater. Ahm, New Year's." I scratch my forehead. It's not far away, but my plans aren't firm. "I doubt I'll do anything. There's a big party that Oliver, Noah, and Liam are going to. But they all have dates." Being the seventh wheel holds no appeal.

"You don't have a date?"

"No." I halfway smile at his funny question. Dating and me are on the backburner.

"Come to Houston," he says.

"What?" It's out of my mouth before I process what he's saying.

"Yeah. Come to Houston. I'm going out with a buddy of mine." His fingers run through his thick locks, and they settle into disarray. "We don't have dates. We're planning on going to a jazz club. It'll be low key, but fun. Besides, you owe me, Sunny. You've been promising to visit for ages."

I narrow my eyes as I consider this offer from the youngest of the three Duke boys. He's always been thoughtful. Inclusive. "You know, you're the only one who calls me Sunny."

"I think you'll always be Sunny to me." His long, dark lashes flutter, and my gaze settles on his brown eyes. Brown with flecks of gold.

"And Oliver will always be Ollie?" That's the name we called Oliver as a kid, and I think Ian's also the only one, besides maybe Patty, who refuses to let the nickname go.

"Hell, yeah," Ian says with a grin. "You can't go changing your name after you go off to college and expect your family to go along with it."

We grin at each other, and his offer hangs in the air. "If you're serious…"

"Absolutely, I'm serious. I'd love for you to finally come visit." He reaches over and squeezes my knee. His touch warms my skin through the jeans, and I pull my hair off my neck, still attempting to cool down from wearing a too-thick winter sweater indoors. "Come have fun for a night. Get away from here. What's the worst that can happen?"

Chapter Three

Sandra

The New Year's Eve before last New Year's Eve

"Yes, Mr. Duke? A Sandra Turner is here to see you."

The older man with kind eyes and a black suit jacket over a white Oxford with a crooked collar checks me out while holding a handset to his ear. About ten charcoal strands stretch across his scalp from one side to the other. He'd look so much better if he trimmed those long strands that do a poor job of covering his scalp.

"Yes, sir." He sets the handset down with an air of authority. "You can go up. Eighteenth floor."

"Thank you." My heels click loudly on the marble as I wheel my suitcase to the elevators.

Rumor has it Ian has done as well as Sam, so a natural curiosity about his apartment and lifestyle exists. Oliver describes Ian to other people as a hotshot workaholic surgeon who made a mint investing in pharmaceuticals and medical devices.

The apartment lobby is nice, but it isn't what I imagined a billionaire would live in, or what I imagine Sam and his family own in New York City. Oliver told me about that apartment once. Two stories with an outside area featuring an enormous gas fireplace and stunning views of the river, Manhattan, and Jersey. Based on Oliver's description, Sam's penthouse sounds television-worthy, and he doesn't even live in it full-time, since he and his wife moved to Connecticut once they started having kids.

As the elevator rises, I fidget with my short dress, tugging it lower on my thighs. The dress code for the night's New Year's party is unknown. I didn't bother asking Ian because he'd probably answer with something like 'anything goes.' I've learned over the years men are unhelpful in many areas of life.

If Oliver hadn't gotten snowed in up in Jackson, I probably wouldn't have come to Houston. He would've convinced me to come out with our group of friends. He would've forced me to because he'd been set up on a blind date, and he'd use that as an excuse to drag me along as a buffer. But without Oliver, my choices were celebrating with two married couples or sitting on the sofa reading a book.

Sitting on the sofa didn't sound half bad. But the prospect of celebrating in a new place won me over. And I have been promising Ian a visit. He's only a three-hour drive away, so it's kind of ridiculous I haven't yet visited. Not that Ian and I talk all that often, but we usually touch base via text at least once a month. Of the three Duke brothers, he's always been the most sensitive and thoughtful. He'll reach out if I don't.

Mr. Duke may have called him a momma's boy, but Mrs. Duke said he just got the blunt end of the stick one too many times and preferred life indoors with her. From what I saw, Ian could give as good as he got when it came to his brothers.

Sam and Oliver weren't wrong when they complained their

mom refused to believe Ian ever did anything wrong. She once found a six pack of beer in his closet and swore that one of his older brothers must have stashed it in Ian's closet. We all laughed hard about that, even Ian. By then, Sam, Oliver, and I were all in college, and Ian must've been a sophomore in high school. Those were, as the song lyrics go, the good ol' days.

When the elevator doors glide on the eighteenth floor, I step out and search for the letter B. After locating the door mere steps from the elevator, I pause, listening. Rock music flows softly out into the hall. I rap against the door and wait.

Footfalls sound distant and resonate more deeply. The door swings open, and Ian fills the doorway. His sandy brown hair has been cut shorter since I saw him on Christmas, and he's shaved his short beard, giving him a more familiar, youthful appearance.

His tight, black, short sleeve sweater hugs the curve of every muscle, showing off a muscular chest and narrow waist. The gold buckle on his smooth black leather belt gleams. The charcoal trousers fit him nicely, not too tight, but just enough to reveal nicely shaped buttocks. The post-college Ian has always dressed well, like a subdued Prada-without-logos kind of man, and tonight is no exception. He excels at classy casual, and I'm so, so grateful I opted to wear a silky crimson cocktail dress with high heels.

"Sunny. Stunning as always." And, yeah, that's another thing that has always been true about Ian. He's the king of compliments. Just a genuinely sweet guy, and I am certain girls will be falling all over themselves to meet him tonight.

"Thanks, Ian," I say. "You look as handsome as ever. I'm sorry I'm late."

He bends down and gives me a welcoming hug, enveloping me in his musky cologne. It's not too much, but rather it's just enough where, when he's close, you can breathe his masculinity in. The earthy scent calls to me. He brushes his lips against my cheek, and his smooth, freshly shaven skin rubs against me, and I close my eyes to revel in the silky soft smoothness.

I grin up at the gorgeous guy who used to be the kid brother down the street. Wow.

"You shaved," I say, suddenly incapable of intelligent conversation.

"I do that from time to time." He winks with a smile so wide his teeth flash.

He opens the door wide and bends to grab the handle of my suitcase. I step inside and take in Ian's bachelor pad. A dark gray wood floor leads down a narrow hall. Black and white abstract art hangs in square black frames along one wall. A small iron table set off to the side holds a wooden bowl and a stack of mail.

An enormous black and white aerial shot of the Duke family ranch is centered on the wall at the end of the hall, framed in a thick, black, wooden frame. I'd recognize the Duke ranch from any angle, but from the air, the trees and winding river and splintering creek border on modern art in photographic form.

"To your right," Ian says from behind me.

At the end of the hall, I venture right, stepping past a contemporary galley kitchen and gape at the floor-to-ceiling curved glass wall overlooking a feast of glittering city lights.

"The view is why I picked this place. And it's within walking distance to the hospital."

"Wow."

A tall man in a dark bespoke suit turns from the window. He's about Ian's height but with jet black slick-styled hair. A slow smile spreads across his face.

"You didn't mention how gorgeous your friend is." He steps toward me, and I take a step back, closer to Ian. "Dr. Ramsey." He extends his hand as he introduces himself. "But, please, call me Harrison."

I glance over my shoulder at Ian and catch his scowl. His expression reminds me of how he sometimes looked at his older brothers when they figuratively pissed in his cornflakes.

"She's off limits," Ian says as I shake Harrison's hand.

It might be because of the expensive-looking suit, or the slicked back hair, but Harrison strikes me as the kind of man who prowls for prey, then disappears before the sun rises. You don't get to be a single woman my age without coming across a few of them.

Harrison presses his lips to the back of my hand in a gallant gesture, and Ian groans. "I just told you…"

Ian's groan causes a few giggles to bubble up.

"What? This is how a gentleman treats a lady," Harrison says with a look of innocence.

"Stay away from her," Ian says sternly, but his lips turn up at the corners. My guess is Ian is messing with Harrison as much as he's messing with him.

"I'm going to put your bag in the guest room. Do you need anything before we get going?" he asks.

"No. I'm good. Sorry I'm late. New Year's Eve is a madhouse at the salon. Everyone wants blow outs."

"Are you a hairdresser?" Harrison asks, looking quite cavalier as he swirls the golden liquid in his highball glass with one hand in his slacks pocket.

"No. I own…well, one is pretty much a hair salon, but the other is a spa. I used to do hair, but I don't now. But on a day like New Year's Eve, I step in and help out where needed. Today I did a lot of make-up. I'm an aesthetician, but not many women want to get a facial on the day of a big night."

"I'm a plastic surgeon. In my private practice we have a medical spa. It's a big profit center for us." Any sign of the flirt evaporates as the businessman emerges. "What certifications do you have?"

Ian claps his hands as he returns into the living area. I assume the bedrooms must be down the hall in the opposite direction of the living area. "Ready? The car is here."

"We're taking a car? I can drive. I'm not going to drink that much."

Ian waves a hand dismissively. "If you saw what we've seen come through the ER, you'd take a car service."

"Spoken like a true orthopedist," Harrison jokes as he deposits his glass in the sink. "This is Houston. Parking is a nightmare. We Uber everywhere. Would you like one for the road?"

"Oh, no. I'll wait until we get there. Is what I'm wearing okay?" I flinch after the words fall out of my mouth, perfectly aware my question comes across as needy.

"You're perfect," Ian answers, and the warmth in his gaze sends a flurry of goosebumps up my exposed arms. "As always." He smiles at me the way one smiles at a friend and offers his bent arm. "Shall we?"

In the back seat of the car, I sit in the middle between Harrison and Ian, but slip closer to Ian's side of the seat.

"How do the two of you know each other?" I ask.

"We were in med school together at Rice. And we both did our residency at Houston Medical," Harrison answers.

"But you chose different specialties?"

"Yes," Harrison says. "I went into med school knowing I wanted plastics. Not sure how Ian ended up an orthopod."

Ian's attention is on the passing city streets, seemingly uninterested in the conversation.

"How'd your ski trip go with your brothers?" I ask Ian.

After Christmas, he and Sam joined up with Oliver for a few days to go skiing in Jackson. From what Patty told me, it had been a last-minute decision for the brothers to get away together, just the three of them. She'd been thrilled to see her sons spend time together, and as soon as she got the green light that her grandkids were better, she and Mr. Duke had been on a flight to Aspen to spend time with those precious grandbabies at Sam's ski chalet.

"You know how it is." Ian shrugs.

But I really don't know. The last time I joined the Dukes on a ski trip was in high school, which was over twenty years ago. "What do you mean?"

"They do stupid shit and try to get themselves killed. If they saw half the shit I see, they wouldn't be such dumbasses."

"You can take the orthopedist out of the OR, but you can't take the memories out of the orthopedist," Harrison says, sounding a bit like a broken record. "If he'd just dedicated his life to improving women's breasts, he would've gone heliskiing. If you ever go on a road trip with him, word of caution, don't let him drive."

"You're so full of it," Ian says, agitated. "I simply don't want a speeding ticket."

"Well, there's no risk of you getting one," he counters.

The car pulls up in front of a concert building decked out in neon blue lights. Similar sparkling blue lights wrap around the palm trees on the street and throngs of partygoers stand in line.

"Is that where we're going?" I ask as the three of us climb out of the back seat.

"No. That's Cleo. You come back another time, and I'll take you there. It'll be a madhouse tonight. It's got dozens of rooms with different tempos and a rooftop pool. It can get crazy. We're going to a more subdued location," Ian says.

"Well, to start out the night, we're going to a more subdued location. Late night, we might end up at Cleo," Harrison counters.

Ian's hand presses against my lower back. The warmth of his breath tickles my ear as he says, "We'll head back to the apartment when you're ready. Harrison will be perfectly fine on his own."

"Thank god we're not planning on standing in that line," I say, leaning into him so only he hears me. The line extends down the block and wraps around the building.

"I'd never do that to you," Ian assures me.

We cross the street and approach a bouncer standing guard outside two black doors, below a sign that simply reads "Jack's Lounge."

Ian hands over three tickets, and the bouncer opens the door for us. No line, no worries.

Inside, tables and booths fill the center room, and a small stage with a piano occupies the back of the room. A man in a black top hat plays the piano, while a woman in a sparkly dress stands on stage, singing a low-key jazz tune. A long bar extends along the far wall. Ian guides me to a booth that has a reserved placard.

"Does this work?" Ian asks.

"It's perfect," I tell him. And it is. Standing all night in heels doesn't appeal to me anymore, and I absolutely love live music.

"I'm glad you came." Ian leans in close enough I get another whiff of his musky scent, and my heartrate rachets up a notch. Silly, really. But I suppose I don't spend a lot of time around men as good looking as Ian.

"Me too," I say, smiling at my old friend.

All the Duke brothers are handsome and have always been the talk of our small town, but Ian has always been the brother with the most penetrating, thoughtful gaze, the kind of gaze that tingles and raises all kinds of insecurities. I run my tongue over the front of my teeth as a precaution, although I haven't eaten since I brushed them before rushing to my car.

"Okay. You two are clearly together. I'm gonna go circle the bar," Harrison says as he raps the table with his knuckle and slides out of the booth.

"We're not—" I protest, but Harrison disperses into the crowd.

Ian stretches his arm across the back of the booth and gives a slight shake of his head.

"Ignore him. He'll find someone soon, and we won't see him again. That's another reason I'm glad you made it out."

I narrow my eyes, judging his veracity. Ian wouldn't have trouble meeting up with someone either, but he's probably too nice of a guy to try for a hook-up when he's playing host to an out-of-town guest. "I hope I'm not messing up your routine."

"Routine? You think this is my normal?"

"Isn't it? Your apartment is…" I search for the right words to describe his voguish bachelor pad without being insulting.

"What's wrong with my place?"

"Nothing's wrong with it. It's just…it's actually…it's very male."

"Male?" He smirks, and I shift in the booth, angling my body in his direction.

"I mean, it's glam but masculine. All the dark wood. Your kitchen cabinets are extremely modern, no hardware, just oak wood panels with stainless steel appliances, and it's–"

"I think the package I chose was called dynamically bold. The apartment complex had finishing options, and I chose one of three packages."

"It's warm and inviting. The windows are—"

"During the day, it's amazing how far you can see. It also makes you realize how sprawling Houston is. You should see it from the top floors."

"You're on the eighteenth floor," I remind him.

"Yeah, but it has thirty-five floors."

"You didn't want the top?"

"Well, I wanted a two-bedroom, and I liked this floor plan. This place is a big upgrade for me. If you'd seen where I lived as a resident, you wouldn't be so impressed."

"You just finished your residency, right?"

"And moved less than six months ago. Picked a furniture package too. Everything from my old place, I gave to Goodwill."

"Well, it's gorgeous. But two bedrooms? Not giving yourself much space for when you meet the right woman and have kids." I meant it as a tease, although my heart stumbles a bit over the kid piece. Not because of Ian, but because for me. At thirty-nine, I am battling a severe case of what they call baby fever. Or maybe it's baby regret. For years, I assumed I'd meet someone. Then I entertained the idea of having a child on my own, but years have passed, and I have yet to move past thinking about it.

Ian dismisses my kid comment with a roll of his eyes and raises an arm to get a server's attention.

"We need to order drinks," he tells the server. Then, to me, he asks, "Do you want champagne? Wine? Cocktail?"

"I highly recommend the Blue Martini. It's our New Year's

special," the server offers. She's young, I'd guess in her early twenties. Her skin is flushed from rushing between tables, but she offers us a gracious smile.

"I'll take that," I tell her, and Ian orders bourbon on the rocks.

The second she takes off with our orders, Ian brushes a loose strand of hair out of my face, his gaze as thoughtful as ever. "I don't have any plans for kids."

"You say that now." He sounds just like Oliver, but if given a chance to bet, I'd bet both of them will end up family men, just like their eldest brother. Sam always wanted kids, and now he has them. His younger two brothers will, too, even if they've been slower to warm to the idea.

"What about you? I always expected you'd have at least three kids by now."

Ouch. His question hits a tender spot. One I don't want to dig into on New Year's Eve. "Didn't happen." I shrug and force a smile as the waitperson arrives with our drinks.

She slides the drinks on the table and hurries off. Ian and I both lift our glasses. He holds his glass out, asking, "What are we toasting to?"

I push my chin out, shake off all sad thoughts, and grin. The New Year toast is one I have down pat. It has yet to work, but that doesn't mean this year won't be the year. "To all our dreams coming true."

Our glasses clink, and our gazes remain fixed on each other over the rims as we sip. The person on stage takes a bow, and a DJ comes on, announcing it is time to get up and dance, and that he's taking requests. The heavy bass in *Something Just Like This* by The Chainsmokers vibrates across the floor, and I tug on Ian's hand. "I love his song. Come dance with me."

Ian and I press close together in the packed area before the stage. He takes the lead, guiding our bodies to the rhythm. The song pulses, and I close my eyes, letting my body absorb the beat.

Songs transition, but Ian and I remain on the dance floor. I lose my sense of time and self, letting Ian guide my body. Every now and then we catch each other's gaze and smile. We are two friends letting loose on New Year's Eve. Often when I dance, I'm hyper-aware of every awkward movement, but with Ian's proximity and guidance, I just move to the beat.

For once, I belong on the dance floor. Besides, I don't know anyone here. There's no one watching. No one here cares who I am dancing with or if his hand accidentally brushes my ass. In the morning, or next week, or next month, women won't be entering the salon announcing they heard I danced with so and so. For once, I am free to be me. I should've visited Houston years ago.

We break apart when the crowd begins the countdown. Television screens hanging from corners display the fireworks across the city.

"Ten. Nine. Eight."

My breath halts as Ian looks down at me, one hand on the back of my neck, his thumb stroking along my jaw.

"Three. Two."

Those probing eyes question, and I close my eyelids and angle my head, poised and waiting. Frozen, mindless, but most definitely waiting and hoping. It won't mean anything. It would just be a New Year's kiss. No matter how ordinary, or how hung in tradition, every fiber in my being alights with desire to be kissed at the stroke of midnight.

His lips lightly brush mine, and my eyelids flutter. Electrical sparks flood my chest, and our eyes lock in the crowded, fog-filled room. I reach up, and my fingers toy with the hair on the nape of his neck, and he dips his head. His teeth graze my lips, nipping, asking for entrance, and I open, pulling him closer until our sweaty bodies align.

Cautious, his tongue flits over mine. I open, and he deepens the kiss, and it flows through my veins like an enigmatic song. He tastes like bourbon and freedom. My blood pulses and my heart hammers and my skin awakens. Inside my heart and head, fireworks explode in a haze of extraordinary color.

An elbow digs into my side. I lurch sideways, breaking our connection. Shouting and the shrill sound of noisemakers explode around us.

"Sorry," someone shouts.

Ian raises his hands, clapping and shouting, just like all the others in the crowd. Dazed, I raise my hands and mimic him, joining in the throng. Someone beside me blows a noisemaker, creating a loud, piercing sound, and I remember I have one, too. As if reading my mind, Ian pulls it out of his trouser pocket, and I put it to my lips and blow through it until my lungs burn.

Chapter Four

Ian

The wise and experienced avoid hospitals on holidays as if they are ground zero for the next plague. On holidays, there's a skeleton crew within the hallowed halls. Residents, namely folks fresh out of medical school and shy on experience, run the show.

New Year's Day qualifies as a major holiday. When I woke to a text from a resident updating me that they caught my patient with four recently reattached fingers smoking, it required a personal visit. I couldn't trust Francisco, a first-year, would convey the full gravity of the situation. The patient claims it was a celebratory smoke since he couldn't have champagne. I told him I hoped it was worth going through life without those four fingers I spent hours reattaching.

Of course, I warned him at the time of surgery. And he claimed he wasn't a smoker. I'd known he was lying by the stains on his teeth, but he had four fingers chopped off by a table saw sitting on ice and he seemed desperate. The carpenter's livelihood was at stake.

Chances were a single cigarette wouldn't hinder the blood flow to the four recently attached fingers, but he was set to be released today, and I had to drive the message home. Otherwise, he'd go home, continue smoking, and he'd be back in a week with four decaying fingers that I couldn't save.

On my way out of the hospital, a second-year resident's slightly panicked voice reaches me with the exit door in sight. "Dr. Duke. Is there any way—"

"I'm not here. You don't see me," I respond without looking back.

"But I've only done two appendectomies."

"It's up to you and your attendee."

"But he's—"

"It's Independence Day, Omar. You got this." He was going to say something along the lines of asshole or incompetent, and I might agree with either sentiment, but appendectomies stopped being my responsibility years ago.

Those nervous eyes tell me he doesn't at all feel confident he has it, and the truth is he might not. But that's how doctors learn. Watch. Do. Teach.

Back in my apartment, I slip off my shoes at the door. Light floods the living area and kitchen, but there is no sign of Sunny. The coffee mug I set beside the coffee machine remains untouched. I peek my head into the guest room.

A riot of golden hair covers the pillow. The comforter has been pushed to the side, and Sunny lies sprawled out on the bed in a silky white chemise. The thin material hugs her breasts so tightly the outline of her nipples peeks through. One milky thigh stretches across the sheet, and from this angle, it seems she might not be wearing panties. The smooth curve of her buttock, the juncture directly above her hamstrings, is a feast of smooth, flawless skin. Her chest lifts and falls slowly in the rhythm of peaceful slumber.

My teenage self would have snapped a photo and savored the

image for years to come. But my adult self simply stands in the doorway, mesmerized, dick twitching, fighting a desire to climb into bed behind her and hold her, or...who am I kidding? I want to do much more than hold her. What I wouldn't give to touch her, to cup her soft breast, to press my lips to her shoulder and nibble the delectable skin along the curve of her neck.

Especially after last night's kiss. It required all my self-control to not grab her ass and pull her hard against my throbbing erection. She'd clearly been turned on, too. Her breath came out in quick, short spurts. Her pupils expanded, turning those blue eyes dark and hungry, and she'd gripped my shoulders as if she needed me for balance. But the celebration noise overwhelmed us, dragging us back into the moment, and with a few blinks and shoulder bumps from other parties, we were apart, clapping and shouting.

I took her by surprise with that out-of-line kiss. I'm not what she wants. She's never seen me that way and never will. She's got me locked in a special kind of friend zone. It's one reserved for the little brothers of your exes.

Less than an hour after the kiss, Sunny sat on the stage, strumming someone else's guitar, singing the familiar *Closer to Fine* by The Indigo Girls. I'd heard her play it ages ago, as it was one she struggled to master way back then.

The after-midnight act didn't show, and John, the owner of Jack's—yeah, go figure—asked anyone who wanted to fill in to come on up and start the new year showcasing their talents.

Sunny blew the whole room away. She only sang two songs, but she earned a standing ovation. And nearly every single man attempted to maneuver his way over to her. But she stepped off that stage and nestled up against me, uncomfortable with the attention. How the hell a woman like her was still single remained a mystery to me. Without a doubt, I'll go to my grave wondering why my brother let her go. Mom used to say it was timing, but no, the guy's a fool.

Sunny's shoulder dips, and her arm stretches across the pillow in a languid movement. Long, golden strands fall over her face, and she rolls, a hand absently brushing them away. Her movements are my cue to back out of the room.

"Ian?"

Busted. "Yeah?" I push the door farther ajar. The shades are down, and the room is dark, but enough light escapes in the gaps along the sides to cast her in a haze of filtered sun.

"Why are you in scrubs?"

I glance down at my navy scrubs and socked feet. "Had to run in and chastise a patient."

She sits up, rubbing her eyes. "What time is it?"

"A little after ten. Sorry if I woke you."

"What? No. I'm just…" She crosses an arm over her breasts as awareness that she's barely dressed filters through her waking consciousness.

"Come on out when you're ready. The guest bath is across the hall, and I set out some towels. I'll be in the kitchen. Coffee is ready."

I chose this layout because the guest room can double as an office. The bathroom across the hall, in my mind, would be a good guest toilet room. But the layout requires Sunny to walk across the hall. Only now do I see the benefits of the en suite bathroom for the second bathroom. That was an option in one of the plans I didn't choose.

About twenty minutes later, Sunny emerges in sweatpants, thick socks, and a tank top. She beelines to the coffee pot and sheepishly peers up at me.

"What have you got planned for the day? I can get out—"

"You are my plan for the day. I figured maybe we could do a movie marathon." Her coffee mug hides her smile, but I know it's there based on the way her cheeks rise higher and the pale skin around her blue eyes crinkles.

"Like old times?"

"Exactly."

Sunny and I watched so many movies together. That was one thing about living out in the country. I didn't have any other friends within walking distance, and, well, all of Sunny's friends had gone off to college.

Of course, she had no idea she reigned supreme as the solo star of my teenage fantasies. That while we sat there watching those movies, I'd been staring at her breasts and her thighs and her ass. And of course, she'd been sitting there thinking of me as the kid brother, cheering me on when I got my permit and later my driver's license. Yeah, I'll be taking those teen fantasies to the grave.

I open a paper bag with the breakfast I brought back from the hospital. Most of the food from the hospital ranks as subpar, but they order the croissants from a local bakery.

I lift one and ask, "Want it heated?"

"No, but do you have jelly?"

"Doubt it," I mumble, opening the refrigerator. "I don't eat here a lot. And when I do, it's usually take-out."

"That doesn't seem very healthy."

"Eh, I eat a lot of salad. The salad bar is about the best thing the hospital cafeteria has going."

"Well, whatever system you have, it's working well for you."

I straighten and cock my head. "Sunny, are you telling me you..." I let my words trail. Does she see me as attractive? I mean, the kiss last night had been hot as hell, but she broke it, and I assumed I'd thrown her because, after all, I'm her ex's little brother. And not just any ex. Her first love. Her first sex. I can't stand thinking about it, so I reach for the butter, since it's all I have, and close the fridge.

"Dr. Ian Duke, are you telling me you don't realize you are all that and more?" Her smile qualifies as flirty, but her tone is more big sister tease. She rolls that pale peach lip beneath her upper front teeth, and I lean against the counter, hiding her effect on me.

"That's all I have," I say, pushing the butter before her.

"You've always been such a cutie pie. I find it hard to believe you don't know it." She slathers on butter and grins like she didn't just re-affirm my position as the kid brother by calling me a cutie pie.

"So, movies. What are you in the mood for?"

"Well, we'd have to go classics, right?" She scrunches her nose and takes a big bite of croissant.

"Oh. So, you're thinking *The Hangover*?"

"No. We watched that one too many times. I can't." She holds her fingers up to cover her lips, since she's chewing as she answers me.

I chuckle. If she only knew how many times I continued to watch that movie, or parts of the movie, through undergrad and med school.

"Let's see." I run through the movie catalog in my head, the ones that probably still sit in DVD cases on my parents' shelves, even though I'm pretty sure they ditched the DVD player ages ago. "*Superbad*?" She wrinkles her nose. That's a no. "Huh. *V for Vendetta*?" The nose remains crinkled. "*Kill Bill*?"

She waves her hand dismissively and sips her coffee, then sets it down on the counter. "*The Notebook*."

I let out an audible groan. She laughs, and I smile. But if it means she'll curl up next to me on the sofa, I'll sit through it one more time. I could always catch up on my medical journals while she sniffles.

"*Sideways*? Or, no, I know! It's still the holidays." She snaps her fingers. "Let's watch *Love Actually*."

She breaks off a piece of croissant and drops it into her mouth. Her eyelashes flutter closed, and she lightly moans. God, I want to step up to her and share in that buttery goodness.

"Does *Love Actually* work?" she prompts. I might have been staring.

"It's good. Let me go change, and we can start up movies."

"Do you have a crock pot?"

"Do I look like someone who would own a crock pot?" She sort of giggles, and my goofy smile breaks out. "Why?"

"Well, I thought I could put on a pot of chili."

"I don't have any of those ingredients." But I have a full drawer of menus.

"Well, the grocery…"

"We'll order lunch in. There are a couple of places nearby that were advertising they're open for New Year's." Sunny's lower lip pokes out, her signature dramatic pout. "Hey, gotta support the small businesses."

"I think I need to make a point of stocking your refrigerator before I leave."

"It would go to waste. I don't cook." Although, that isn't completely true. The freezer holds a pack of chicken breasts and frozen smoothies from the health food center down the street.

She tucks a loose strand behind her ear. She opens her mouth to speak but closes it. I lean forward, closer to the breakfast bar. Her gaze falls to her plate.

"What is it?" She can say anything to me. I hope she knows that.

"Last night. John." My muscles tense at the lounge owner's name. "He said he'd love to have me come back and play. Like play a set one night. He said Sunday nights he does all acoustic."

All my muscles relax. "You should totally do that. You enjoyed it, right?"

She lifts her eyebrows and looks at me like I must be out of my mind.

"I can already hear what people would say." She adjusts her tone and feigns an annoying female. "Who does she think she is? Like she's going to get a musical career at her age? Like people launch careers in Houston."

"First, who gives a damn what they say?" I air quote *they* for effect, but I have a vague idea of who qualifies from her perspective. "You've got one life. You live yours and let those folks live theirs. And two, why would anyone from back home know? None of those people venture to Houston. I've lived here for, what, ten years? I have yet to run into anyone from home."

The faint chorus from the Beatles *Blackbird* echoes down the hall.

"My phone," she says and jumps off the stool.

Her loose sweatpants fall lower on her hips with each step, exposing a slim riff of skin. I like that she used a Beatles song for her ringtone. I do, too, only mine is *Here Comes the Sun*, and my phone is always on vibrate.

She answers the phone in the guest room, and while I can't hear exactly what she is saying, I can tell from her tone it isn't good news. A few minutes later, she reenters the kitchen, holding her phone up against her waist, her expression pensive.

"What's wrong?"

"Polly. I think I need to head back."

Neither Ollie nor my dad are home, so I can't get them to go check on her horse for her. "Who called?"

"Frank."

I scowl. She'd said she wasn't seeing anyone, not that I have a right to be upset if she is.

"He's one of the ranch hands at your family ranch. Nice guy. He offered to swing by and check on her and feed her, since it's on his way to work. She didn't eat."

While not eating is a universal sign for something being wrong, the equine in question is ancient. She was old when we were young.

"Polly is the reason you've stayed in that house, isn't it? You've been taking care of her all these years."

"What was I supposed to do? No one else would take a horse that old."

"Oliver would have."

"Polly can't be in a herd. They'd be too mean to her." I think they'd probably leave her alone. At the very least, Ollie would set her up in a paddock where she was safe, but there was really no reason to debate the topic.

Surgeons have a reputation as being cold and heartless, but the stereotype rarely fits. You don't work hard saving lives without caring, and you don't deal with patients' families without developing a sixth sense for when a person is hurting.

I step up to Sunny and pull her against me. Her head falls on my shoulder, and I caress her. Polly is her family, and the worry coming through Sunny flows deep. "Hey, she's lived a full life."

Sunny sucks in a breath and nods. Her glassy eyes, filled to the rim with emotion, catch the light pouring through the windows and reflect the skyscrapers in the distance. I hold her close, rubbing my hand along her back, breathing deeply, and loving every single minute of holding my friend close. And I don't feel guilty for it. Or at least, not that much. She's not Sam's anymore.

With a deep breath, she pushes up and pats my chest like a dog. "Thanks for that. I think I'm going to have to take a rain check on movie day." A hint of a smile plays on her lips. "What is that smell?"

I smell my hands. "Hospital?" She gives me a look that says she's calling a bluff, but I'm not bluffing. I sniff my pit for a quick check. Nothing. I just left the hospital. "Antiseptic? Hand sanitizer?"

"Chemicals." That nose crinkles in disapproval.

"You don't like it?"

"Way too harsh." She shakes her head. "You need something more uplifting. And at home, something more relaxing. When I come back, do you mind if I bring you some lotions and soaps? Maybe a few candles?"

"As long as you come back, you can bring as much foo-foo as you want."

"It's not foo-foo. It's aromatherapy. It's important for the psyche. For your aura."

"If you say so."

That radiant smile nearly knocks me back. That's one thing about Sunny, and the reason I first gave her that nickname. She could get the worst news, absorb it, and turn around with a brilliant smile, ever the eternal optimist. The world could use more people like her. No matter what happens in her life, she'll focus her attention on the beauty in the world. Always.

"Don't you worry. I'll fix you up." She pats me again. *Yep, trapped in the little brother cage.*

"When will you be back?"

"John said he'd call me about booking a date. We'll see if he does."

"Even if he doesn't, I'd love for you to come back." I point at my kitchen. "Clearly, I need you."

And there it is. The brilliant, megawatt smile that hits me right in the sternum. Every. Single. Time.

Chapter Five

Sandra

Polly's head hangs over the fence, and her loose skin around her nostrils quivers as she whinnies. Her long, speckled, gray ears point forward, intent on my approach.

"Polly girl, are you not feeling well?" She brushes her head against my chest, and I scratch near her ear as she nuzzles my other hand. "It's not like you to skip meals."

A milky white appearance glosses over her pupils that, back in the day, were jet black. The vet suspects she sees only shadows. Her once shiny black coat is now heavily salted, and all the whiskers around her muzzle gleam white. She scratches her head up against me, using me like a post as I rub her neck.

"Such a sweetheart." She smells my pockets, hoping for a treat. "I jumped right out of the car, baby. I'll bring you some carrots. Is that what you want? Something special? Maybe an apple?"

My phone rings, sending Beatles lyrics across the countryside, and Polly sniffs at the phone as I lift it out of my pocket and read the unknown number.

"Hello?"

"Hey, Sandra?"

"This is she."

"Hey, Sandra. I hope you don't mind me calling. Jocelyn told me I should check with you."

"Oh. Okay. And who is this?"

"Aw, I'm sorry. This is Cindy, a friend of Jocelyn's. Oliver and I were supposed to go to the New Year's Eve party last night, but he got snowed in. And, well, he said that he'd have to take a rain check but… do you know, did he just not want to go with me?"

"Oh, hun. I don't think that's it. I… ahm." Shit. How would I know if Oliver blew her off? "I just got back myself. I haven't spoken to him. But he mentioned getting snowed in." Actually, Ian said he'd been snowed in, but it's not like I'd tell this woman the chain of communication.

"So, you weren't with him?"

"No. I wasn't." A silence fills the air as I decline to expand on exactly where I was. If I mention Houston, that could unlock a flurry of rumors.

"Jocelyn said you weren't with him. But I just… I wasn't sure since you both missed the party."

"No, I wasn't with him." I grimace, wondering how many other people questioned both Ian and me being absent at the same time. "If I tried to keep up with him skiing, I'd break my neck." And then I'd need an orthopedic surgeon. "Hey, hun, I just got out of the car. I haven't unpacked yet. I came home early because my horse isn't doing well. Can I call you back later?"

"You don't have to call me back. Unless, well, if you find out anything. Or, no, you don't have to call me. He'll either call or he won't, right?"

"That's one way of looking at it." I laugh. "Pretty much sums up a lot of my dating life. How about this? I'll give you a call or text you if I learn anything. That's if I run into Oliver. I don't see him all that much."

"You don't? Jocelyn said you guys are always together. That's why I wondered if maybe…"

"He's like a brother to me." I roll my eyes. *This town.* "I wouldn't say we're always together." *What the hell, Jocelyn?* "I guess I can reach you at this number?"

"Yes. Thanks so much, Sandra. Jocelyn said you'd be cool about it."

"Absolutely. Any time." I hang up with a shake of my head. "Polly, it sounds like our friend Oliver is fishing on the younger side of the dating pool." She rubs her head against my chest, knocking me back a step. "No, I'm serious." Polly listens intently. "Those Duke boys. They've caused an awful lot of heartache over the years."

I pat Polly's shoulder and step past her, headed to the barn so I can check out her uneaten food for myself. Before I reach the paddock, my phone rings again.

An image of Patty Duke from maybe fifteen years ago shows up on my screen. Her hair is a mix of steel gray and white, she's smiling wide, and her full cheeks are flushed pink.

"Happy New Year," I say.

"Sandra, Happy New Year to you." Mrs. Duke's gentle tone always warms me up from the inside. She's been the mom down the road my whole life.

"Are you having fun with those grandbabies?"

"Oh, you know I am. I'll send you some photos. They're growing like weeds." I reach Polly's open stall and inspect her hanging bucket. Most of the oats are gone. Maybe she just hadn't been hungry when Frank stopped by and fed her. "Ian told me that Polly isn't feeling well. Are you back home? Is she okay?"

"Just got back."

"Was traffic bad?"

"Not bad at all."

"And how is Polly?"

"Well, she seems okay."

"That's a relief. Usually, with Frank, it's a horrible situation and he downplays it."

"Well, she looks okay, and most of her oats are eaten." Polly stands out in the pasture, her muzzle hovering over the grass, one ear pointed in my direction.

Mrs. Duke and I chat a bit more and hang up when one kid calls out, searching for Gigi, their chosen word for grandmother. Within seconds of hanging up, my phone vibrates and three photos of two gorgeous girls come through. They have darker hair than their father. Actually, they don't resemble Sam much at all. Mrs. Duke loves to say they look like Sam, but based on these photos, Sam's daughters took after their mother.

As I tuck my phone away, my dad's words float through my mind. "You and Sam will make me some good-looking grandbabies. But that doesn't mean I want them right now."

God, I'd been mortified when he said that to me. I'd been like eighteen or nineteen years old, and Sam and I had been having sex, but it wasn't something I shared with Dad.

Years later, before he died, he'd sung a different tune. He'd say things like, "Now, Sandra, I need you to stop looking after me and go out there and meet a nice young man so I can meet my grandchildren. You never know how much time I have before it's my turn to meet our maker."

Partially thanks to his pressure, along came Henry. But then I had to give Henry back to his mother, and one month later, Dad died. My future shriveled into nothing.

A heaviness weighs down. I delete the photos of Sam's kids and slip my phone into my back pocket, then call out to the pasture, to Polly. She's been my confidante forever. The one living being I could say anything to and she'd never tell a soul.

"Didn't happen, did it, Polly?"

She meanders up to me and knocks me a step back with her head, asking for a scratch. With a heaviness in my heart, I oblige. Loving on Polly gives me comfort.

After a good rubdown, fresh water, and hay, I close her in for the night and return to the house to prepare for bed. My thoughts stray from my dad, and like they often do, to Henry. When you take in a foster child, the goal is reunification with the parents. Only I failed at absorbing that part of the training, because I ache for him. I ache for that little boy and for all the things in my life that didn't come to be.

The phone rings, and given the well of emotion in my throat, I seriously consider letting it go to voicemail. But Aunt Nora's smiling image shines up at me, and I answer.

"Happy New Year."

"Sandra. Happy New Year to you. Are you hungover?"

"No." If I had more pep, I might laugh at my raucous aunt.

"Well, that's a shame. Don't tell me you didn't do anything."

"No, I did." I plop down on the sofa, fully aware I sound sad, but sometimes the best way to handle sad is to let it be.

"What's wrong?" Aunt Nora's concern coats the line between us, and my index finger rubs the back of the phone.

"Nothing." The automatic answer is met with a grunt. Then silence.

"Honey, I think it's time you consider seeing a therapist." I close my eyes and tilt my head back, letting my gaze roam over the ceiling. This is why I didn't go to Washington for Christmas. Aunt Nora jumps to drastic conclusions all because I'm feeling a little down. This isn't the first time she's suggested a therapist, and it won't be the last. "It's perfectly natural. You lost your child and your father close together."

Tears well in my eyes, and I thrust a nail between my teeth. He wasn't really my child, but I certainly loved him like he was. I'd been so sad all the time, and Derek couldn't deal, so he ended things the week before I found Dad in the woods. The rule of three held true for me. Three shitty things all at once. Wham, bam, thank you, ma'am.

"Did you get my email?" Aunt Nora loves to forward articles.

"Maybe?"

"It's an article about all the options available to have a child as a single woman, or as a gay couple." As a gay woman, even though she didn't have children of her own, my aunt's friends with plenty of alternative families traveled down a nontraditional path for their children.

I explored all the options. That's how I originally ended up as a foster parent in the state's foster care program. As a single woman, I wasn't an ideal candidate, but there's always a shortage of foster parents. I'd thought it might be a path to adoption, and in theory, it could have been.

For those first few years after the rule of three, I wasn't in the right mindset to pursue alternate options. Regardless of this tidal wave of sadness that came out of nowhere, I am doing better. I went out for New Year's Eve. I traveled all the way to Houston.

The pads of my fingers touch my lips, and a searing heat fills me as I remember the New Year's kiss.

Aunt Nora jabbers away, highlighting the options, including freezing my eggs, which seems crazy to me, given my age. It feels like another window I waited too late to open. Something I thought about but haven't moved on. And now, here I am, driving to Houston and getting kissed by my ex's brother.

And boy, can Ian Duke kiss. I mean, he's a Duke brother. There's no surprise there, really. It meant nothing. He's a long-time friend. Without a doubt, interested women line up for him, all living a lot closer than Whispering Creek. And besides, there's an unspoken rule... you don't date your ex's brother. It's just not done. So, I need to wash that kiss right out of my head.

Yes, he might've been flirty at times. But the youngest Duke brother has always been a flirt. Even back when I dated Sam, he'd been a flirt.

Ian and I have known each other so long, we're like siblings. Just like me and Ollie. Which I suppose is why we'd both been a little shell-shocked after the unexpected kiss. Or at least I was.

But it was New Year's. Everyone was kissing someone. The kiss didn't mean a thing. And the way my body reacted was just a sign that, if anything, I might need to force myself back to my dating app.

Aunt Nora might push therapy and artificial insemination, but there are other ways to move forward. Dancing in my living room and shaking off the bad vibes, for one. A solid orgasm would also do wonders. But, my god, I don't want to do the dating app thing. I'd probably need to upload a more recent photo, and that's an exhausting notion.

"Will you at least tell me you'll consider it?" Aunt Nora is still going on about motherhood.

"Yes, I'll consider it."

"Promise?"

"Promise. Love you, Aunt Nora."

"Love you, too."

After the line goes dead, I set the phone down, pull a pillow into my lap, and mull over the mess of my life. Derek helped me to realize I didn't need a man to be happy. I'm happier without him. Truly. The craving that makes my core ache is for a child of my own. A dream that passed me by. Or did it?

Maybe Aunt Nora is on to something. It took me a few years to get my heart and head back on straight, but this is something I should pick back up and evaluate. If I had a child of my own, maybe the ache from Henry's absence would lessen.

My phone rings, and I flip it over, screen side up. A grin breaks out.

"Hey, you," I answer. My fingers automatically touch my lips, and yeah, I roll my eyes at the girliness.

"Mom told me you got back okay. You forgot to text."

"Oh. I'm sorry. I just—"

"No worries. How's Polly?"

"I think she's fine. I didn't see a reason to call the vet. But maybe I should."

"Don't they charge you for the visit?"

"Don't you charge a patient for a consult?"

"No. Actually, I don't. But a lot of my patients don't have a choice with surgery."

"So, what did you do for the rest of the day?"

"Not much. Why?"

"Just curious what a big-time surgeon does on his day off."

"Big-time?" He chuckles. "You and my family love to give me shit. Well, let's see. This hotshot surgeon stopped by the hospital to check on his patients after my plans hopped in the car to check on her horse."

"I thought you had the day off."

"I do. But pretty much only first years work on New Year's, so since I had the free time, I stopped in to check on things. And then I ended up spending a couple of hours playing Uno."

"The card game?"

"Yep. I had one pediatric patient. She was with her family. But there was another kid. Young boy, all on his own. Everyone else had visitors, but his mom had to work. So, I hung out with him."

My heart melts like a tub of hot wax, envisioning Ian on a rare day off, spending his time with a kid who isn't his patient, just because. Of the three brothers, he's always been the kindest. "Look at you. A surgeon with a heart."

"Don't tell anyone."

I smile and curl back onto the sofa. "Your secret is safe with me."

"Of course, it is. We always keep each other's secrets."

His reference to our past makes me smile. I not only caught him red-handed in high school mixing Mr. Duke's bourbon with soda, but I'd helped prevent him from getting caught by teaching him how to mix in water so he wouldn't notice some was missing. I was probably the worst kind of big sister.

"Hey, you know, I had this crazy thought. And I can't get it out of my head."

I hold my breath, waiting for him to finish. Has he been thinking about our kiss? If he suggests we go out on a date, I can't say yes. There's simply no way.

"You still there?" His question kicks me back into the moment.

"Yeah. Still here. Waiting to hear what crazy thought you had."

"Have you not been with anyone since Sam?"

"What?" I curl forward. That is the last question I expected. "Ian, you know I've dated other people."

"Yeah, I know. But like I said, it's crazy. And it's not my business."

Of course, that's all he'd think about. Me and Sam. Oliver, being the brother closer to my age, had always been my dating confidante. I've never spoken much to Ian about my dating life. So, of course, he'd still think of me and Sam. And that New Year's kiss, which strayed from platonic, probably disgusted him. Or didn't register.

"I shouldn't have said anything," Ian mutters, his words laced with apology.

"Ian, do you have any idea how old I am?"

"Of course, I do. But every time I ask if you're dating someone, the answer is no."

"Well, I dated a guy for several years in my late twenties to early thirties."

"Why don't I know about him?"

"You were in the thick of med school and, I guess, maybe residency. I hardly ever saw you."

"That makes sense. I was just—"

"And there was this guy who was a total gaslighting narcissist. Things ended with him about three years ago. And thanks to him, I learned I am happier on my own. And when I forget that, I go out on a date, and ten out of ten times my memory is refreshed before dessert arrives. A woman does not need a man to be happy and fulfilled."

"I completely agree. And it was a crazy question. A woman like you would have, of course, dated."

"You're like everybody else in this town, aren't you?"

"What do you mean?"

"You think I never got over Sam?" I swear, it's so frustrating. To this day, women in the salon whisper about Sam as if they can't speak about him for fear of upsetting me. It's like we're the Brad Pitt and Jennifer Aniston of Hill Country.

"Forget I asked. But for the record, I'll never understand how he let you go."

"That's a nice thing to say. Sweet, but…it was a long time ago, Ian."

The truth is, Sam and I grew apart, plain and simple. And when we broke up, it was pretty amicable. Neither of us said much to others about what happened out of respect for each other. And I'd been petrified I'd lose my connection to his family. But, in hindsight, maybe I should have been more outspoken. But the past is the past. I put it behind me, and at some point, everyone else would, too.

"What about you? We never talk about relationships. Have you had any serious ones?"

"No one I'd ever bring home."

"What kind of women are you dating?"

"Busy ones. Good ones. I didn't mean they were bad, I just meant I've never gotten close to anyone. I have colleagues who are married, and I can't even fathom. Some got married during residency." A heavy sigh crosses the line. "Others got divorced in residency. The hours, you know, they pull at you."

"I guess that explains why your mom hasn't ever mentioned anyone. But, you know, Ian, there's more to life than work. There's got to be."

"Maybe. I could've chosen a life like Dad's. Dinner every night with the kids, present at every game or awards ceremony."

"Our dads were ranchers. They had a good life. Doesn't mean you can't, too."

"I do have a good life. I'm doing exactly what I wanted. What about you?"

"Yeah," I say automatically, but at the same time I feel a little itchy and squirm on the sofa.

"You never wanted to leave Whispering Creek?"

"I kind of did," I answer with a little more defensiveness than is maybe warranted. "I have a business in Austin. I spend time there. And no…I mean, I know my five acres is nothing compared to the Duke ranch, but I love this land." There are so many memories, and I'm close to my dad out here.

"You and Ollie. Love that land."

"And you don't?"

"Too many mosquitoes." That has me snickering. The mosquitoes really do seem to love Ian's blood type.

After saying goodnight, I open my stickered laptop to do some research. I'd meant what I said to Ian. A woman doesn't need a man. And, as I close in on forty, the one regret I hold about my choices so far in life is that I didn't have a child. Maybe it's Dad's voice speaking to me in my head, or maybe it's the pang of missing Henry, or maybe it's the knowledge my other child out in the pasture might leave me soon, but as I click through Aunt Nora's article and related links, a different possible path for my future crystallizes.

Chapter Six

Ian

March Last Year

Burning eyes, sore muscles, neck pain, a dull headache, and an omnipresent bone-deep weariness plague me. The intense exhaustion weighs more heavily after eight hours of surgery. A surgery I argued against performing.

My phone rings as the powdered electrolytes float to the top of the glass of water. Mom's face in a photo from ten years earlier flashes on the screen. Patty Duke possesses a sixth sense. All her sons swear to it.

"Hey, Mom."

"Lots of surgeries today?"

"Why do you ask?" With one hand, I pop the Tylenol lid and shake out three tablets.

"You sound it."

"One surgery. Eight hours."

"Oh, my. What was it?"

"Hemipelvectomy. Cancer patient. Seventeen. Female."

"Oh, dear. Were there complications?"

A sigh I've been holding on to escapes, and I rub my forehead, hoping to ease the ache.

Mom was a nurse before she had kids. She continued working after she had Sam, but by the time she had me, she worked full-time as a mother of three boys. My older brothers more or less followed in Dad's footsteps, but Mom gave me her love of medicine. Throughout my career, she has been my sounding board. The one I go to when frustrated or defeated.

"In theory, the surgery was a success. But god, Mom. What that poor girl is going to go through? I advised against the surgery. She has an aggressive form of cancer. Less than five percent survival rate after five years. Why the fuck we did this to her..." I grind my molars, remembering my disagreement with the oncology team.

"You advised against it, but she chose to fight for her life?" Mom's words oversimplify the case.

"I removed half her pelvic bone, Mom. Plus a leg. Think about that. Think about her rehab. She could have had maybe another year of a good life. Now, she's got a year in hell." Mom can complete the equation.

"But she chose it."

It's not that simple. "Her parents did. Based on her oncology team's advice." *Fuckers.*

"Oncologists are at war. They attack cancer, especially aggressive cancer, with nuclear options. You know that."

I exhale heavily. Mom is right. I couldn't be an oncologist. They lose too many battles. I chose a specialty that allows me to go in, see the problem, and fix it. Almost always, I deliver a better quality of life. As a general rule, I don't decimate lives right before death.

"But it is possible to lose sight of the big picture." My goal isn't to argue with my mother. I was raised better than that. But I can't shake the vision of her mutilated body. My hands mutilated her.

"It is. But it wasn't your call. And you did what you were asked to do. She's lucky she had you as a surgeon. You performed a difficult surgery successfully."

I briskly run my hand over my face, then over my hair, then haul my ass up on my kitchen counter.

"How are things there?" I don't want to talk about work anymore.

"We're back at the ranch."

That's unexpected. This is prime beach weather. "Did you miss home?"

"No. Polly died. You remember Polly? Sandra's horse?" *Fuck.* "Dad brought the backhoe over today to bury her. He's going to build a nice marker for her. Poor Sandra. She's taking it pretty hard."

Damnit. Sunny and I have exchanged random texts over the last couple of months, but I've been working nearly seven days a week. I've thought about her. Hoped she'd plan to come back for another visit.

"You should call her. I'm sure she'd love to hear from you."

I nod in agreement, not that Mom can see. "What happened to Polly?" Given the horse's age, the question feels nonsensical.

"She found her in the woods. It's fascinating, you know, how animals handle death. Sandra buried her near the back property line. It's a peaceful area in the woods." Sunny found her dad in the woods, too. But there's no need to bring that up. Mom is fully aware.

"I'll call her. How long are you staying out there?"

"Not too long. Your brother has a friend who is going through a rough patch, and we'll probably be clearing out soon. Don't want to be in their way."

My pager beeps, and I groan. Motorcycle accident, en route.

"Mom, I gotta go. Motorcycle accident on the way in."

"You're on call? After an eight-hour surgery?"

"It's a madhouse tonight, and the attendee went home sick. Covid. Gotta run. Love you."

As it turned out, I scrubbed in but never operated. The patient never stabilized. The organ transplant team took over to recover the organs, and I joined the resident while she informed the waiting family.

After the resident let them know we did everything we could, I mention to the family they can request an autopsy. The man cocks his head at me and says, "I think we pretty much know what killed him. Unless you're trying to say you guys fucked up?"

"I'm not saying that. This is a teaching hospital. This is how we learn. Examining what went wrong is how we become better doctors."

The man accepts my answer. I leave before the family decides on the autopsy and without hearing which organs were harvested successfully. An SUV sideswiped the motorcyclist, and he sustained serious injuries. If the team had stabilized the internal hemorrhaging, he would have required significant surgery to piece together his shattered femur, at a minimum.

On my drive home, I call Sunny.

"Hey, you." Her cheery voice throws me. It's such a stark contrast to my mental state.

"I heard about Polly."

"She's in a better place. Running around like she used to without any arthritis."

"Well, you sound better than I thought you would." A car honks, and I raise my middle finger. "I didn't realize Polly had been sick."

"Well, I mean…" There's a pause. If I actually picked up the phone and called, as opposed to sending short texts, maybe she would've mentioned it to me. "Your parents have been wonderful."

Sam and Patty Duke are good people. There's no doubt about it. "I'm sure they have. But I'm calling to find out how you're doing. It's gotta be hard losing a childhood friend. Polly has been with you almost your whole life."

"She has." I'm pretty sure she sniffles, but her tone remains bright. "But life was getting hard for her, ya know? The arthritis, she couldn't see."

"You gave her a wonderful life."

There's a weighted pause. Definitely a sniffle from the real person beneath the upbeat effervescence.

"I'll never forget the time you and I both rode her bareback through the trails all the way to Main Street."

"You wanted to get ice cream." The smile in her voice comes through the car's speaker.

"Yep. And we bought it, and she reached over your shoulder, and with one bite nabbed the top half of your cone."

"And then opened her mouth to spit it out. I don't think she expected it would be cold."

Sunny and I rode a lot of trails together over the years. At least, after she and Sam split. Sam moved away for college and never returned. Sometimes Ollie would join us, but during that time period, he spent most of his free time at his fraternity. Sunny always rode Polly. My horse varied, but more often than not, I rode a bay quarter horse named Pepper.

"She was a good horse. Sometimes more like a dog than a horse. Remember how she used to follow you around the pasture and the barn? Wherever you went, she'd be a few feet behind you."

"She was the best." Sunny blows her nose. When she returns, her tone is bright and forced. "What's going on with you?"

"Not much. Just living the dream."

A text comes through. The notification flashes long enough for me to read that the chief of surgery wants me to call her.

"I'm not buying it." Sunny says. "Your tone is off. Tough day?"

"You are perceptive." Sunny and Mom are both perceptive. "It's been a long day."

"Your aura is off. That's how I can tell."

"My aura," I repeat. *Only Sunny.* "Maybe I need you to bring some of your aromatherapy my way."

"You're into aromatherapy now?"

"Didn't you tell me I needed better smelling soaps and lotions? Something less harsh and more, what did you call it? Hopeful?"

"I forgot all about that," she says.

Because it was months ago.

"Maybe we can barter." She sounds tentative, which is odd.

"Barter? I'd give you anything. You know that."

"Well, you remember John? The owner of Jack's Lounge?"

"Yeah." The older man had been taken with Sunny. Like every other man within her radius.

"Well, he'd like for me to come play one Sunday night. Not for the whole night, but as part of an acoustic rotation he's planned. He's been asking for a while, but I couldn't get away. I'll bring you lots of goodies for letting me crash at your place."

"Sunny, you can stay at my place any time. And that should be easier now, right?" I cringe at the unstated implication. It's too soon to be pointing out the advantages of Polly's death. "Seriously, Sunny, I'd love for you to come visit. Any time." Silence fills the distance, and as I pull into my apartment complex, I sweeten the deal. "You weren't wrong about my aura. I need some of your sun. It's been a tough few weeks." My phone vibrates, and there's another text. "Sunny, I've got to run. But seriously, any time."

I disconnect the call and click over to call Leida, our chief of surgery. It's late, and she's calling me from her cell phone, so it's probably not good news, but if I need to return to the hospital, she wouldn't be the one calling me.

"Hi, Leida."

"What exactly did you say to Mr. Moerman?"

"Who?" I stretch my neck to the side, open the car door, and pick up my phone.

"The father of the motorcyclist. He initially refused to donate organs. He wanted to see video of the surgery. He was somehow convinced Houston Medical was to blame for his son's death."

Jesus fucking Christ.

"I offered an autopsy. That's it."

"What exactly did you say?"

The elevator door opens, but I remain in the parking garage. I'll lose signal if I get in. I cover one eye, pressing against it, masking the pain and trying to remember the conversation.

"I don't know exactly what I said." It's not like me to forget, but my thought processes are shutting down. I need sleep. "It was over in sixty seconds."

"Ian." It's a reprimand. "You know how autopsies can be interpreted. Why were you even there? He wasn't your patient."

"I was helping out."

"You're spreading yourself too thin. Doing too much. You can't do it all, Ian."

Leida's been around for decades. She's right. I don't want her to be, but she's right.

Chapter Seven

Sandra

April - Last Year

The packed folder on my desk goads me. Color coded paper clips hold together each potential path forward. Green for sperm donor. Blue for adoption. Yellow for IVF. Yellow is a last resort.

The center I found in Austin won't see me for IVF, as I haven't had a baby in the past, but there are others that will gladly take my money. Unfortunately, my health insurance doesn't cover IVF for single women. The company probably didn't intend to be judgmental, but the policy smacks of judgement.

Adoption isn't much more realistic. It's incredibly expensive unless I attempt another round of adoption via foster care. It's always an option, but it'll take years, and there's no guarantee anyone would choose me among a host of couples to choose from. If I pursue adoption, then the green door effectively slams shut by virtue of my age.

The scary hot pink clip reminds me the green door might already be barricaded shut. The facts and figures about getting pregnant as a forty-year-old woman are safely ensconced behind the pink clip. I don't need to flip through the printed pages, as the stats remain stuck in my head. Five percent of women my age will have a successful pregnancy after one year of trying. That figure takes into account the fact that forty to fifty percent of women my age miscarry.

It's a bit naïve and ridiculously hopeful to believe I'd fall into the five percent category. I've never won a lottery ticket in my life. Why would I win with this?

Years ago, adoption had seemed like the obvious choice. But after meeting with one local center, I feared I would never be chosen. Women searching for parents for their child often envision a traditional family, or at the very least, a pair. International adoption is slightly more promising, but exorbitantly expensive. The pandemic hit my small business hard, and my savings isn't what it used to be.

The edge of my nail snaps against the blue clip. Successful adoptions originate from the foster care program. But can I handle returning another child to his parents after falling in love? If I had a child of my own, maybe I could be that strong. But social services driving Henry away gutted me.

My palm flattens against my sternum, and nausea stirs in the pit of my stomach. My head hits the back of my chair. Ian says he needs my aura, but my aura needs a good cleanse. Or maybe a different approach, something like realigning my chakras. Getting back in touch with my soul. A regrouping of sorts.

Three light raps on the slightly ajar office door announce Kara before she enters, and I flip the folder closed.

Kara's bright blonde hair artfully curls around a thick black head wrap. Her black jeans, black sweater and black cowboy boots are well worn. Black is our chosen uniform color, and everyone tends to rotate the same black outfits throughout the week.

As the owner, I don't adhere to the dress code in our Main Street location unless I am seeing clients, and then I choose black scrubs.

"Whatcha working on?" Kara asks, closing the door behind her.

With her back to me, I stealthily slide the floral folder beneath a stack of manila folders. When she turns around, eyes bright and arms folded loosely over her middle, I rest in my office chair, smiling, ready for whatever requires a closed-door session.

"Tomorrow is bill day, and I'm preparing. Makes it go faster. What's up?" There's a bounce in Kara's step as she approaches. A smile plays across her lips. Something is definitely up.

She sits down and leans forward. "Noah is moving out of the house."

Her eyebrows move as she speaks. She leans back in the chair, arms crossed with a big-as-the-ranch smile.

I slowly nod.

Noah discovered his wife, Jocelyn, was cheating on him. She says her baby is the other man's. I haven't said anything to Noah, but given all my research on getting pregnant, I question how she knows this. Unless she and Noah were not having sex. But in all my conversations with him, and I've had plenty because he's needed a friend, he was shocked. His degree of shock led me to suspect they hadn't been going without sex, but that is a personal question I chose not to ask.

"You don't look surprised. You know everything before I do." Kara's foot stomps playfully.

"I actually didn't know he was moving out of the house. But I'm not surprised." *Come on, Kara. Did you expect he'd continue living with her while she dated someone else?*

"Well, I heard she's pregnant. I'd think they might try to work things out if she's pregnant." Kara cocks her head and looks at me expectantly. I never divulge my friends' business, and Kara has worked here for years. She should know better. "Unless it's the other man's baby."

And there it is. Her head tilts, and I don't miss the way she narrows her eyes, studying my reaction.

"Kara, why does it matter?" I place my elbows on my desk and link my hands. "This has to be a shit time for both of them."

"Oh, I know. I'm just… I mean, if it's really the end, and you know why I'm saying that." She reaches across my desk and taps my desk planner. "They are the drama king and queen. Any woman with her wits would steer clear of Noah on their breaks because, as sure as the sun rises, they'll get back together. But…" Kara points an almond-shaped coral painted nail at me, "if that baby isn't his, then this really could be the end. And Betty Marshall told Marissa that she heard the guy Jocelyn's seeing is moving into the house after Noah moves out. That means it's definitely over."

Noah crashed with Oliver at his ranch house for at least the past month. Once he found out about Jocelyn's affair, to my knowledge, he never slept in their house again. Liam mentioned he'd been showing Noah some of his spec homes that were for sale, but I hadn't heard that he'd found anything.

Liam, Oliver, and Noah are all my good friends. Not only did we go to high school together, and our time at UT overlapped, but they moved back to Whispering Creek after college.

Jocelyn and I were, of course, friends too, but given the volatile nature of her relationship with Noah, and my loyalty to Noah, our friendship was what I'd qualify as a hug-when-you-see-her and leave it at that. Liam's wife, Jada, was one I really did like, but she was a working mom, and she and I grew apart when she had kids. Not because I don't like her; I really do. But a working mother with two young kids doesn't have a lot of free time. Liam tends to be available a lot more than she does, and that little fact should have me seriously questioning my desire to venture into single parenthood. Maybe I should print additional pages and use an orange warning clip for the pitfalls of single parenthood.

"What do you know? I can tell from that face." One perfectly manicured nail draws circles in my direction. "You've got deep thoughts. Are they already getting back together? Did Oliver say something?" Kara taps her nails in quick succession against my desk. "You think I should wait and see what happens? Not approach Noah yet? Is that what you're thinking?"

"Kara." I half-laugh. "Girl. Slow your horses. I would say that no matter what is going on with Noah and Jocelyn… and no, I do not know any details… they're in the middle of a separation. A painful separation. And if you are really interested in Noah, you will be there for him as a friend."

"But he's going to rebound. And what if he falls for his rebound?"

"Kara…." She's so eager. How best to guide her without unearthing Noah's mess?

Noah's been on a rebound fury. All just sex, from what I can tell. His mental space simply isn't open to a relationship.

"Has Oliver said anything?"

"No."

"If you were dating Oliver, you'd say something, right?"

"If I were dating Oliver, I'd tell you."

"You'd better. I tell you everything."

I let out an exasperated sigh. Yes, she does tell me all about the men she dates. But where is this Oliver questioning coming from? "You know he's just a friend."

"Right. That's what I told Annabelle. But, you know," she flaps her hand around, and I don't know, but she's annoying me, so I fold my hands in my lap. "And nothing new on Noah? 'Cause, I know it's kind of crazy, but I really think…well, he's different, you know?"

"He's a good guy," I say. I mean, he's my friend. I'm not married to him, so it's easy for me to say that. "Give him time, Kara. He's not about to leave a twelve-year relationship and jump into another relationship. It's just not going to happen."

She scrunches her glossy lips together. "That makes sense. He's probably going through a lot."

"Yes," I say, nodding to reinforce my agreement.

"You probably know a lot about that." Her face contorts into a pity-face, but before I can get my head around the conversation swivel, she jumps up and heads to the door. "My three o'clock will be here any minute. Need to run to the ladies."

I stare after her, head spinning. I know a lot about what? Break-ups? By the end of the day, she'll be talking about something else or someone else, so there's nothing to do except shake it off.

My phone vibrates, and I check the incoming text.

Oliver: Up for birthday drinks after work? Noah is in tow.

Me: Sure. Where?

Oliver sends me the details, and after finishing all my to-dos, I turn off my lamp and close down my computer. In the salon, one hair dryer blows, finishing up our last client. A woman checking out at the register turns to me, and her eyes widen as she smiles in recognition.

"There's my favorite aesthetician."

Mrs. Margaret Womble was one of my aunt's longtime clients, and she proved her loyalty through the years by sticking with me when I took over the salon. She is also one reason I continue to work on Tuesdays at this location. Mrs. Womble loves having her facials at the beginning of the week. In her navy slacks and pastel silk blouse, she looks like she walked out of the pages of a Talbot's catalog. For years, she'd come in here wearing pumps. But some-time over the last decade she switched those out for flats. Thick gold jewelry decorates her wrists, neck and ears.

"Betty Johnson looks fantastic. And I mean years younger. Are you holding out on me?"

I laugh as her hand falls to my wrist, and I place a hand over hers and squeeze.

"Mrs. Womble, I promise you, I give you the best treatments available."

"But now, is she going to that needle doctor of yours?"

Again, I laugh.

My clients create fantastic terminology. Meena visits my Whispering Creek location two days a week and sees clients in my treatment room while I work at my Austin location. She does the injections I'm not certified to offer, such as Botox and filler injections.

"I'm honestly not sure. But Mrs. Womble, you know I don't treat and tell." There's no society governing what aestheticians can and can't tell, but as a matter of ethics I keep it all close to the vest, giving my clients the confidentiality a therapist would provide.

She leans in after glancing around the space, as if someone might try to hear what she has to say. "I think she had a facelift."

"Well, if she did, and she looks as good as you say she does, then good for her."

Mrs. Womble's spine straightens and her lips purse. But something takes hold within her, and those lips stretch into a cordial smile.

"Well, if you could find out who she used, I'd be in your debt."

"Why don't you just ask her?"

"Well, that might make her feel uncomfortable, don't you think?"

I pat her arm and shake my head while smiling.

"You sneaky dog." Mrs. Womble and I both turn our attention to Kara. She stands at her station holding her phone.

"What?" I ask Kara.

"I was just scrolling through my alerts. And it's someone's birthday." Mrs. Womble's mouth opens slightly, and, resigned, I force a polite smile. "I never go on Facebook, but I do scroll those alerts. Look at you, trying to sneak by without telling us."

I wave dismissively. "When you get to be my age, it's not a big deal."

Mrs. Womble folds her arms over her middle. "Well, when you get to be my age, every year's big."

I roll my eyes. She isn't that old. Maybe sixties or seventies.

"We're going out!" Kara exclaims and claps her palms together.

"Maybe another night? I've already got plans."

"With who?"

"Just meeting up with some friends."

"Oh, my god, are you meeting up with Noah?" Dang it. Me and my mouth.

"Oliver and Liam." I feel Mrs. Womble's eyes on me. "Just for a drink. Not a big deal"

"You're still close with that Duke family?" Mrs. Womble asks.

"Yes. I am."

"I don't know how you do that. When I got divorced, I cut all ties with his family."

Kara's client joins in on the conversation. "Me too. I never keep in touch with my exes. The day we split is the day we say goodbye."

"Really?" Kara asks. She smooths out a section of hair and wraps a curling iron around it. "I'm friends with all my exes."

Of course, Kara generates a new crush monthly. To my way of thinking, they don't qualify as boyfriends, exactly. She'll have someone she seems to be dating exclusively, and then a couple of weeks later she'll be on to someone new. I wish I'd been like her when I was twenty-five. That thought right there punches me in the gut. Twenty-five was fifteen years ago. I mumble something about needing to get work done before closing, but I'm not sure anyone hears me.

"Was she engaged to Sam Duke? The billionaire brother?" Kara's client asks. She can't see me because I am in the hallway, and she probably isn't thinking about how sound carries in an open room with dividers that don't go all the way to the ceiling.

"They weren't engaged," Mrs. Womble answers authoritatively.

"But they were close to it. His momma thought for sure. But now, was she talking about Oliver Duke?"

My eyes close as my hand rests on my office doorframe. *Dang. It.*

"Yeah, they're close friends," Kara answers.

"Just friends?" Mrs. Womble asks. I can't see her, but I'm pretty sure her eyebrows are sitting high above the line of her eyeglass frames right about now.

"Well, you know," Kara answers, in that way she has when she wants to leave implications to the wind. *Jesus, Kara.*

The sound of laughter makes its way down the hall. My legs trudge forward. In the office, I can only hear snippets of conversation.

"She missed the boat. A billionaire. Can you imagine?"

"Maybe…"

"He's so freaking hot."

"Can't blame a girl for trying. But really, two brothers, that's poor taste, if you ask me."

"If it were me, I'd move on. Put that history behind me."

I close the office door and shut down my computer. Kara will close down the salon tonight. I pick up my flowered folder and my pocketbook and head out the back.

Half an hour later, Oliver waves me over to our standard table at Old Town Bar.

"Where's Noah?"

Oliver shrugs. "He bailed. These days, he's about as reliable as the rain. But Liam is gonna make it."

As if called to appear, Liam weaves through the crowd looking dapper as ever in a deep purple suit with a paisley tie.

"Where's Jada?"

"She's picking up the kids from daycare." My chin dips at the expected answer. "Have you seen my kids lately? Shonda starts kindergarten next year."

He pulls out his phone, and I snatch it from him, flipping from photo to photo of an adorable toddler.

"Shonda's lost her baby fat," I moan. He chuckles. "But she's still adorable. So sweet looking. And look at those cheeks on James. I just want to pinch them."

"He wouldn't like that at all. Shonda pinches them all the time, and he wails."

"She's just loving on her younger brother."

"If that's love, I think he could do without."

Oliver leaves to get us beers from the bar while Liam beams like a proud papa. He nudges my arm.

"You want one, you know you do." He winks at me.

"If I had a kid, I couldn't meet up with you guys for beers."

"Why?"

"Where's Jada?"

"Oh, well, get yourself a wife too." I shove his arm, and he chuckles. He removes his suit jacket, rolls up his sleeves, and transforms into a semblance of the college student I used to know. "Nah. It is a lot of work. And this is just an after-work beer. I'll be going home to help her right after this. But Jada understands it's your birthday." There's no point in reminding him it could be a Tuesday and he'd still meet us for drinks after work. "By the way, birthday girl, Jada mentioned she knows someone she'd like to set you up with. Divorced dad. Insta family." He raises those eyebrows and looks at me as if to say I should give it some serious consideration.

"Thanks, Liam, but I don't do blind dates."

"Why not? You know Jada wouldn't do you wrong."

"I stopped doing blind dates circa two thousand and twelve."

Oliver joins us and slides beers across the table.

"I second that," he says. "It's much easier to go onto an app and find someone. You go on a blind date and you gotta explain everything to your friend who set you up."

"Cindy still asks me about you," I say and raise one eyebrow pointedly. I don't even really know her, given she's maybe twelve or thirteen years younger than me, but she still reaches out.

Oliver holds his hand out as if I have presented him with evidence. "See! This is what I'm talking about. I say, sure, I'll go with your friend on New Year's Eve. And half a year later, I'm being asked about going out with her again."

I give Oliver the stink eye, because I am pretty sure he was doing someone else on New Year's Eve.

Oliver continues to text someone. Likely the girl he's been seeing. I haven't pushed him too hard for information, but if he continues being secretive, I sure as hell will. We tell each other everything. Or top line everything.

Liam excuses himself like a dutiful husband, and I pull out my phone to text Noah.

Me to Noah: Sure you're not up for a drink?

There's no response. He could be busy working. He's in the restaurant business, and it's Friday evening.

"Can you stay out for one more round?" Oliver asks.

"I don't know. It's late."

"Come on. It's not that late. One more round, then we'll pick a spot for dinner."

I cock my head, questioning his persistence, but he's already up and heading to the bar. His head is down over his phone, texting away.

I scroll through Instagram, liking everything from everyone, until Oliver returns with three beers.

"You thirsty?"

He just grins. "How've you been since Polly?"

"Huh?" Oliver's a good friend, but he's not one to bring up uncomfortable topics.

"I haven't asked," he says a tad defensively.

"I miss her, but I'm doing good."

"You want a new horse?"

That question makes me laugh. "No. I mean, maybe one day, but for right now..." Right now, what? I want a reprieve from the obligations of caring for a horse, but yet I want to be a single mom? That's about as clear as mud.

Oliver picks up his phone and stands, scanning the crowd. "Back toward the wall. Outside under the lights."

I scan the crowd, searching for Noah. He must be here.

But the smile breaking through the crowd doesn't belong to Noah.

No, it's the youngest Duke. Ian.

Chapter Eight

Sunny

My Fortieth Birthday Surprise

Only, as Ian cuts through the crowd, there's really nothing about him that says little brother. The sleeves of his navy button down oxford are rolled up and tight on his forearms. The fabric stretches across his shoulders. His light brown pants are a cross between jeans and slacks and they fit him just right. His golden-brown strands are brushed back, and a five o'clock shadow strengthens his jawline. There's truly nothing little about this thirtysomething version of Ian Duke.

"Surprise," Oliver says, waving in the direction of his brother.

"And here I thought you were just trying to get me drunk, coercing me into one more beer."

"What is that?" Ian asks as he steps up beside me. He wraps his strong arms around me and lifts me a couple of inches off the ground. "Are we trying to get the birthday girl drunk?"

"Not on beer," Oliver answers. "But I can bring a round of shots over."

"I can't believe you came home. For me," I say to Ian, completely disregarding Oliver. Shots are not on the agenda.

"I'm not going to miss your big day." Ian straddles the bench I've been sitting on with one leg under the table and one leg on the outside, so he's facing me. He lifts his pint, taps it against my glass, and sips.

A single black braided bracelet rests below his watch. It's sexy. It's also the kind of jewelry I'd imagine a woman at some point purchased for him. He sets the glass down and lifts a fist across the table and butts it against Oliver's held out fist.

"I've been a bad friend. MIA for the last few months. There's no way I could miss the big four-oh."

"Let's not use those words." I wrinkle my nose, and he chuckles.

"You don't look it."

Oliver grins. "Yeah, every guy I meet is surprised to learn you're older than me."

I point a finger at Oliver. "Not by much."

He grins. Back in high school, to tell the truth, all of our age differences mattered a lot more. It's not something we think about now at all...except, you know, at the turn of an effing decade. How that happened, I'm not sure.

"You'll be there before you know it," I tell him.

Oliver's two years younger than I am, but he jumped ahead in first grade, whereas I did kindergarten twice. It looked like I might have to do second grade twice, but Patty Duke stepped in. Dad was fighting too many demons at the time to help me with homework. I can only imagine how she knew I needed help. I've always suspected my teacher, Mrs. Taylor, must have told someone the Turner girl was really struggling, and that person told someone, and so on until the tidbit eventually found its way to Patty. Mrs. Duke turned it all around for me.

"What're you planning for your birthday weekend?" Ian asks.

I look to Oliver, who is looking down at his phone. He glances at us and holds the device up. "Noah, man."

"What's he up to?" I ask.

"He's in Austin tonight. Wants me to come out. You guys up for going the rounds tonight? Make your fortieth unforgettable?"

"You mean the college circuit, don't you?" There are a lot of bars around UT that cater to the college crowd. Some hold fond memories, but I aged out of those places a good decade ago. Jeez Louise, it's painful thinking like that, but still… "Noah's hitting on the college crowd?"

"Eh, I don't know if it's strategic. He hangs out a lot with the waitstaff from his restaurants, and they hit those places. You up for it?" Oliver asks with a nonchalance that's typical Oliver.

With a quick shake of my head, I decline. "No. I can't imagine a more depressing place to be on my…." I can't force out the word *fortieth*, so I don't. I chug my beer.

"You go." Ian tilts his beer in his brother's direction. "I've got this one."

Oliver shrugs and tosses the phone down on the wood tabletop. It hits with a *thunk*. "He's a big boy."

"Who's he with? You trust him to Uber?" Ian asks him.

Oliver's index finger scrolls through texts on his phone.

"If you're not sure, just go," Ian says.

"Man, I miss the days when he was with Jocelyn. As sure as shit easier. When he's on the prowl, sometimes you can barely get one beer down before he's ready to get to the next bar." Oliver's complaint rings true. I've shared in that experience.

"You want us to believe you're not prowling right alongside him?" Ian asks.

Oliver looks up and shrugs. "Believe it or not…" He holds his phone up again and taps away. "All right. I'm gonna go."

"You good to drive?" Ian checks.

"Yeah. This is only my second. I'll be fine."

"Did you guys already blow out candles?" Ian asks.

"Candles?" Oliver's expression is classic. Scrunched up face with a what-the-heck-you-talking-about look.

"You didn't order her dessert?" Ian asks with a bewildered shake of the head. "Go. Just go."

Ian waves him on, and after giving me a quick hug, Oliver is on his way. He exits the patio with his trademark cowboy-boot-wearing swagger.

"I suspect he's seeing someone." I raise an eyebrow like I'm a snooping detective, and I want Ian to spill. Which is behavior that is very similar to Kara. That thought churns my stomach.

"Oliver?" Ian lifts his shoulders in a way that says he couldn't care less about his brother's dating life. "Maybe. It's your birthday. Pick a dessert. Let's get you a candle, and you've got to open a present."

"A present? You got me a present?"

"Yes. I got you presents."

"Why?"

"Did I miss something? It's your birthday, right?"

"Yeah, but…why are you in town?"

"Are you trying to be obtuse?" He opens his jacket and pulls out two small, wrapped gifts from his inside pocket. "I haven't been a good friend. And I'm going to change that. Or at least try to."

"Do you want me to open these here?"

"Nah. Let's go back to your place."

On the drive back to my house, I keep checking my mirror, half-expecting Ian's Tesla to disappear from the rearview. But it doesn't. It stays right there.

He's always been a good friend. When my father died, he was the one who waited at the gravesite and drove me home. I'm not sure what he means by being a better friend, but it's possibly something that's going on in his world. Maybe he's the one who needs a friend.

He follows me into the house, and I flip on lights as I kick off my heels.

"Can I get you something to drink?"

He holds up a wine bag. "Already got it." He bypasses me for my kitchen. Drawers open and close.

"Wine opener is in the everything drawer. Small drawer by the dishwasher."

I set my tote bag from work on a kitchen chair and join him, watching as he fills two glasses with red. The two small, wrapped presents sit on top of the folders I brought home from work.

It's been years since anyone gave me a gift on my birthday. Well, no one has since my dad passed. At work, someone might show up with a cake or we'll all go out for drinks. I lift the presents out of the bag and gently set them on the old kitchen table.

"This is one of my favorites from Napa. Let me know if you like it." Ian hands me a glass of red wine, and I swirl the dark, maroon liquid.

"Hhmm. Full-bodied. Robust. It's good. Really good."

"Harrison recommended it. He's a member of their wine club."

"He likes to spend money, doesn't he?"

Ian laughs. The fullness is disarming. He brushes a hand through his hair, messing it all up, and then gives me that boy-next-door grin.

I'm helpless to do anything but grin back.

"Open your presents." He pointedly looks to the gifts and pulls out a chair. It scrapes the linoleum floor as he does so, but the floor is so damaged it doesn't matter.

He sits down, and I set my glass on the table. I carefully open the first present, peeling back the tape slowly so as not to rip the paper.

"Sunny. Come on, now. Don't tell me you're planning on re-using that paper." He smiles over the rim of his wine glass, and my defenses rise.

"It's the planet." But that's not really it. I just don't receive many presents, and care feels like the natural approach.

As I peel back the paper I suck in air. It's a small silver frame, and the photo inside is a gorgeous photograph of Polly. She's galloping in the pasture, but it's not my pasture. It's the pasture by the tree line on the north end of the Dukes' ranch. She's younger, and her ears are forward, and the image captures her just like I always want to remember her.

"Where did you get this?"

"It's a photograph I took of her."

"When?"

"Oh, you'd ridden her over and taken off her tack so you could eat dinner. She was out running wild."

"It's really..." My thumb glides over the smooth glass. "Gorgeous."

My heart softens in my chest. I have plenty of photos of Polly, but none that capture her in her youthful glory, a free spirit running through the wind. My eyes moisten because it's just so thoughtful and sweet.

He shifts in his seat, and if I didn't know better, I'd say he looks a tad uncomfortable. I blink rapidly and shake off that emotional spillage.

"Did you take the photograph of the ranch? The aerial hanging in your apartment?"

"I did." Those amber eyes sparkle in the kitchen light.

"That's gorgeous, too," I tell him.

"Sam rented a helicopter one day. We took it up to get an aerial view. The plan was to take photos for Mom and Dad." He swirls the wine in his glass. "Did that. But Sam framed some for us."

"But there isn't one of those hanging in the ranch house."

"No." He shakes his head, and his eyes almost disappear in a thoughtful squint. "They took their portrait back with them to the beach house." He straightens and tilts the wine glass in the direction of the other present. "One more."

The remaining present is a much smaller box. This one, too, I open slowly. I can't bring myself to rip through it. Presents are too rare. Beneath the bright blue paper is a velvet box. A jewelry box.

"It's not much," Ian blurts.

I flip the lid open, and it's a short gold necklace with a golden sun pendant.

"I saw it and thought of you. If you don't like it, it's from a little jewelry store near my apartment building. Next time you come to Houston, you can trade it and get whatever you want."

"I love it." It's beautiful. And thoughtful. My insides go gooey.

I lift it out of the box and hold it up to my neck. The chair scrapes against the floor as Ian moves to stand. He comes around behind me, lifts my hair, and brushes it over my shoulder. His warm fingers caress my skin. Tingles run freely along my spine.

"There." His palms cover my shoulders, and he gently squeezes.

I turn, and his gaze falls to the necklace. He's so close his energy pulses through me. It's as if he's performing reiki on me, and his heartbeat pulses through my veins, awakening my chakras.

"Looks good. Do you like it?"

I step aside, my fingers clutching the smooth gold charm. "Let me go see." I step into the bathroom and stand on my toes to get a better look in the mirror over the sink. The charm hangs over my clavicle. It's the perfect length and, in truth, it's perfect for me.

When I return to the kitchen, he's holding a folder. *The flowered folder.*

"What is this?"

"It's just…research."

I move to take the folder from him, and he lifts it higher in the air, out of my reach.

"You're looking into IVF?"

"Well, I researched it. My insurance doesn't cover it. Since, you know, I'm single." I still get irked over the unfairness of that bullshit policy. "But I don't know that IVF will be needed. I'll try, you know, the old turkey baster approach."

"You want kids?" Familiar brown eyes wash over me, thoughtfully but without any hint of judgement.

"Yeah, I do." I move to take the folders out of his hands.

He narrows his eyes. "Who's the…"

"Sperm donor?" I ask, since he seems to be at a loss for words.

"Yeah."

"I think I've picked this one." I pull out the paper-clipped papers, and he takes them from me. Like a good friend, he sits back with his wine and studies all the information with a fervent intensity.

Chapter Nine

Ian

Last Year in May

Weekends aren't a part of my regular work routine, but twice a week the hospital schedules me to be on call for emergencies. Orthopedic surgeries are often planned and scheduled, but many are not. Accidents happen.

And, as luck would have it, a three-car collision on Highway 59 happens Sunday afternoon. A text from Sunny saying she was one hour out arrived as a nurse found me and told me I'd need to be on standby. Fortunately, there wasn't much for me to do other than surgically repair a fractured wrist. Still, by the time I scrub out and arrive home, a silent apartment greets me.

I smell citrus. With a deep whiff, I confirm the scent, kick off my shoes, and drop my keys and ID card on the entry table.

"Sunny?" I call.

A brown wicker basket with an oversized white bow sits on my kitchen counter. I peek in the basket and pick up a funny-looking bar of soap. Chunks of lavender and rosemary protrude from the uneven surface. With one sniff, herbs invade my nostrils.

The label on the spray-top bottle reads All-Natural Cleanser. I pull the trigger, and lemony water droplets glisten in the air. A white contraption sits on my counter, plugged into the wall. I lean over it and inhale citrus.

Sunny brought me aromatherapy products. Personally, I prefer disinfectants that are scientifically proven to kill germs and microbes. Besides, there's an argument to be made that the world is better off with minimal use of anti-bacterial disinfectants.

After showering and getting dressed, I call Harrison and ask him to meet me at Jack's. Given he's always up for a night out, it's no surprise he agrees.

"Why didn't you tell me she was singing tonight?" Harrison asks as we approach the lounge. "I would've been there on time."

"I thought I'd be home to drive her." And not that I will admit this to Harrison, but I hadn't decided if I wanted to invite Harrison to join us.

The lounge door opens, and adrenaline spikes as Sunny's sultry voice wraps around me. The light shines down her lithe jean clad form creating a half silhouette, half golden ray effect. The stool she's sitting on is slightly off-center. Her fingers strum her beloved acoustic guitar, and her long, straight, sunbeam hair is tucked behind her ears.

The modest Sunday night crowd sits mesmerized, sipping their beers or cocktails, leaning back in their chairs, entertained.

Harrison and I find a small booth off to the side near the front. Sunny gives a soft, friendly smile in recognition as we pass the stage. She's wearing a tank top with lace along the edges, and her faded denim jeans tuck into her lucky cowboy boots. It's the kind of outfit she wore in high school. Beaded bracelets line her wrists, and the necklace I gave her dangles from her neck. The golden sun pendant glints in the light, and a flush of warmth comes out of nowhere. *She's wearing my necklace.*

"So, how long have you had a crush on your brother's ex?" Harrison's question pulls me back to our booth.

"Don't be ridiculous."

"Yeah. I'm the one being ridiculous." He waves down a waitress and orders us our usual Sunday night elixir.

Sunny finishes her song, and the place breaks out into subdued applause. I blow out a whistle that sounds a lot like a cat call.

She laughs and speaks into the microphone. "Thanks, everyone. That song was called *Merry Go Round* by Kacey Musgraves. It's all about having traditions passed down to you that you don't want to keep. This next one is a bit more fun. It's an adaptation of The Rolling Stones, *Waiting on a Friend.*"

I hold my beer in the air to salute her.

"You're really going to sit there and tell me you don't want to fuck her senseless?" I slam the glass down, and golden ale sloshes onto the table. He can be as crude as he wants, but not with Sunny.

Harrison shrugs off my warning glare. "What? She's hot. I'd fuck her."

Jesus. "She's like a sister to me. Next subject." I knock back a deep swallow and focus on the stage.

"Like a sister. Good to know." He angles his body so he can better watch Sunny. "I bought myself a full membership."

"Isn't that like a million dollars?" Harrison's partner gave him two passes, and he took me once. Something I'm sure the partners didn't appreciate. A place like that tries to limit the male attendees to those who pay.

"It is. And I'm on a payment plan, so I'm limited as to how many guests I can bring, at least, you know, straight men. But I'm stoked. It's the best way on the planet to blow off steam. Healthier than this stuff." He holds up his glass of bourbon.

"Is that where you went last night?"

"Believe it or not, they're closed most Saturdays. But Friday night when your lame ass was working, that's where I was."

I run a hand over my face and then through my hair, thinking back over Friday night in the ER. The place had been a madhouse. And they'd had a newbie nurse in admissions.

"If you picked plastics, you'd never have to work weekends."

"And like my brother likes to tell me from time to time, if I'd picked gynecology, I could look at tits and ass all day."

"So, you're finally in agreement you picked poorly?"

Despite my annoyance with Harrison, a grin breaks out, and I just shake my head. "I like my career just fine." I down another swallow of beer and add as an aside, "And I sure as hell wouldn't pick gynecology in this state."

Harrison disregards my comment. He's fully aware of what I'm referencing, and there's no point in digging into it when we're aiming to relax.

Sunny sings about how she's been waiting for a friend, and I wish I hadn't brought Harrison. If given a choice, I'd listen to her soulful tunes all night, uninterrupted.

"I have to tell ya man, you're not looking at her the way a man looks at his sister."

God, he has a one-track mind.

"I don't get it. Why aren't you going for her?"

I tear my gaze away from Sunny. Harrison looks genuinely puzzled. He's not trying to be a jerk; it just comes naturally to the guy. "She's my brother's ex," I answer. He knows this.

"Wife?"

"Girlfriend."

"Which brother was that again?"

"Sam."

"He's been married as long as I can remember. Olivia, right?" Harrison scratches at his jaw, looking thoughtful, but his gaze stays fixed on Sunny.

"He's married to Olivia. Now. But Sam and Sandra were together in high school and college."

"And how long ago was that?"

I shrug and let my gaze fall back on the golden blonde.

"Dude. You can go for her now, you know?"

It's not that simple. And if she gets her way, she'll be pregnant soon. Hell, she could be pregnant right now.

Sunny ends her song and speaks into the microphone. "That's it for me, folks. I really appreciate you all listening." Subdued sporadic clapping sounds in fits and bursts. "Shane Wilcox is up next, and I hope you're as good to him as you were to me. Thank you all. And if you'd like for John to put me on the roster again, be sure to ask for Sandra Turner." She places her hand to her lips and blows out a kiss to the audience. The action wins another round of applause and even a couple of catcalls from the back.

She steps down from the stage and strides straight to our booth. She leans across the bench and gives Harrison a hug, then slides in next to me.

"Great show," I say.

"You made it for two songs." Her smile is teasing, but guilt slices.

"Three-car collision." I search her expression, hoping for understanding. I'm not like others. I don't have a choice when work calls.

Her light arched brows draw together and her lips tighten. "Oh, no. Everyone okay?"

"They will be." To my knowledge, they will all be okay. My patient will eventually be fine, but she may set off security alarms for the rest of her life.

"So, Sandra or Sunny?" Harrison butts in.

"Oh, Ian's the only one who calls me Sunny. Everyone else calls me Sandra."

Harrison narrows his eyes, and I prepare for the inquisition.

"Why do you call her Sunny?"

"Yeah, why do you call me Sunny?" She seconds, and her nose wrinkles up in that adorable way she has when she's both teasing and asking.

"Apropos, I guess." There's not a chance in hell I'll admit that back when I was crushing hard, it used to feel like the sun came out whenever she entered a room. Harrison, of all people, would never let me live down the cheese in that sentiment.

"Blonde?" Harrison guesses.

"Exactly," I say. "Sunny, what would you like to drink?"

"Honestly, I'm exhausted. And I drank enough water before the show that I might float out of here if I drink more." Water. Hmm. The turkey baster approach might have worked.

The guy on stage begins singing. We're sitting a mite too close to the amplifier.

"What song is that?" I ask Sunny, raising my voice to a near shout.

"Oh, he sings all his own work."

Harrison lifts his arm and checks the time. "I know you two kids don't have work tomorrow, but I do. I'm gonna head on out."

I lean down so my lips are closer to her ear. "You want to stay, or you ready to call it a night?"

"I'd love to get home and get comfy."

"Looks like we'll head out with you," I tell Harrison. His sophomoric smirk says plenty, but I ignore him.

Sunny steps backstage to collect her guitar and to thank John, then we all head out together. Harrison jumps into his Uber, and after a brief discussion, we agree to walk the couple of blocks back to my place.

My fingers graze hers as we stride side by side down the sidewalk. The touch is jarring and possibly overly friendly, so I shove my hand into my pants pocket.

"I really loved listening to you tonight," I tell her. She cocks her head, and a ghost of a frown plays across her glossy lips.

She bumps her arm against mine. "You should really play again.

We could play a duet at Jack's."

"Maybe. I'd have to re-learn everything." It's been a long time since high school.

"You can't be all work. You've got to have some downtime."

"Playing for others was never really my thing." I glance sideways at her. She'd always been the one who treasured time on stage. She got a thrill out of it. She won the school talent show her senior year.

"You loved to play," she insists, pushing up against me again. My hands remain firmly ensconced in my pants. Her guitar case bumps against the back of my legs.

My guitar interest stemmed entirely from spending time with Sunny. I'd been a young, horny teen stoked to spend time with the college girl with perfect tits. I only played for her.

"What about you?" She obviously loved the stage and the mic. "You could do more of this."

"It's fun. It's not a career or anything."

"So, it's not something you'd move to Houston for?"

She laughs hard. Too hard. I pause, waiting for her so we can continue down the quiet Houston streets.

"Yeah. Like I'd move for the twenty bucks he paid me." I flinch. Twenty dollars seems like resident pay, an hourly pay so low some liken it to indentured servitude. I'd have thought she'd make more. "No, this is fun, but–"

"Are you pregnant?"

Her gaze falls to the ground, and she kicks a loose rock. "No. Didn't take." She lifts those hopeful blue eyes, and the ends of her lips turn up into a forced smile. "It's not guaranteed. At my age…"

Her mouth continues moving, but I absorb only bits and pieces. I shouldn't be shocked. I did a little research after I saw her last. At her age, pregnancy isn't guaranteed.

The kicker is Sunny would make a great mom. It hadn't surprised me to learn she wanted kids. I guess when she was doing the foster care thing, I understood that. What surprises me is the unwanted reality time forces down on us. In my head, Sunny has all the time in the world. I still see her as that college girl I obsessed over, but her anatomy continues aging. But still…

"You're sure you want to be a single mother?" It's a question I've been mulling over since I saw her last. My colleagues seem to really struggle balancing parenthood, marriage, and careers.

"I mean, that's where I am." She raises her shoulders and holds out her hands like a ray of sunshine. Why would something as silly as not having a partner get in her way? That's Sunny. She'll make the best of what she has… always. "Lots of people do it."

I nod, absorbing her expected words. She is right. I work with quite a few single parents, people with demanding jobs who make it all work. Modern families come in all flavors and varieties. Her child will be a lucky kid. And one way or another, she's going to get that kid.

I remove one hand from my pants pocket and wrap an arm around Sunny's shoulder, pulling her against me as we approach my apartment.

"It's all going to work out," I tell her, not that I need to. She's an optimist.

Back at my apartment, she heads into the guest room and comes out wearing loose cotton pajama pants and an old, ratty UT sweatshirt. We sit on the sofa, and she picks up the remote, flipping through channels with it on mute. I reach for her socked feet and pull them up into my lap.

There's one thought that's been going back and forth in my mind. Her sperm donor is someone she doesn't know, an absolute stranger. And, to some extent, that makes sense. But would there be advantages to it being someone she knows?

I see the unexpected happen all the time. Statistically, Sunny should exceed the mortality average. But accidents happen. Wrecks. Falls. The body fails. The only family she has is an elderly aunt in Washington State.

"Would you consider…maybe…letting me be your sperm

donor?"

Those glossy pink lips form an open-mouthed gape. She thinks I've lost my mind. And the analytical portion of my psyche agrees with her. Parenthood isn't something I desire. I do not envy my colleagues with children. No, I've always been grateful I didn't have a neglected family sitting back at home. I've been grateful I don't have to carry that guilt.

Her facial expression softens from bewilderment to warm appreciation. I half-expect the words "bless your heart" to fall from her lips. She has this way of not taking me seriously that used to hurt.

"Ian, you are such a sweetheart. But—"

"But nothing. It's a consideration. Rather than jumping into this with a random sperm donor…Think about it, Sunny. I have. I've been thinking about it ever since your birthday. You know my family. Hell, you're a part of my family. Your child would have grandparents who loved it like crazy."

"Oh, my god. Now you've lost your mind. Can you imagine? I could never tell your parents."

"Really, Sandra?" My use of her real name grabs her attention. "You think you're going to hide a pregnancy?"

"Well, no. When the time comes, I'll tell them I did artificial insemination with an anonymous donor."

I breathe in deeply to control a stir of frustration. I don't have the right to get frustrated. I am simply proposing an alternative route for her consideration.

The truth is, my parents will be all over her baby no matter who the father is. They love Sunny. They'll be so thrilled to have a grandchild in Texas they'll probably move back to the ranch, or at least move back for most of the year. Mom will insist on helping her out, especially given she'll be a single mom.

History would repeat itself. Mom insisted on helping Sunny's dad out, because he'd been a single dad. People said all kinds of things about Sunny's dad. I'm not sure how much was true, but he drank a lot. Mom didn't care. She said people didn't know what they were talking about, and he was a good man who needed good neighbors.

"I'd be honored if you would consider me. We're friends. I'd like to do this for you. That sits better with me than a stranger."

Sunny chews on the corner of her lip. I can practically see her considering the future. And then her nose crinkles, and those eyes sparkle, and I brace myself because she's going to tell me I'm a fool. And I probably am.

"Think about what you're saying, Ian. One day, you're going to find the love of your life, a woman who means everything to you, and are you going to want to tell her that there's another child out there that's not hers? Oh, and that child lives down the road from your parents and is in the mix of all the grandbabies?" She waves her hand in the air. "No. I appreciate your offer. I do. You've always been the sweetest. But no. That's crazy."

"Sandra." My doctor voice comes through, probably because I need to mask the mental gymnastics leapfrogging strange emotions. "Please think about it. You can still tell people the father is anonymous. But I have no intention of getting married or having a baby. My hours are not conducive to family life. Parenthood is purposefully absent from my life plan. But, as you go through this process, I can be a supportive friend. I mean, no matter who you choose, I'll be a supportive friend. But life can be full of the unexpected." I think about what I'm really saying. Does it matter whose sperm impregnates her? No, it doesn't. If something happens to Sunny, I'd still step in. If she needs me, I'll be there for her.

I should do more research.

"Thank you, Ian. I do appreciate your offer." Her voice, syrupy sweet, wraps around me as I breathe in her light floral fragrance. Her lips brush the side of my cheek, blindsiding me with the lightest of touches, igniting heat and hope, until she murmurs, "You're a good friend."

Chapter Ten

Ian

Last Year in May

The sun peeks over the trees in Hermann Park. The humidity lies dormant this early, and the city has scarcely begun to stir. My feet pound the pavement. My lungs burn. Thoughts and emotions coalesce.

Relationships among my medical peers do not have a high success rate. At least, in medical school and residency I heard about more splits than unions. About half the surgeons I look up to are divorced.

It's one of the reasons I've never invested time into a relationship. Chances are it will end. And time is the most valuable asset I possess.

I've been exploring spine fellowships and am in the process of applying to one in Minnesota and one in New York, as well as one here in Texas. Fellowships are competitive, and chances are great I will not have a choice in location.

I might want to offer Sunny my DNA, but realistically, I won't be present to help her if she needs it.

Sunny wants to be a single mother. She claims she doesn't need or want a man in her life. And there's no reason to not believe her.

She'll be an exceptional mother. I wouldn't be an acceptable father. I could never live up to my dad. Sam Senior never missed a single event in his sons' lives. He joined us at the dinner table for every single meal. Most mornings, he woke us up. When I think about what a father should be, of what a good father is, I think of my dad, and I'll never have that kind of availability.

Sure, I can continue being Sunny's friend. Call her on the phone or check in via text. We've been friends our entire lives.

Sunny is practically a Duke family member. I wasn't bullshitting her when I said my parents would treat her kid like a grandchild. It won't matter who the father is.

But is there a reason to not give it Duke DNA? I'm not the most fantastic candidate, but I can give more than those anonymous sperm donors.

She'd never want anyone to know. She'd be mortified if it got out that her anonymous donor was her ex-boyfriend's younger brother. But wouldn't she feel better knowing the dad? When her child grows up playing with Oliver's kids and being treated like a family member, wouldn't she feel better if she knew the child's biological connection?

Sunny worries too much about what other people think. She's always been like that. People used to talk about her dad, and it embarrassed her. She said nothing to me, but I remember hearing stories. I overheard Sam talking to Mom. He'd wanted to protect her, and I'd silently rooted for him to do so.

With this kind of situation, keeping it under wraps would be easy. I live in Houston. Out of sight, out of mind to that closed-minded small town. Whether it's my baby or an anonymous donor, people are gonna talk. But her answer of an anonymous donor will settle the discussion. Although I'd imagine rumors will start. No matter what, who, or how. People in our neck of the woods gotta have something to talk about. I'm so damn glad to be out of that town.

Of course, Sunny isn't one to focus on the negative. She's not a glass half empty kind of girl. But, without her saying it, it's clear her biggest concern, much bigger than what people will say, is that it won't happen. She tried once; it didn't take.

It could take a lot of tries. Even with IVF, there's no guarantee. I wonder if she's visited a fertility clinic. If she's checked her estrogen levels or considered any other potential issues. When it comes to fertility, I'm not a subject matter expert.

One thing I can do, as a friend, is connect her with the best medical professionals, even if that means getting her out of state, and help her weed through research. Take a specific interest in helping her dream of motherhood become a reality.

As I pause at a sidewalk, stretching a calf while I wait for the pedestrian crosswalk light to turn, a memory from med school hits me. There was a study. Harrison found it. Of course, he did. Back then he was the king of sophomoric humor. But the study concluded fertility rates increase when orgasm is achieved.

Now, there were all kinds of issues with the study. For one, the study was one hundred percent dependent on self-reported survey data. Harrison made his normal cracks about it.

I wonder if Sunny would laugh if I told her about it. Probably not. The study might convince her that her sperm in a cup approach won't ever take. It's not like she could try the real thing with one of those donors from the clinic.

My thoughts ramble on as I re-enter my apartment with a

sweat-soaked shirt and achy muscles from pounding the sidewalks. After toeing off my running shoes and heading down the hall, I halt, slack-jawed.

The morning sun reflects off Sunny's golden strands and cast a halo around her. Coffee mug in hand, she's taking in the sunrise in a tight, cropped pajama top and loose, low-slung pajama pants, exposing a smooth, creamy, slim waist.

When she turns, her pale pink lips slowly blossom into a warm, from-the-heart smile. Her blue eyes stun beneath barely-there light eyebrows.

"So, you go running like that?"

I glance down at my running shorts and white ankle socks. The hand with my balled up wet shirt shifts, holding it away in case she smells it, but her gaze remains locked on my midriff.

"Took my shoes off at the door." Sunny's tongue traces her top lip. "And my shirt got wet."

She blinks rapidly, as if waking up, and gestures to the coffeepot. "Would you like coffee?"

"Already had some. Thanks, though." I lean against the wall, watching as color floods her cheeks. Is she flustered because of me? If this buzz of attraction is mutual, then I might have a fantastic proposition for her.

"Don't you have work?" She steps past me into the kitchen, grabs a kitchen towel, and wipes away at nothing while still holding that coffee mug in one hand.

"No. Like I told you yesterday, I worked the weekend and didn't schedule any surgeries today. You said you were coming to visit. I'll go in this afternoon to check on a few patients who are recovering." Her attention remains on the dish towel. "I'm going to go shower."

She nods, and her hand stills.

I force myself down the hall, leaving her to her thoughts and whatever flustered her.

In the shower, I lather up with the minty body soap she brought and afterwards apply a woodsy smelling lotion. If I stink now, it'll be her fault.

But what did that blush mean? Was it a blush? Her cheeks bore as much color as on New Year's. We'd been dancing then, both of us hot and sweaty. But that kiss had been some kind of hot, too. I'd brushed it off as a New Year's one-off. Assumed she didn't think twice about it. That it had meant more to me because she'd always played a starring role in my fantasies.

And yeah, that had to have been it. Sunny Turner isn't interested in me. She probably didn't feel comfortable with a smelly, half-naked man in the kitchen. Discomfort doesn't equal attraction.

Oliver mentioned a few years ago that he thought Sunny still wasn't over Sam. The fact she refuses to be in the same room with him lends credence to his theory. Mom's hinted that she shares Ollie's theory.

Her heart might belong to my older brother, but her attention definitely focused on my body. In biology classes, they cover attraction in medical terms. While literature describes it as a force akin to gravity, science explains it as an increased blood flow to the ventral segmental area of the brain, or the VTA. When ignited, the VTA produces dopamine, also known as the "feel good" neurotransmitter.

I don't require a brain scan to confirm my attraction to Sunny. She's the first girl I jerked off to. Yet another piece of personal history I plan to take to my grave. But now, so many years later, is it possible my presence is igniting her VTA? Probably not, but all things considered, the question warrants an observational test.

I wrap a white towel around my waist, brush my teeth, and run a comb through my wet hair. My wet hair looks like I applied too much hair gel, so I grab a towel, run it vigorously over my head, then use my fingers to put it back into a semblance of order. Then I exit the bathroom and cross the hall to the guest room.

She sits on the narrow twin bed with a magazine spread out. Those blue eyes travel from my face to my chest, then dive a little lower. *Interesting.*

"Can I take you out to breakfast? It's Monday morning, so my favorite place won't be packed."

"Sure."

I stroll over, mindful of the wrapped towel, and sit near her. The mattress sinks with my weight, and her torso leans in my direction. I could be mistaken, but I suspect her chest is rising and falling more rapidly. A light glow of color blossoms across her cheeks.

"What're you doing in here?"

"Just reading."

"About?"

She closes the magazine, and those blue eyes settle on my abdomen. "How do you have time to work out?"

I half-laugh. But damn if I'm not socked with a touch of euphoria. My little observational experiment indicates an active VTA in my proximity. "I find working out makes everything sharper and improves my focus. For a surgeon, that's important. So, I make time. I schedule it."

She nods, all doe-eyed, and those top teeth sink into her lower lip. My cock twitches below my towel.

"You obviously work out, too."

"Well, I mean, until recently, I had a barn to take care of. Still have a lot of grass to cut and yard work to do."

"Hhmmm." The thin cotton of her pajama top hints at the shape of her areolas with the darker shade showing through.

"And I do yoga and Pilates. We offer those classes in my Austin location. So..." She tilts her head like that answers everything. A loose strand crosses her cheekbone, and I brush it away with my thumb.

"Why do you want a child?"

She leans back on her arms, palms flattened behind her,

creating space between us. "It probably seems silly. Especially to someone who doesn't want children. But I've always wanted to be a mother. It's just, something…" She pushes up and leans over her legs, bent at the waist, gaze dropped to the floor. "Who knows? Maybe because I didn't really have a mom, I focus on it more. My favorite pretend game growing up was with my babydolls." She clucks her tongue. "You'd think the craving would diminish the older I got, but it's only intensified. Maybe it's hormonal. After Henry and now Polly… I just want to try. If it doesn't happen, I'll be okay. I'll survive. But I want to try."

"Polly was like your baby." She nods. I try to register Henry. The name sits on the fringe of my brain, familiar, but… "And Henry?"

"The little boy I took care of." That's right. Mom mentioned him. She'd become a foster parent.

"I have all this love inside me, and I want to give it to someone. It's lonely in that house by myself." She sits straighter and smiles, but the smile doesn't fit. She's attempting to be her upbeat self, but her glassy blues undermine her effort.

"Being lonely probably isn't the best reason to have a child." I don't mean it as a slight to her. To be honest, I find it difficult to comprehend why anyone would want to have a child. It's so much responsibility.

"I'm not lonely." The indignation in her expression effectively scolds me. "That's not what I meant. I decided years ago I'm better off without a man. And I mean it. Don't look at me like that, Ian. I mean it. Really. And, you know, a child might not be in the cards for me. It's not a done deal. I waited to the point that it might not even be possible. I don't really know. But I just want to try. Deep in here." She flattens her palm against her breastbone. "I feel a need. I can't really describe it. But it's like… it's like my soul is speaking to me and telling me that this is the time for me to try. That there's someone I haven't met yet who will be the most important thing in the world to me, and I'll be the most important thing in the world to her. But only if I try." She falls back on the bed and places the back of her hand over her eyes. "You probably think I'm crazy. Talking about the soul doesn't jibe with your analytical mind."

"Sunny, I understand." I wrap my hand over the curve of her thigh to assure her.

"Really?"

"Sure. A similar perspective isn't required for understanding." I squeeze her knee. "Listen to me, and then I'm going to go get dressed. You don't need to respond. But I want you to give what I say consideration, okay?"

She lifts her hand off her face and looks me over. Her gaze falls to my chest, then lifts quickly back to my face. I purposefully keep my stoic doctor face on and refuse to smirk.

"I've been thinking nonstop about this. Ever since you said the first donor didn't take. Well, maybe even before then. I want to be the father of your child. I want to give this to you. It would be an honor to give this to you. And if you want me to pose as a friend, as an uncle, or whatever you choose, I'm good with that. I can be there with you every step of the way. Through the pregnancy—"

"I might not get pregnant."

"Through it all, I can be there for you. Through the difficulties and the uncertainty. I can promise you no one will comb through the medical aspects more thoroughly than me. And if you want to it to be a secret, I'll take it to the grave." She doesn't know exactly how good I am at keeping secrets. "Just promise me you will give it consideration."

She slowly nods, and I rise from the bed. That conversation felt heavier than I intended, and somehow, by saying the words out loud, the truth in them reverberates through me like a punch to the gut.

I entered the guest room with a towel wrapped around my waist and a juvenile curiosity about whether Sunny found me attractive. Yes, I want to help my friend. But mostly, I was curious. My teen self is inquisitive.

But as I exit the guest room, the pressure in my chest drives home the truth. I really want this. If she's going to have a baby, I want it to be mine with a bone-deep desire.

But there's no point in delving into it further. I put it all out there for her consideration, and the decision is hers.

Chapter Eleven

Sandra

Last Year in June

My thumb grazes Paul Rudd's messy hair, which strikes me as similar to Ian's. Only Ian's is slightly longer on top and flaunts golden highlights. *People Magazine* has Paul Rudd in a leather jacket. It's an old issue from last November. Just one of the many dog-eared copies lying around the salon.

Paul's hot, but I bet if they had a photo of him shirtless, he wouldn't rank anywhere close to Ian. A sweaty, shirtless Ian with low-slung gym shorts. Gah. What a beautifully proportioned body. Lean and toned. A vision of my fingers trailing the dips and valleys springs up. That light sprinkling of dark tendrils below his belly button that trails lower…I lift the magazine to fan myself. Jesus, I might be going through early menopause.

It's been one week since my visit to Houston. Flashes of sweaty Ian haunt me. Well, the images rotate between sweaty, shirtless Ian and night club Ian. And then sometimes those images blend with our New Year's kiss, that slow, drugging kiss that tuned out everyone and everything. A kiss that left me gasping for air and had my heart beating double-time.

God, talk about the little brother all grown up. I mean, I'd known he had matured into an attractive person, but I hadn't *known*.

Of course, Ian does his thirties right. He's a fitness disciple, and his dedication shows in all the right places. He isn't overly muscular. He's what I would describe as *fine*. Toned biceps, pecs with shape but that aren't bigger than most women's breasts, and a washboard stomach fit for a magazine. His forearm muscles flex with the slightest movement, probably because surgeons need forearm strength to hold surgical tools for hours on end. As a matter of course, one would expect those talented hands and long fingers to wield a certain precision.

And that train of thought is precisely why I need to switch magazines. I pick up this week's *US Weekly* and flip to stars with lives like mine. They always look washed out and pudgy. The fact my brain short-circuits to visions of Ian is proof-positive I need to go with an anonymous donor. His volunteering to be my baby daddy has somehow shifted my sex drive into high gear and is pumping all kinds of hormones through my body that are playing tricks on my brain. And that can be problematic for our friendship. Not to mention, for my sanity.

"Whatcha reading? Is it that the article about how the Brits hate Meghan Markle?"

I glance down at the magazine laying across my lap, open to a spread of an unrecognizable reality star pushing a shopping cart.

"No, I'm just wondering if this photo is staged or if Taylor Swift really buys her own groceries." I close the magazine and slip it below the *People*.

The client getting her highlights done looks up from her

phone. "I don't know why they hate Meghan Markle so much. She's gorgeous."

"It's that Oprah interview. Pissed 'em all off." Kara sets the timer on the counter, asks her client if she needs anything, and sets about cleaning her area. "Have you heard anything more about Noah and Jocelyn?"

I'm pretty sure Kara's question is directed at me, but her client answers.

"Only that the guy she cheated on him with is Hispanic. He works with her, and he's younger. And get this. He reports to her." Her eyebrows lift emphatically. It's the this-is-juicy- shit-and-I've-got-all-the-info look.

Kara grins. "Go, Jocelyn."

Her client goes slack-jawed. "How can you say that? She cheated."

"Yeah, but it's about time women started banging their underlings."

I open a *Vogue* and zone in on a moisturizer that minimizes wrinkles within four weeks of usage.

"Kara, you are bad."

"Just telling it like it is." Kara grips the broom and sasses her way around the chair. "My neighbor across the street. He cheated on his wife with some assistant. And my neighbor farther down the street... let me tell you. That baby don't look a damn thing like it's supposed daddy."

"Well, now, doesn't that mean the mother cheated?"

"Yeah, but I guess my point is that cheaters are all around, and it feels a little better when it's the woman who bangs the assistant."

"What?" The question forces its way out. I don't even want to be a part of this conversation.

The client laughs, and then in a full-on southern drawl, goes on to reprimand her beautician. "Kara, darlin', it's horrible. So sad. My heart goes out to all those people and what they're goin' through."

My phone rings. Kara's eagle eyes narrow as she hones in on my phone screen.

"I'm going to go in the back," I tell her before swiping and answering. "Hi, Patty."

"Sandra, how're you doing, sweetheart?"

"Oh, I'm good. How's the beach?"

"Good, good. I know you're at work, dear, and I don't want to take up much of your time, but I wanted to see if I could ask you a favor."

"Oh, of course."

"I bought a couple of cakes and some casseroles from Henrietta. You know, she lives on Tapioca, in that cute little pink and gray Victorian?"

"Yes, I know where she lives." Henrietta is semi-retired, but she bakes cakes and sells them from her home.

"Would you mind picking them up and dropping my order by the house? Ollie said he'd take it to Noah, but I don't think he'll remember. And it's kind of on your way."

"Of course. No problem."

"I've been ordering from places that will deliver, but I feel like they're all frozen, and I think Noah could probably do with something fresh."

"That's so sweet of you."

"Well, you know, I don't live there full-time anymore, but I still care about all of you."

When our call ends, I re-emerge from my office with a smile on my face. I love Patty Duke.

"I think it's so great you are still so close to your ex's family. A little weird, but it's great." Kara's comment stuns, and all I can do is look at her. There's really no response to that.

"Was that Patty Duke?" her client asks, stopping me in my tracks. I don't even know the woman in the chair, but she pieced together from that conversation who I'd been talking to?

"Yes, ma'am," I respond in my most polite southern dialect.

"How is she?"

"Doin' good."

Bianca, our stylist-in-training—meaning she mainly washes hair, runs the register, and answers the phones—pipes in. "I heard Ian is in town."

Her statement confuses me. "Ian who?"

"The surgeon." She looks at me like I've asked for mayo on my fries. "The youngest brother."

"Ian Duke is in town?"

"Yeah. Marley saw him in the parking lot at the Dollar General."

All right. This is a case of mistaken identity. "He lives in Houston." I state it like that proves she has her information wrong.

"You're still friends with him, right?" Kara asks. "You're friends with the whole family. But you and Sam don't speak?"

All the women stare at me, and it feels like I'm a performer and there's a spotlight over my head. "Sam and I still speak. I just don't see him often. He lives in Connecticut."

"It's gotta be hard," Kara says as her face morphs into the pity face. The timer beeps, and she lifts a flap of foil to check the color.

I stand there, flustered, torn between clarifying exactly what she means or just letting the sleeping dog lie.

"There he is. Told you," Bianca says then leans over the trashcan and promptly spits out a piece of gum.

I can't stop staring at Kara. What, exactly, is so hard that I deserve the pity face?

The salon door opens, and the man of the hour strides straight to me, completely ignoring the other women who are all gaping as if he sprung from the pages of *GQ*.

"Hey. You guys close soon?" he asks.

"Yeah, we close at five. What're you doing in town?"

"Had a meeting in Austin. Figured I'd stay in town for the night. You don't have work tomorrow, right?"

"We're closed on Sunday and Monday." The wheels churning in

Kara's brain are so loud I can't even look her way. "Did you come to check on Noah?"

Ian's brow crinkles. No one speaks, because everyone is listening to us. He nods as he looks in Kara's direction, the first sign he's aware there are others in the room.

"That's really so sweet of you. Since you're home, can you run an errand for your mother?"

"My mom?" he asks as I gently guide him out of the salon and to his car.

"Yes, she called. She needs something picked up."

"Well, I wanted to see if I could talk you into dinner."

I glance back at the salon. The door is closed. No one can hear, but they might be able to read lips.

"Dinner?"

"The meal at the end of the day?"

"You realize that every single one of those women is going to be talking about you coming into the salon?" How can he waltz into my place of work? Doesn't he realize there will be theories circulating all over Whispering Creek before nightfall?

"What would they talk about?" Before I can state the obvious, he adds, "And who cares?" Ian is right, of course. People can say whatever they want. Words will never hurt me. I get all that. I understand it. But understanding it and falling in behind it are two different things. "We're friends, Sandra. Just tell them we're friends."

Right. My brain sometimes completes unorchestrated flips. Of course, he is right. I shouldn't care what people say, and the truth is we're just friends.

"Now what errand do I need to run before dinner?"

"Huh?" He looks at me like I'm a dull knife, and only then do I get his question. I wave my hand dismissively. "Oh, I'll do it. And I have to take it by the ranch house. Is that where you're staying?"

"Yeah."

"Well, I'll see you then."

He glances back at the salon. The setting sun shines against the glass, and you can't really see inside, but I'd bet money those women are all watching us.

"Should we give them something to talk about?" He leans down, as if going in for a kiss. My hand flattens against his chest, which is remarkably firm, as expected, and push him back.

"Ian." I glare, and he just chuckles.

"I'll see you soon," he says at the same time I say, "See you later."

The moment I step into the salon, Kara asks, "What was that about?"

"Nothing."

I am seconds away from ripping into her for what she is implying with her facial expression, when she asks, "Is Noah taking everything really hard? Are you all worried about him?"

Jeez Louise. "He had a meeting with a doctor. You just heard him tell you that." I walk away, shaking my head, acting like she is a looney tune with a one-track mind. Even though, in reality, I seem to recall that's the excuse I pushed out there when he first walked in.

As I venture through the salon to my office, the client whose name I don't know says, "I heard Noah is taking it really hard."

Lordy. Yeah, he's taking it so hard he's slept with half of Austin. Not that I will share his secrets with any of these women.

After closing up the salon and stopping by Henrietta's, my car winds around the packed dirt road I know almost as well as my own. Lights stream over the grassy back yard, so I walk around the side of the house to the screened-in back porch.

Ian jumps up as I approach and lifts Henrietta's cake box from my arms.

"I brought home takeout for us."

"This is for Noah. Oliver is supposed to take it to him. It's from your mom." He carries it into the kitchen, and I follow along. "Where's Oliver?"

"Saturday night. He's out." That's right. The guys mentioned going out. Ian crosses his arms across his taut chest. His button-down Oxford fits snugly along the shoulders but otherwise conceals the muscular lines of his arms and chest that I ogled like a schoolgirl back in Houston.

"Did you have time to consider your options?"

I back away and pull out a kitchen chair.

Chapter Twelve

Ian

Last Year in June

Sunny crosses her long, jean-clad leg and flexes her ankle, sending the pointed end of her tan high heel in my direction. Her white blouse beneath a loose blazer and matching heels gives off a casual business vibe. Two long gold necklaces adorn her chest, and the pendant on one dips between her breasts. The necklace I gave her glimmers in the light. Straight, silky-smooth locks cascade down her shoulders, and her makeup artfully highlights her cornflower blue irises.

The woman sitting in my parents' kitchen chair represents the grown-up version of the teenage girl I once lusted after.

I lean against the counter and cross my arms, waiting for whatever serious conversation she wants to have. And yes, having a child together deserves a serious conversation.

I'd like to think I'm preferable to an anonymous donor. If I vow to keep our arrangement secret, there really shouldn't be an issue.

I count Sunny as one of my closest friends. I would be honored to do this for her. Admittedly, unlike myself, she has an extensive social circle. The possibility exists that within her circle of friends someone else more fitting exists.

When I threw myself into med school and residency, she remained in our hometown, fostering friendships. But, to my knowledge, the only other guy she is close friends with is my brother Oliver. He crossed my mind as a potential donor, but he would likely settle down with someone. He's already been engaged once. And Sunny referenced the future-wife scenario as a concern. And in Oliver's case, he lives down the road from her. There's no way Oliver is ever leaving this ranch.

I live three hours away. I could be completely absent from the child's life if she wanted, or I could be there to assist periodically. Financial and emotional support are elements I could provide from any location.

She mentioned worrying I would marry and my wife wouldn't like this arrangement, but a wife isn't something she has to worry about with me. I've seen enough relationships fizzle and die, a sort of collateral damage from the time-intensive job. Relationships that are constantly placed in lower priority status simply don't thrive. And the life on the operating table will always be my highest priority. I took an oath.

"Ian," she says, but the tone and her apologetic smile say it all, "I am so touched you want to give me this." A chill falls upon my hands, and I shove them in my pockets for warmth. "I truly appreciate your offer. It's incredibly sweet of you. But it's too much to ask, and it's just not a good idea."

"I think you're missing one important point here." She tilts her head, observing me. "I want to do this. I really want to do this for you."

"But I'm not looking for a man to step into the father role. I want to do this on my own."

"There are contracts for these arrangements. You can stipulate exactly what interaction you want me to have with the child. You can have full parental rights. No one needs to ever know who the father is. You can tell everyone you chose an anonymous donor. But should health problems arise in the future, you'll know the family personally."

"Health problems?"

"You never know. The baby might need a blood donor or a kidney."

She waves her hand dismissively, as if I'm being ridiculous.

"You may think I'm being an extremist, but I'm not." The unexpected happens every single day.

"Ian," Sunny scolds, "you don't want to be a parent. You told me so."

"True. I can't be the traditional dad." My dad spent time with me every single day. Ate dinner with me every day too. That's not the life I chose. "But you're saying that's not what you want. In this situation, I'm the best of all worlds. We're close. We've been friends pretty much our whole lives. You love my family, and my family loves you. And I will let you completely call the shots. You dictate how you want to structure the arrangement."

"And what would I tell my child about her father?"

"Whatever you want. If you go with an anonymous donor, what will you tell him?"

"The truth."

"Well, the truth is an option. When he's old enough to understand, you can tell him that two close friends wanted a baby, and that we chose an admittedly nonconventional path forward, but that those two friends love him very much and will be there to support him."

She narrows her eyes, and her lips purse. "That sounds really nice."

The tiny pucker of a frown warns me she's thought of another rebuttal. "What about your family? Think about what they would say. Ian, I love you for wanting to do this for me, but it's just not a good idea."

A frustrated sigh escapes. Sunny is one of the most magnificent people in the world. She's kind and unassuming. Loyal. Trustworthy. Giving. But her constant concern about what others think or say frustrates the absolute hell out of me. However, her mention of my family leads to a topic worth probing.

"Is this about Sam?"

They broke up almost twenty years ago, yet she remains single. She avoids him. She never talked about what happened between them. Admittedly, I'd been fourteen years old and probably not a likely confidante, but still. She never talked about it to Oliver either, and they were in college together.

Her chest rises, and a loud, dramatic sigh fills the room. I'm sighing, she's sighing, there's a lot of sighing in the room tonight. I suppose that's par for the course when she's disappointing me and I'm exasperating her.

"No." Those blue eyes look directly into mine.

Doctors discover early in their careers that patients lie. Often, patients lie for fear of being judged, and they will put their lives at risk in order to escape judgment from a physician who doesn't give a damn about anything other than helping them live.

I study those honest, cornflower blue eyes and her blank expression. And an older professor, with thin gray hair and bushy black eyebrows, speaks loudly in the recesses of my mind. "People lie."

"Can I tell you something?" she asks.

"Anything."

"I don't know if I ever loved your brother." My lie detector blares. "I mean, sure, in the way one does at that age. But... everyone acts like he crushed me. Like I've been mourning him. You want to know the truth? I ended things with your brother. Or at least… it was mutual. We grew apart. He went off to Boston, and I stayed here. I didn't even live in a dorm. We were in such different places. Why can't anyone get that? The 'poor Sandra' routine drives me batty. Why can't people just accept that I love your parents like I loved my own. You all were family to me before Sam and I ever dated. And Sam and I probably would've never dated except he literally lived down the road, and back then we really lived in the middle of nowhere."

I consider her words. Her dad worked for my dad on the ranch. Our parents were close. We all hung out together, rode bikes and horses together. Built forts in the woods.

"When Sam and I broke up, my biggest fear was that your parents wouldn't want to see me anymore. That our parents' friendship would splinter. But your parents were wonderful."

"That's because they care about you." I scratch my jaw, considering her perspective and concerns. "When you worry about what my family would say, you realize it will thrill my parents if you have a child, right? It won't matter to them who the father is. And if they found out we did this together, as friends, that would only make them exultant. They only want their kids to be happy, and, as you know, you're like one of their kids." The cake box on the counter catches my eye, and I point to it. "Noah is like one of their kids. Liam is too, but he's married and on solid ground, so it's not as evident these days. But their love is unconditional. That's what love is, you know? Unconditional."

I could push my point home and tell her that if she lets me be the father, the child would be born into a family with unconditional love, but no matter who she chooses, that child will be a part of the Duke family. Just like no matter who she chooses, I'll be a support throughout her pregnancy and ensure she gets the medical care she needs, wherever she needs to travel to get it. If there are complications, Texas has become a state you don't want to be in, but I'll help her get the medical care she needs, no matter what.

"Statistically, it's likely I won't conceive. We're going 'round and 'round about something that's..." She exhales loudly, and her gaze travels to the ceiling.

As a physician, I agree with her that, statistically, a positive result isn't likely. After one year of attempting to conceive, only five percent of women age forty will deliver a baby. Part of the problem isn't conception, though. Depending on the study, between forty to fifty percent of women her age will miscarry. And I don't have access to Sandra's medical records, but they would need to be reviewed. Her mother died in childbirth. It was forty years ago, and there could be any number of mitigating factors, but I would definitely want to research any genetic causal factors.

"I have access to a wide variety of doctors. We can visit someone–"

"Obviously, but that's..." She waves her hands as if I exasperate her. "Why do you care who I choose? Parenting isn't on your life wish list."

"Because you're my friend. And I want to do this for you. I want to be there for you. It might not be easy, and I don't want you to go through it alone." I mean, as much as my schedule allows, I want to be there for her. "It's probably going to be a long process."

"It's crazy talk." She half-laughs, and it is in that instant hope surfaces.

"Yeah, I suppose some might call it crazy. But it feels right."

"It's lunacy."

"Nah, it'll be fun." Of course, I'm thinking about the sex, but when her eyelashes flutter, I backtrack. "There's a sign one nurse has hanging near her station. Life doesn't have to be perfect to be wonderful. Maybe this isn't the perfect scenario you envisioned, but there's no reason it can't be wonderful... for both of us."

"Well, if you're really serious, I'll get you a jar..."

"No, no, no. That's not the best way."

She blinks in startled astonishment. Okay. Having sex with me never crossed her mind. "I think, given your age, we'll have the best results if we do it the way Mother Nature intended."

And she laughs. Hard.

Well, damn. Talk about a bruised ego. Her eyes tear, and she wipes the corners with the tips of her index fingers.

"Ian Duke, think again." She wags her index finger. "Oh, my god."

The side door opens, and heavy footfalls bang against the wood floor.

"Sunny! What're you doing?" Noah comes in with his fist out to bump mine in greeting.

"Thought you guys were going out tonight?" I ask, annoyed he's here.

"We are. Come join us."

"Grabbed dinner for us to eat." I gesture to the take-out.

Oliver sticks his nose in one of the brown paper bags. "Mac's barbecue. There's enough here for all of us. You don't mind, do you?"

"No. Sure. Go ahead," I grumble.

"Oh, Noah, that pink box is yours. Mrs. Duke bought it for you," Sunny says. "Plus that bag. It had casseroles in it."

"Patty." He draws out my mom's name and rubs his palm over his stomach. "She is one in a million."

"Barbecue and cake. Then we'll hit Zack's." Oliver sounds pleased with himself and commences opening drawers and pulling out utensils.

Zack's Bar & Grill has a dance floor, and it's one of the few fun places to go in Whispering Creek.

"Hey, Sunny, did you see the stack of photo books Mom dug up? Last time she came through, she was rearranging the shelves and cleaning out closets. Found those in the top of the hall closet." Oliver points to the painted blue shelving against the wall. Sunny gets up and fingers one of the books. She opens it and laughs as she flips through the pages. "Look at your hair."

I step up behind her and see a photo of Oliver, back when everyone called him Ollie. It's short on the sides, long in the back, and it's probably the worst haircut he ever had. She flips the page again and stills.

She's in a sky-blue prom dress that almost matches the vivid color in her eyes, and my brother Sam stands beside her in a tux. In the photo, he's holding a plastic box with a corsage inside. Mom cropped me out of the photo, but I stood to the side of my brother. I ran to get the corsage out of the refrigerator and had just handed it to him when Mom snapped the photo. Later that night, he gave her a promise ring. A promise for the future, for forever.

Yeah, this is why Sunny laughed at my preposterous suggestion. All that happened twenty years ago, but it's still there, in these photo books, in every room. Memories haunt the house, the pastures, the stable, the woods. She was my brother's first love, his girlfriend. His. And I was the little brother. Some things don't change.

Chapter Thirteen

Sandra

Last Year in June

"How was your weekend?" Kara slides into my office chair with her coffee in hand Tuesday morning, which is Monday for us. Only, whereas other people are sometimes slammed on Monday, our Tuesday is a little slow, and the days ramp up to Saturday madness.

"Fine." I throw her a smile and pointedly flip open my desk calendar. On Tuesday, I open the salon on Main Street in Whispering Creek, then drive into Austin and cover closing there. "How was your weekend?"

"Good. Went out in Austin. Nothing too much. Ran into Cindy. She said you were out at Zack's Saturday night with Noah, Oliver, and Ian."

"Yep. Normal night." I pretend to be focused on my computer screen.

"You and Ian line danced."

I side-eye her. "It was a line dance. We all did it."

"Hhmmm. And here I thought you might be secretly going after Oliver."

"What rumors?"

She shrugs. "I don't know if you'd call them rumors. Just…you know. He hasn't been dating as much as he used to, and you're not going out as much. You've always been friends."

"Still friends. Why don't you tell me about your love life instead of digging into an old lady's nonexistent love life."

She grins at me. "You're not old."

I appreciate her stated assessment, but I remember my twenties. There's no way she doesn't think I'm old now that I'm forty. "So, let this chick without a love life live vicariously through the you."

"Really nothing much to say." She puckers her lips. "I might go out for coffee with a guy I've been texting on Bumble."

"Oh. That's interesting." I personally have never used Bumble, but I recognize it as the latest dating app Kara and the others have been trying out. "What's the maybe?"

"Eh." She waffles her hand. "I'm just not so sure." She pulls her phone out of her back pocket and thrusts it into my hand. "There he is."

I look down at a photo of a guy wearing a baseball hat that shades many of his facial features. He has a beard, and he looks nice enough. How exactly are you supposed to judge by a photo? Maybe that's why me and dating apps never worked out.

I hand her the phone back. "Coffee can't hurt, right?"

Her face contorts. "You'd be surprised." She takes her phone back and asks, "Did Ian go home on Sunday?"

"Yeah, I think so." Oliver, Ian, and I went for a trail ride Sunday morning, and Ian headed back to Houston after lunch, but I purposefully sound ignorant. "Where's your nine o'clock?"

"She texted. She's running late. Great start to the day, huh?"

"Exactly. I rescheduled my Saturday no-show for this morning, so my day's gonna be crazed, too." I schedule client appointments on Wednesday, Thursday, Friday, and Saturday, but clients who've been with you for years expect flexibility. So much for reserving Tuesday solely for office management. I click open a spreadsheet to get to it.

Kara takes the hint and heads out of my office, but I feel her inquisitive gaze on me the entire time I tap away on my keyboard. She pauses at the doorway and tosses her hair over her shoulder. Those long, loose curls cascade in waves down her back. "You know, you should've held out for Ian. Or Oliver. They're both hotter than Sam by orders of magnitude. Of course, Sam is the billionaire, so..." She angles her head back and forth as if weighing the men. "I suppose you aimed for the biggest fish. Human nature." She shrugs. "It's not like you have a crystal ball and could see you were wasting your time on Sam and the smaller fish would end up being much tastier."

"Can you not talk about them like that? They're my friends." She gives me a look that says she isn't buying what I'm selling, and it really kind of pisses me off. "They're like family. And, for the umpteenth time, I wasn't aiming to bag the billionaire. He was a broke college student when I dated him."

"You know, I always forget about that. You broke up with him after he dropped out of college, right? He must've seemed like such a loser back then."

I grit my teeth and breathe in deeply for calm. "Sam dropped out of MIT because he had an idea he believed in."

"Sandra, you know, it's okay to bash on your ex. Really, it is. You might feel better if you do." She nods with all of the authority of Gen Z.

"Kara..." Exasperated, I can't even finish. I'm her boss and want to tell her that she needs to adjust how she speaks to me, the boss, but there's just no way to get it out without sounding like a bitch, and the last thing I want is a negative workplace vibe.

Thankfully, the outer door chimes, announcing her client. She wiggles her fingers at me, flashing her impressive ombre nails.

I can't blame her for dredging up Sam Duke from time to time. Since reaching the elusive billionaire status, he's become our small town's most notorious former citizen. If we had royalty, he'd hands down be the king of Whispering Creek. I suppose if someone like Matthew McConnaughey had been from our town, he'd probably be more infamous. But while our little alcove of a town lacks a Hollywood connection, we do have a whiz kid who created a business most people don't even understand and made a mint. And given the fact said newly minted billionaire grew up on one of the few working ranches remaining in our section of suburban sprawl and was one of three hot, sexy brothers, of course the whole town fixates on him. Lucky me, I happen to be the last local girl to have dated him. Actually, the only local girl who dated him. Almost twenty years later, folks around here haven't forgotten, and I truly don't know if they ever will. You'd think we were Brad Pitt and Jennifer Aniston.

One thing Kara did get right is that I would've been better off to have waited for the youngest Duke. But how could I have known that? How could I have known the scrawny teen with acne and buck teeth would grow into a fit, focused surgeon who can also line dance and remembers birthdays?

Here's the thing about hindsight. People say it's twenty-twenty, but really, that's because all the details are vague and muted when looking backward. When you're looking forward, into the future, all the details are technicolor and emotions are clear. And back in high school, I'd been insanely attracted to Sam Duke. His presence meant an overload of butterflies and the inability to process thought. And then, I honestly don't know what happened. People want a heart-wrenching drama story, but that's not what happened with us. We simply grew apart. The butterflies disappeared. We had nothing in common and nothing to talk about. The distance meant we saw each other like twice a year at a time in our lives when we were evolving at warp speed. And yes, Ian had been my friend, but let's be real. Six years is a big age difference when you're in college and he's in junior high. Now, at forty, sure, six years is nothing, but back then, that age difference was prosecutable.

If I could go back and do it all over, starting at, say, sixteen when I went out on that first date with Sam, I'd do it all the same. Because I followed my heart. That's what teenage girls do. And we don't have crystal balls. And our hearts can lead us astray. It's all part of life's journey.

As Ian said, life doesn't have to be perfect to be wonderful. Which leads me back to my situation with Ian. Ian isn't offering a storybook ending. He's offering to give me his sperm. Sure, for years I said I wanted to focus on growing my business and I didn't need a man or a family. And I do not need a man. I really, truly do not. But I'd really love to have a baby.

And if I'm honest with myself, at this point in my life, there's no one I would rather have a child with than Ian Duke. Now, yes, in an ideal world, we'd be madly in love and married. But in this world, we're not madly in love. I mean, yeah, I am attracted to him. A girl would have to be blind not to be. But he's not looking for a relationship, and neither am I.

If we are able to conceive a child, we'd most definitely have to keep the true parentage under wraps. Lordy, I can only imagine all the gossip our baby agreement would stir. Kara and her cohort would have yet another reason to look at me with blatant sad eyes, thinking I tried to snag me another Duke and failed. Yeah…that little fact right there is one reason to stick with a truly anonymous donor.

The chime on the door sounds, and I enter the salon to greet my client. She removes her sunglasses, and I instantly place her. She's dressed for a facial. No make-up, hair pulled back, and she's in leggings, a tee, and sneakers. "Barbara? It's been ages."

"Well, I moved away after college. We moved back about a year ago. I've been meaning to schedule forever, and then I scheduled so far in advance I forgot all about it. I'm so sorry about that." Barbara's mother is one of my regular clients.

"No worries. You're here now." Barbara follows me down the hall to the private treatment room. "We're doing a luxury facial today, right?"

"Or, well, whatever you think my skin needs."

"We'll take a look."

Barbara is around ten years younger than me, but I know her through her mother. She used to come in and get her hair done at the salon, but she wasn't my client. After I get her situated, her arms rest outside the spa blanket and an enormous set of diamond rings glisten on her left ring finger.

Barbara's an attractive woman, but she has dark, puffy circles below her eyes, plus the beginnings of fine lines around her eyes and nasolabial area. She lets out a deep sigh and visibly relaxes with each cleansing swipe on her skin.

"That feels so good."

"You seem tense." I brush upward, massaging as I go. "Are you tired?"

"Stressed. I got into law school."

"Congratulations."

"Thanks."

Satisfied with the cleanliness of her skin, I dab a cotton ball on the toner.

"But the enrollment forms are due. With payment. And then, it's like…commitment. I'm scared."

"Of what?"

"I have a young child. My husband is worried about how I'll

manage family and school. I'm worried about the extra debt. And then, what if I don't make it?"

"What? Through law school? Don't be ridiculous. You can do anything you set your mind to."

"I'm old, though."

"What?" I glance down at her skin. "You can't be older than twenty-eight."

"I'm thirty-two." She sounds deflated. "That's old for law school."

"So? If it's something you want to do, go for it."

"That's what everyone says, but then when I go to put the envelope in the mail, I freeze. Maybe it's a sign it's not what I really want to do."

"I don't know about that." I move on to a light conditioner to prep the skin before applying steam. "I think sometimes we give our worries more power than we should. Sometimes you have to envision the future you want, think through all the steps to get there, and take that first step. Think about how proud your child will be when you graduate from law school. A boy or a girl?"

"A girl. Five years old. She'll enter kindergarten this fall, which is why I thought..."

"Tell me about her."

By the end of Barbara's facial, she has moisturized, clean skin, and I learned all about her adorable daughter named Maple after the tree her husband carved their names in when they were in fifth grade, and how after having Maple they tried but hadn't had luck getting pregnant again. She came to terms with it, and now she really does want law school, but she's scared to take that step.

She gives me a hug before leaving the treatment room. While we hug, I tell her, "Just go for it. Don't let the worries hold you back."

It's not bad advice. Fear and worry hold too much weight. It's advice I could give myself. Like Barbara, I want a baby. This is my year to try to do this. And, if I'm aiming for a dream, I should just do it. Maybe not conceiving after the first anonymous donor is a sign. I pull out my phone and, before I can second guess myself, shoot off a text to Ian.

Me: If you're really serious about this, I'll take you up on your offer.

Chapter Fourteen

Ian

Last Year in June

Sunny: If you're really serious about this, I'll take you up on your offer.

Astonishment strikes first. I reread the text. Over and over again. She's going to do it. Breathing becomes more difficult each time I read the text. We're going to do it. I'm going to do it. Or, well, my sperm will. Procreate.

"Dude. Did you get bad news?" Harrison returns from the bar and slides a beer across the table.

We both had early morning surgeries and finished up early. Or somewhat early. It's almost five. The humidity and heat outdoors surpass one hundred degrees for about the tenth day in a row, so we're sitting in the air conditioning, by a picture window staring out onto the empty baking patio.

I check the time of the text. She sent it a few hours ago. My response is late, but she knows I store my phone in a locker when I'm in surgery. I got caught in a conversation with a patient's wife that put me late meeting Harrison, and I ended up rushing here.

Harrison, like the nosy ass he is, leans over the table and reads the message upside down. "What offer?"

"Sperm donation." I swallow my beer and avoid Harrison's open-mouthed face by watching the baseball game on the television over his head.

"Dude."

My beer hits the table with more force than intended. Harrison leans back against the booth, giving us some much needed room.

"Is there a reason you sound like a surfer today?"

He shrugs. "I watched *Bill and Ted's Excellent Adventure* last night."

The Houston Astros hit a homerun, and the bartender shoves his fist in the air.

"You're not going to expand on what's going on?"

Harrison's mouth opens and I stop him with, "Do not say dude again."

"Message received. But we're best friends, right?"

I give a quick jerk of my head in response. Truth is, he's closer to me than my brothers. Maybe partially because of age, but also because we went through med school and residency together. That's a shit ton of bonding.

"And this," he motions to my phone and raises his eyebrows, "seems discussion-worthy."

I let out a sigh. As much as I hate to admit it, Harrison is probably right.

"It's not a big deal. Sunny...you met her?"

"Your brother's hot-as-fuck ex that you are completely and totally jonesing to fuck?"

The disapproving scowl I throw his way doesn't register. He lifts his glass, taps the rim against mine, and drinks.

"Sunny is her name. And she wants to have a child. I volunteered to be the sperm donor."

"Could be fun," Harrison says. He waffles his head back and forth, lower lip jutting out, weighing the idea. "Do you want to be a dad?"

"She's looking to be a single mom."

"Do you want me to tell you what I think about this?"

"No."

He stretches back, places one arm against the booth, and focuses on the game. "Thought so. If, on another day, you want someone to talk to, I'm always here."

I return my attention to the phone. I need to respond to her. I know Sunny, and if I go too long without responding, she'll read into it. She'll second guess her decision. So, I tap out a response.

Me: Good.

I delete the word good and start over.

Me: Great.

I stare at that word. I don't like it, so I hit the delete key until it's gone.

Me: Excellent. Do you have a date for your next visit?

. . .

That response sounds like a professional, business response. I jam down the delete key.

Me: That's good news.

Ugh. That's even worse. Delete.

Me: You made my day yet again. What do we do next? When are you coming back here?

There. That feels real. I hit send.

I glance up and meet Harrison's steady, judgmental gaze. "What?"

"Dude."

I ball up a napkin and throw it at him. Three little dots appear on the screen. Applause sounds from the overhead speakers, and Harrison lets out a, "That's the way you do it."

Sunny: Do you have plans this weekend?

Me: Nope. It's a great weekend for you to visit.

Chapter Fifteen

Ian

Last Year in early July

The elevator dings, and I lean against the doorjamb, arms crossed, heart noticeably palpitating beneath my sternum, waiting. My palms sweat and my fingers and bare toes ice over in the overpowering air conditioning. It's either the freezing AC, or it's a spike in adrenaline. Probably a combination of the two.

The doors slide open, and cornflower blue eyes peer down the hall. She's wearing a long off-white t-shirt dress that falls off one shoulder with a light brown woven belt. The loose dress is just tight enough to hint at the nubile curves beneath. Strappy high heeled sandals with braided leather the same light tan color as her belt give her height and accentuate toned, shapely calves.

Her gold bracelets glisten under the fluorescent light as she adjusts the overnight tote on her shoulder. Her blonde hair cascades softly over lightly tanned shoulders, and her glossy, rose-colored lips curve into a smile.

With one arm, I hold my apartment door wide, gesturing for her to come on through. In my eagerness, I didn't grab a key, and if the door closes, it will automatically lock, so I stand there, glued to the spot, gawking at the woman who may bear my child.

There's nothing strange at all about that thought.

As she passes me, I lift the straps over her overnight bag, a multi-colored cloth bag that surprises me by its notably heavy weight. She saunters down the hall, and my gaze falls to the sway of her hips and the way the cotton dress drapes over the globes of her ass. I'd like to push her up against the wall, lift the hem of her dress, caress her curves, and find out why she doesn't have any panty lines, but I shake that line of thought away as I flick the lock on the apartment door. I'm getting ahead of myself. Way too ahead of myself. She's still expecting a jar.

"How was the drive?"

"Fine. No traffic on a Saturday evening." She gives me that girl-next-door, blushing smile, and the rest of the room fades to black. "Well, on good days," she amends.

Congestion in this city can occur at seemingly any time, but yes, the traffic gods favor drivers in off-times like the weekend.

"I'll put this in the guest room." As I say it, I wonder if she might be expecting me to deposit her things in my room. Does me putting her stuff in the guest room communicate I'm fully expecting to hand her my jar?

I return from depositing her overnight bag in the guest room and find her standing at the end of the hall where I left her. The corner of her lip moves up and down ever so slightly, a sure sign she's chewing that corner of her lip. The awkwardness between us needs to be resolved or she'll be backing out and driving back to Austin before we share a drink.

"Have you eaten dinner?" She shakes her head, and I say,

"Good. I'm starving. Let me get some shoes on and we can head out. Make yourself at home."

When I return with socks on my feet and shoes dangling from my fingers, she remains in the same spot, leaning against the wall that separates the galley kitchen and the entry hall. She opens her pocketbook, which could double as a small overnight bag. It's in the same light color leather as her belt and sandals.

"I've got a contract. We can review it at dinner if you want. Everyone says that in situations like this, it's important for the arrangement be agreed to in writing, so we don't have any misunderstandings."

She holds the papers out to me, and I simply stare at them. *A contract between friends?*

"This removes any parental obligations. You won't need to pay child support. That kind of stuff."

A memory of her sense of fairness hits me hard. "Is this another situation where you want to outline the parameters of the contest?"

We used to do our own homegrown version of barrel racing, but she and my brothers were older, and she'd always insisted on adjusting the rules to create an equal playing field regardless of our differences in sizes.

"This isn't a game."

Her words slap like a well-deserved reprimand. Of course, she's right. I take the papers from her and set them down on the kitchen counter.

"Why don't we talk about it over dinner?" I propose.

Her gaze cuts to the discarded papers.

"I'll agree to anything you want. And I agree, this is important. It's not a game. We should talk about it, and then you can mark up the contract in any way you wish."

On the way to the restaurant, she asks about work. As a matter of principle, I never share specifics on cases. Even in the cloak of anonymity, it slips into murky waters, and a non-medical person would rarely understand, anyway. But I share that it's been a good week. Mostly scheduled surgeries, with one exception. A construction worker fell from a building about five stories high. Before I entered the OR, he'd been stable, or so I had been told, but the staff didn't catch internal cranial hemorrhaging and he died on the table while I worked on repairing his pelvic bone.

I spent a good amount of time reviewing the case today and determined there were few signs, and even if someone had picked up on it, there was little chance we could've saved him. The bigger miracle was that he'd made it into the OR at all.

"How were things at the salon?" I ask as we are seated in the Asian restaurant across the street from my building.

"Fine." Her glib response is less than I gave her, and I wonder if she's nervous or there isn't much to tell.

I can only imagine what women do in a salon, or what she does as an aesthetician. I expect that, like me, her goal with each client is to improve their lives. I do so with bones and muscle, and she does so with a focus on the epidermis.

Over the years, Harrison and I have had enough conversations about the world of plastics that I understand feeling good about oneself has tremendous implications to the quality of one's life. Sandra has, for as long as I've known her, cared about making other people feel good.

We agree to split beef Szechuan and vegetable fried rice. After the waitperson leaves, Sandra runs the pad of her finger up and down the condensation on her water glass.

"Sunny…what's going through that head of yours?"

She breathes in so deeply her shoulders lift.

"I don't want to risk our friendship. I need you to take this seriously. That contract might seem silly to you, but it's important we go through it so we're on the same page." Her forearms rest on the table, and she splays out her hands, palms open to the sky, visually augmenting where words fail her.

I reach across the narrow table and capture one of her hands, clutching it and tightening my fingers around her slim, chilled hand.

"It doesn't need to be awkward."

She tilts her head and raises her gaze. The flush of color through her cheeks and neck could be interpreted any number of ways. Longing, desire, nerves. Uncertainty is a probable emotion.

"We're both adults." I weave my fingers through hers. "And we're friends. We've been friends for decades. This isn't going to change that. If anything, going through this together will strengthen our bond."

"Well, that's the point of the contract." She pulls her hand from mine and places her hands demurely in her lap. Her gaze falls to the table, and I get the distinct impression she wishes she had the contract with her. "If I'm going to do this with you, or anyone, I want sole custody. That's important to me."

I get it. She's thinking of Henry. The foster care child. The little boy she never gained custody of. The mother moved out of state, and Sunny has no idea what happened to him.

"Why would you even want to do this?" she asks.

And that's the million-dollar question. Why do I want to do this? I'd like to believe it is a completely selfless act. That my friend wants a baby, and I want to give it to her. But Harrison wasn't so off the mark. I'd be lying if I didn't see this as an opportunity to have sex with someone I fantasized about for ages. But I still want to do this for her, just because.

The food arrives and gives me time to formulate my answer. An answer that should come easily.

Sunny sets about spooning out our shared courses, and my foot taps the floor.

"Sandra." As always, my use of her first name grabs her attention, and she lifts her head, a large serving spoon held out midway across the table. "I told you, you're my friend, and I want to give this to you. But there's more."

She sets the serving spoon down and straightens her shoulders, waiting for me to share my reasons. She probably sees me as a respectable surgeon, a friend she can count on, and an upstanding, dependable citizen. She's probably never viewed me as a potential sexual partner, given I am the youngest brother of her first boyfriend.

"What is it?"

"I'm not doing this solely out of the goodness of my heart. In some ways, my offering, or, well, my request that you consider me, is one hundred percent selfish. You were always my fantasy. You probably don't realize this, but I possess a stash of photos of you. Some I stole from Sam, some from my mom, some I took when you weren't looking. And then, of course, there's the mental stash." Her eyes widen. My knee bounces frantically up and down beneath the table, under the weight of the knowledge this share could prove to be a colossal mistake. "I don't mean to freak you out. I don't want to sound like a pervert." Those blue eyes finally gaze up at me, reassuring me she doesn't find me so disgusting she can no longer look at me. "But it's the truth. I don't think I've ever fantasized about a woman more than you. For me, this is a dream come true." It's a win-win scenario, but I have the wisdom to refrain from using business terminology to describe this situation. "We live three hours apart. I don't want children. I don't want marriage." She nods as she absorbs my statements. I'm not normally so forthright with women, but she deserves to hear the truth. She's been my friend for over a quarter of a century. As much as I would love to have sex with her, I don't desire it enough to throw away our friendship.

She fidgets with the napkin in her lap.

I take a swallow of water. A waitress walks by, and we exchange a glance. I offer her a smile.

I can't take the silence or her downturned gaze, so I ask, "Does that bother you?"

"Reality never lives up to the fantasy. You know that, right?" She smirks, subtly mocking me in a manner reminiscent of how she used to when we were kids—or, well, when I was a kid and she was a college student. "You know, back then, I knew you were flirty, but I didn't think–"

"Anything of it. I know."

My gaze wanders down to her breasts. The scoop line of her dress offers no cleavage, and her bra conceals the outline of her nipples, but I fixate on the hint of curves.

She kicks me under the table. "Stop it." Her smile is a cross between bashful and amused.

The vise on my rib cage loosens under that smile, probably because she isn't treating me like a silly teen. The secret I shared isn't my deepest, darkest secret, but it's the source of all of the deepest secrets.

"Ahm, Ian, we already talked about this. We're not doing it. The plan is you'll–"

"Your chances of conceiving are higher if we do it the way nature intended." Her fingers fly over her mouth, her cheeks flush and her eyes sparkle. "Seriously. I'm not joking. I'll show you the studies." It's not a huge difference in odds, but it's there. She breaks out laughing, losing her battle to rein it in. Her laughter is contagious, and I grin but still push forth with my argument. "If you have an orgasm."

She bowls over laughing, lying on the booth, and I can no longer even see her. Yep, that went well.

When she finally controls her laughter, with one arm over her ribcage as she gasps for air, I'm already digging into the meal, although her humor sapped my appetite. Our conversation meanders back onto a normal path, even with her constantly breaking into fits of laughter and regularly wiping below her eyes.

The second we exit the restaurant and step out onto the city sidewalk, I take her hand possessively and pull her against me. She can laugh all she wants, but I remember New Year's Eve. I'm a good friend, but I'm no saint.

Startled, those blue eyes search for an answer. Why can't she see it?

Blood rushes thick and heavy in my veins. Want. Need. With us, it wouldn't be just sex. She has to sense it. And all the things she fears are a world away. Here, in Houston, we can have this.

Her cheeks flush and those full lips part. My pulse thrums. Her palm caresses my chest. The light touch resonates through my body.

My fingers graze her arm. Along the side of her breast. She shudders. Her breaths come out short and choppy. Her pupils darken, overshadowing the crystal blue.

I dip my head lower, tasting her, nipping at that lower lip. She tastes sweet as honey with hints of spice.

My hand curves up behind her neck, angling her head to allow a deeper kiss while holding her in place. Her hands wander, over my back, in my hair. My skin tingles with awareness and a desire for more. I back her up against the building, pressing into her. My lips recapture hers, demanding more. Her thigh lifts, allowing me closer, and I rock against her with a savage intensity. *Fuck, I want her.* She releases a long, sexy moan that has me throbbing with need. Her chest heaves as she sucks in air.

A horn beeps in the distance, reminding me of our present situation, on the street with her pressed against a brick wall. The pad of my thumb gently soothes her soft, swollen lips. I press my forehead against hers and ask, "Still funny?"

Chapter Sixteen

Sandra

Last July

Heat radiates off my skin all the way back to his apartment, and it has nothing to do with Houston humidity or the sultry summer night. Lust surges in my core as physical need overrides all logical thought. Through his lobby, riding in the elevator, his hand brushes mine, or grazes my wrist, or warms my lower back, nurturing the conduit of energy coursing between our bodies. Always touching me, ensuring the heated urgency never cools.

At his apartment door, he fumbles with the key, and my brain kicks back into gear. Ian isn't the young, gawky teen from down the road. Decades have passed, and he's gorgeous. Sexy and desirable.

Ian Duke could have anyone he wants, and he probably does. If his friend Harrison is any indication of his activities when I'm not here, they prowl the bars at night. We don't chat about our dating lives. Oliver and I do, but I know little about Ian's sexual history. Our sex life has always been more or less a mutually agreed to taboo topic.

The lock clicks. *Am I really doing this?*

His molten gaze has me squirming, in good and bad ways. He said he fantasized about me, back when I was in college. A twentysomething younger version of me. My body has changed in twenty years, even without the markings of childbirth that are so common in others my age. My breasts are mostly the same shape and size, my skin elasticity not as tight. There's no way I can live up to whatever his teen imagination concocted.

He extends his arm against the door, holding it wide for me to enter. The bluish haze of city lights brightens the end of the long hall, beckoning. I inhale deeply, centering my wayward chakras, and enter.

He toes off his shoes at the door, and I slip off my heels. Midway down the entry, he pushes me up against the wall. His fingers tug at my hair, and his cheek roughly grazes mine just before he plunders my lips. Desire unfurls as he presses his pelvis against me, rubbing my throbbing center, stoking all that simmering desire into a roaring flame. The soft material of my dress provides little obstruction, and I mewl as the movement of his hips strokes me.

My body thrums with anticipation. His smooth fingers roam over my body, along my hips, my back, and my ass. He's everywhere, and I follow his lead, exploring his body over his clothes. The long, muscular lines of his back, the curve of his shoulders, the tips of his hair.

He breaks the kiss and runs the tip of his nose against mine, and the rough pad of his thumb tenderly strokes my chin.

"Bedroom?" As if he needs to ask.

I'm clinging to the man like he's a trellis and I'm a vine, and he's asking. I don't want him to ask. I don't want to think. But I should be thinking. This isn't just a hook-up. We're doing this with the goal of getting pregnant.

"Sunny." He breathes out my name, and the heat in those warm, golden-brown eyes melts the percolating second guesses.

"Yes." Nerves stir, and I force a timid smile. "Let's do it the natural way. Take me to your bedroom."

"You won't regret this." He caresses my cheek, and my heart palpitates from the intensity in his gaze, in his presence. "I'm going to make you feel so good."

It's a sinful, delicious promise, and I'm pretty sure I whimper.

He bends, there's pressure behind my legs, and my feet lift off the floor. I cling to his shoulders as he speeds through his condo. The tips of my fingers run over his trimmed beard. He grins. It's more of a bad-boy smirk, but there's a still a touch of a boy-next-door grin.

We're doing this. I want to do this. But we can't lose our friendship. We can't lose touch with who we are to each other.

"I burn for you." I wiggle my eyebrows, hoping he gets I'm joking. It's an infamous line from a television show I forced him to watch.

He cracks up, bypassing the guest room, and I let out a snort of laughter. It's not sexy at all, but it's natural. And it's important we don't lose this, no matter how sexed up we get for this little window in time.

I half expect him to toss me on the mattress in his bedroom, but he lowers me with care, gently setting me back onto two stacked pillows.

The hallway laughter subsides. I suck in air as realization sets in that we are really about to do this. Ian Duke. And me.

"I want you to tell me what you like."

He presses his lips to my knuckles.

"You don't have to do—" He covers my lips with his, probably to shut me up. I'm not sure why the urge to tell him we can just do it quick and fast rose, but our open-mouthed kiss has a drugging effect causing an entirely different set of urges to course through me. The warmth of his fingers travels up my leg, over my knee, to my inner thigh. He palms my mound, and my hips roll into his touch.

"No panties. I wondered."

"Panty lines always show—" I gasp as the cool skin of his finger slips inside my folds. His finger plunges deeper while he massages my clit, his gaze locked on me.

"Feel good?"

My hips fall into the rhythm set by his hand, and my eyelids flutter closed.

"Sunny?"

"Yes. Very good."

He pulls his finger out, then sucks it clean.

"I knew you'd taste good." He gathers the hem of my dress and lifts. When it reaches my shoulders, he says, "Lift your arms."

I comply, and he tosses my dress over to a chair. The only piece of clothing remaining is a smooth bra picked for its discreet features beneath my dress.

I reach for the buttons on his shirt, and his arm disappears behind me. As I fumble with the series of buttons down his shirt, my bra unsnaps, and the straps loosen around my shoulders. The bra meets my dress in a pile on the chair.

"Fuck, you are beautiful." His intense focus has me imagining he's holding a camera, clicking away, photographing me. It's sensual and intimate.

Heat blossoms along my cheeks. The lights are dim, but one thigh crosses over the other in a weak attempt to hide.

"Take off your clothes. Join the naked party." It sounds ridiculous when I say it out loud, but it's a reference to our pajama parties of yore. By middle school, I no longer received invitations to join the boys, but they had them for years, a bunch of boys running roughshod over the house and pastures. The boyish smile playing out on Ian's lips tells me he gets my reference.

He finishes my unbuttoning job with his gaze locked on me. His shirt sails to the chair. As he unzips his trousers, I pinch one of my nipples while my other hand drifts down my stomach. I press four fingers flat over my center, letting the heat of my hand warm my sensitive, needy core.

"Fuck," he groans, pausing with one leg out of his slacks, watching me with an appraising, appreciative, and yeah, I'd say burning stare. "Damn."

He kicks off the remaining pants leg and moves to the foot of the bed, watching me while stroking himself with a slow and steady motion, up and down his engorged flesh, from the base up to his tip.

I spread my legs and curl my index finger, motioning for him to come to me. Because, fuck, he's long and thick, and I really want to feel his full length inside me.

The mattress dips with his weight as he climbs on, one knee at a time. His lips find my ankle and press against the hard bone.

"Talus." He says and shifts forward. "Fibula," he says, moving higher up my leg and pressing his thumb into muscle. His lips press flat against my knee cap. "Patella." His eyebrows rise, and he smirks. "Breathe." His command lurches my lungs into action. "Spread your thighs."

I'm already open for him, but I comply, spreading farther, and he feathers soft kisses up the sensitive skin. The rough hairs of his jaw scrape, bending the line of pleasure.

"There are two hundred and six bones in the human body. Did you know that?"

I force myself to swallow. I think I did know that. I had to study anatomy for my aesthetician training, but... His tongue swipes through my folds, and all thoughts flee.

Holy fuck. The good doctor knows exactly what to do with his tongue and those long, dexterous fingers. In the salon, we sometimes joke about men not knowing where the clit is, but that joke does not apply to the surgeon between my legs.

"Oh," I gasp. "That feels good."

"Yeah?"

My fingers tangle with his longer strands, and I push him back down.

"Very good."

He chuckles against me. "I aim to please."

And fuck me if he doesn't. He works me over for what feels like forever as I tug his hair, groaning until my muscles tighten and release culminating with a mind-numbing explosion.

"Holy shit." My head tilts back, and I take in the ceiling. "That was…" I don't have words. He crawls over my body, trailing kisses from my hips, along my belly, and pausing to administer warm, languid attention to my breasts.

"Do you have any idea how many times I wondered what your breasts looked like?" He nuzzles the valley between them. "Felt like?" His warm, wet tongue circles my sensitive, peaked nipple. "Taste like?"

A cross between a moan and an *uh-huh* comes out. I tug at him, wanting to push him onto his back so I can return the favor. But he rises on his forearms, nudging my thighs wider.

"I need you now. Is that okay?"

My core clenches. I'm soaked, and fuck if my whole body doesn't throb. "I'm ready."

So, so ready.

The tip of his erection probes at my entrance. His hand grips his base, and he guides the tip, up and down, just the tip, in and out, with the sexiest peekaboo on the planet.

"Please." Yes, this little game of his is sexy, but I need him inside me, stretching me, filling me.

Satisfied with his position, he lets his cock go and shifts over me. His tongue plunders my mouth as he pushes inside. His hips thrust, back and forth, and my hips mirror his movements, rocking him deeper inside me.

He slows and hovers over me, seated inside me completely. Our foreheads touch, and he stills. "Christ, you feel good."

My hips buck up to meet him, begging for movement.

"Shhh." He sounds strained. "Give me a moment. I've never… not without a condom. Just, this too…let me adjust."

He lowers his head near mine, and I nip along his jaw. His arm muscles strain, his chest expands, and he holds himself still, eyes closed in concentration. The intimacy strengthens when he pulls back and gazes into my eyes. Something undefinable passes between us, and for that second, we are frozen in time, joined together as only a man and woman can be.

And then he moves. He lifts one of my thighs, resting my leg over his shoulder, and delves impossibly deeper, slamming against me, hitting just the right spot. I tighten my core muscles, and he releases a guttural groan as I purposefully coax him, tightening my core, massaging his length as he pounds into me.

He releases my thigh and lowers himself over me until his chest rubs mine. My hands grip his ass, pulling him deeper into me, and he kisses me with a passion unlike anything I've ever experienced. Like he wanted this, me, more than anything.

Sweat coats his chest, and with each slight movement forward he coaxes my clit. My toes curl, and his movements increase in frequency, building me up, until all that tightness explodes. My nails drive into his damp skin, and he quivers, pulsing inside me, veins bulging, until he collapses over me. I cling to his sweaty back as we both gasp for air.

His head falls to my shoulder, and he kisses the damp skin, then proceeds to place kisses along my throat, below my ear, my cheek, my nose, my chin, and my lips.

"Thank you," he whispers, then slips out of me and rolls onto his side. "I don't know how much you've researched this, but chances are, we'll need to do that over and over. You know, in order to achieve pregnancy."

My teeth clamp down around his nipple in a playful bite, and he chuckles. What just happened was beyond incredible and fantastic and all the words, but we're still us. Thank god, we're still us. He palms the back of my head, smoothing what must be a frightful mess, and I rest my ear against his chest. The pounding of his heart pushes out all thoughts, and I relax into him.

Chapter Seventeen

Ian

Last Year in July

A light, whispery touch brushes over my erection, drawing me out of a relaxed sleep. The fan overhead whips cool air over my chest. A warm body presses to my side. Her heat contrasts with the cool air. The quiet of the room makes it tempting to drift back into the comfort of sleep, but my stiff morning wood begs for alternate plans.

The sheet moves lower, and long hair tickles my abdomen. Hot wetness surrounded the head of my cock, and my eyelids blink open. Daylight leaks in through the cracks in the shades. And I groan as the blonde head lowers, her mouth taking me whole.

Fuck.

She grips the base of my cock, and those full lips glide up and down. Crisp blue eyes catch my gaze, and she smiles around my shaft. She rises, and her lips leave me with a pop.

"Never got to return that favor."

My fingers brush through her hair, and I gently guide her back down. I rest my head back on the pillow and take in the rapid circular motion of the ceiling fan. *Holy fuck.* Another fantasy come to fruition. And yes, I dreamed of this. Me, lying on my back, just like this, with her blonde head bobbing up and down. She cups my balls and squeezes, and almost instantaneously the familiar pressure at the base of my spine builds.

I tug her elbow, and she gives me a questioning squint.

"Oh, I want to come this morning, but I want to come inside you." Yeah, last night, going bare had been out of this world. We had another repeat in the middle of the night, but I'm greedy.

I maneuver her onto her hands and knees, push her knees wider, and lick her while using my thumb to rub her clit. She's soaked. Did sucking me off turn or her on, or did she wake up wanting me? Either scenario fuels fantasies.

I straighten, directing my tip to her center. She rocks back on her knees, partially enveloping me with her tight heat. With a groan, I grip her hips and thrust into her.

"God, you feel like heaven."

I reach around and knead her breast, tweaking the nipple. Her blonde hair falls forward, pooling over the sheets. Her muscles tighten, coaxing me, and I lower my hand to find that precious nub, loaded with nerve endings, and work her into a moaning frenzy, her body pushing back as I drive forward. Her arms collapse, and her cheek presses against the mattress, ass still in the air. Her muscles quiver all around me, milking my cock. Her legs flatten, and my body molds around her, remaining inside her as I chase my release and nearly black out as the orgasm rips through me.

I shower kisses all over her shoulders then roll off her, and she presses her back against my side. We lie there, wrapped around each other, as our breathing and pulses calm.

Bliss completely envelops me. Sure, I've had plenty of sex.

Some with random women, some with colleagues I liked quite a bit. But never have I ever had sex with someone I fantasized over throughout my teen years and embarrassingly sporadically throughout my twenties. That kind of obsession leads to a level of sexual satisfaction I never imagined. While we fucked, I wanted to kiss her. Holding her afterward is the most natural thing in the world. I need her close, skin on skin. It's mind-blowing how youthful obsession triggers an astounding level of hormones to pump through my body. I cling to her, needing her near.

She stretches against me, her butt cheek against my groin, which leads my cock to twitch, threatening to come back to life and beg for another round. Unaware of the reaction she is stirring, she reaches behind her and pats my thigh.

"I'm hungry. Let's shower and get breakfast."

She jumps off the bed, and I move to follow her, but she holds up her bossy index finger, stopping me. "Nope. You're not seeing me in bright lights. It'll destroy your fantasy."

My bedroom door closes before I can respond, so I shout so she can hear me through the door. "You're out of your mind."

In less than twenty-four hours, she's shifted my Earth's axis. But I won't explain to her exactly how much she upended my world, because I don't want to scare her. She only wants my sperm, and I need to remember that. Besides, while this is more than sex to me, as a doctor, I understand there's a scientific explanation for the deeper emotions impacting me. I also know that over time, with enough sex, the hormones will stabilize, and fucking her will be like sex with any other woman.

I sling my legs over the bed and stumble into my shower. Even with the knowledge these emotions will eventually normalize, I want mind-blowing sex for as long as possible. Of course, with my luck, she'll be one of those rare women who becomes pregnant on the first attempt.

Under the spray of warm water, I run through the stats. About fifty percent of women attempting to conceive in their early forties do achieve pregnancy eventually. The risk of having a baby with Down's Syndrome at age forty is one in one hundred, or one percent. At age forty-five, that risk increases to one in fifty, or two percent. All manageable numbers. According to my research, if she's not pregnant within six months, we should see a fertility specialist. But the research didn't say what the odds are of a pregnancy on the first try. I hadn't cared. But now I'd like to know. I want what we had last night and this morning over and over again.

I find Sunny in the kitchen. She's wrapped her wet hair into a low-hanging twist. Her tank top shows off the outline of her luscious peach-tinted nipples. Her loose sweats cup her ass, and I palm the curvy globe.

She laughs and scrapes her nails through my scruff before pulling me down for a chaste kiss. She slaps her palm against my pec and says, "Go. Sit at the bar. I'm going to make you breakfast."

I cock my head to the side, reluctant to step away from her. There's a visceral need pulsing through me, and I'm not sure what to do with it. "But I was going to take you out."

"No. Let's stay in and have a lazy morning."

Since once again she isn't wearing panties, I let her win.

My phone rings. It's charging on the kitchen counter where I left it the night before. Sunny turns back to the oven and cracks eggs in a bowl.

Sam's name flashes on the screen, and I unplug the phone, quickly stepping out of the kitchen and into the living area.

"Hey," I answer in the den, next to the windows overlooking the sprawling metropolis.

"Morning. Am I waking you up?" My brother's tone is all business. He's probably calling from his office, hours into his Monday morning.

"Nope." I glance back at Sandra, and she throws me a warm, vibrant smile that I attempt to return.

"Did you get a chance to look at the company info I sent you?"

"I looked at it. But they don't share any of the research."

"They say it's proprietary. Once we invest, we can see more."

"Smells like BS to me. I'd sidestep it if I were you."

"That's your professional opinion?"

"Yep. If you want me to do more research, just say the word. I'm basing that on their site and what you sent me."

Sunny stretches on her toes, reaching for something in an upper cabinet. Her tank top rises with the stretch, exposing a smooth stomach and her delectable belly button. The cabinet door slams shut, and she mouths, "Sorry."

"What are you doing?" Sam's question hits like a bullet of guilt. He has me feeling like a kid who has been doing something wrong and has just been called out.

"About to eat breakfast."

"Are you entertaining someone?" Sunny's blue eyes meet mine from across the room.

"Yeah, I am."

"Who?"

I shift around, turning my back to Sunny. He's better off not knowing. There's no reason for him to ever know. "Do you need anything else?"

"Can she hear you?" I glance over my shoulder at Sunny. It's not like he can see her. It's an audio call.

"Yes."

"Okay. I'll call you tomorrow."

"Tuesday. Call me Tuesday. And if you want me to look into anything else, just text me." Sam's a good guy. He's got an army of analysts at his VC firm, but he throws questions my way. I'm not a fool. I mean, sure, I have insights some of his analysts don't have, but he's doing it as a favor to me. He paid off my medical school loans in exchange for the completion of several research evaluations. The last few years, I've turned his payments into investments that have done remarkably well.

I end the call and meet Sunny's questioning gaze.

"Everything okay?" she asks, probably assuming it's the hospital.

"Just fine." And it is. Sam and Sunny were together two decades ago. He's happily married. But that doesn't mean he wasn't crazy about her back then. That we didn't tease him for running when she called. For spending all his extra time with her. What we're doing isn't wrong, but it's probably a good thing Sam will never know. No one will ever know.

Sizzling egg mixes with the morning playlist. I more or less waltz over to the chef, loving how relaxed she looks with her hair up, barefoot and beautiful in my kitchen. The stretch of smooth skin between the bottom of her tank and loose, hip hugging pajama bottoms tantalizes me. Her hips sway to the beat of *Sunday Morning* by Maroon 5.

I want to pull her against me, trail kisses along her neck, and maybe lift her on the counter to christen my kitchen. But that might be too couplish, especially while a song about being all I need is playing. This is just sex, and it's not even just sex. This is sex with a purpose, and knowing Sunny, she'll never visit Houston again after the birth of a child. She stayed in Whispering Creek for years for a horse. So, I let us cool a bit and heat up toast and set out butter, jelly, and plates on the breakfast bar.

As far as Sunday mornings go, even without kitchen sex, this one ranks as near perfection. When she joins me at the breakfast bar, she combs her fingers through the back of my hair. A fission of energy spreads across my shoulders and down my arms and spine. It's enough to eliminate rational thought, and I pull her to me and press my lips to hers. It's a closed mouth, nothing kiss, but it feels like something two people in a relationship would do. My eyes snap open, searching her face for concern or trouble. She pulls away to sit on the stool, but I don't register any cause for concern.

Her phone rings, the *Blackbird* ringtone jarring with the

morning playlist filtering through the apartment. "It's my aunt." She scrunches her nose and lifts her shoulders apologetically.

"Answer," I tell her, squeezing her thigh to reassure her, and, well, if I'm honest with myself, to touch her, to placate that visceral, hormonal need.

She speaks to her aunt for a while. Most of the conversation seems to be from her aunt's end. She eats through the call, every now and then glancing at me with a sexy as fuck smile. I get up and clear the dishes. We didn't have much to eat, just eggs and toast, so it didn't take us long to finish.

"Aunt Nora, I'll call you next week. Sound good?" She hangs up the phone, and it clatters on the counter. "Sorry about that. Aunt Nora can talk."

"No worries. She doing good?"

"Yeah, I think so. She finished reading a book she knows I won't read so she wanted to tell me all about it."

"What book?"

"Women's fiction. You've never heard of it."

"Why won't you read it?"

"Because I prefer romance. I like happy endings."

"You do, do you?" I wink at her, joking around, but not at all surprised by what she's saying. Sunny and happiness are synonymous.

She joins me by the sink, her hip nudging me out of the way so she can put her hands on the pan I'm scrubbing.

"No, ma'am. You cooked, I clean."

"I can't just sit back and watch you clean." She tugs on the Brillo pad in my hand, and I use my shoulder to block her.

"Go sit down."

"No. I want to help."

I toss the Brillo pad in the sink, shake the extra water off my hands, and bend to scoop her off the floor. She tosses her hair back, giggling. It's the best damn sound. My plan is to place her on the sofa, but her squirms threaten my balance, and I settle on the far end of the counter, stepping between her legs and claiming that joyful mouth. The kiss begins playfully, but when she tilts her head, our kiss deepens. I crush her to me, and her fingers dig into my back and my scalp. Her eager response urges me on, and I trail kisses from her lips down her throat as I palm her breast.

I lift that little tank over her arms, setting it down on the counter beside her, and stand back, taking in those luscious breasts in the daylight. She has truly fantastic tits. Fuller on the bottom, the perfect size for my hand, with round, pale nipples that beg to be sucked. The sunlight brightens her blonde, sex-tangled hair, and those blue eyes, well, that's the most fantastic sight of all, because she's looking at me with desire.

"You are incredible." *Stunning*.

Her cheeks flush with a light pink, and self-consciously, she raises an arm to cover those gorgeous breasts.

"Nooo," I scold, brushing her hands away.

One by one, I cup her lush breasts and lavish attention on the pale pink areolas with my tongue and ever so gently with my teeth. When my mouth covers one, my thumb flicks the sensitive skin of the other.

Her fingers cup my jaw, and I pause. Her lips turn up on the ends in a cautious smile.

"You said you wondered what my breasts looked like. Did you fantasize about doing this?"

I straighten, move a wayward golden strand off her face, and place a quick kiss on her nose. "I did. But can I tell you? These breasts are actually better than I imagined. More full. I love the color of your nipples. The way they taste. Sweet. Like honey." My palm presses her stomach, asking her to lean back. She complies, and with both hands around her pajama bottoms, I tug them right off and let them fall to the floor.

With her legs spread, my gaze falls to her bare pussy. "I also wondered about this. If you trimmed or if you were bare. I figured as much time as you spent on your nails, there was a good chance you didn't have a full bush."

Her gaze tilts up to the ceiling as she attempts to close her thighs, her cheeks aflame with rosy blush. "Back then, I probably did have a full bush. Is that what you prefer?"

My thumb flicks over her mound, then I snap my index finger over her clit. Her back arches, and she let out an *oh*.

"I like this. Smooth. Bare. Perfect for dessert."

I bend, bowing before her, nipping and kissing my way up her thighs to her petal-smooth center.

"Ahm…" Her back arches, and her fingers tease my hair. My erection throbs, peeking out of the top of my pants, but I ignore that need, because the desire to have her writhing on my kitchen counter is far greater. "Pretty sure I can't get pregnant this way." I pause, glancing up at her, my lips soaked with her essence. "As awesome as it is," she breathes out on an exhale.

"Do you want me to stop?"

"No." Her top teeth sink into her lower lip as she gives me a sultry smile, and I return my focus to her, slipping two fingers deep inside while my tongue worships her. Within minutes, her heels beat against my shoulders and she screams out my name like I always dreamed she would. Another fantasy come to fruition. I press my face into her stomach, giving us both a moment to catch our breaths.

"Did you request the counters to be this height?" Her fingers both tease my hair and massage my temple. The sensation is divine.

"I've never done this in a kitchen." Truth is, I haven't yet brought anyone back to this apartment. My hospital hook-ups happen at the hospital, and I've had a few hook-ups on nights out with Harrison, but for whatever reason never ended up back here. Those encounters were pretty far between, a side effect of residency and long hours post-residency.

"No?" Her thumb presses against my furrowed brow.

I brush my lips lightly over hers, and answer, so close my lips graze hers as I speak. "No."

My cock pulses, pre-cum dripping from the end. I grip my shaft, flicking my hand up roughly from the base, and position my tip at her soaking wet entrance.

"Now, let's get you pregnant."

Chapter Eighteen

Ian

Last Year in July

"You missed out this weekend," Harrison gloats with a conceited grin.

"I had a good one, too." I keep my facial expression as muted as possible. His gaze narrows, and I lift my water bottle and chug.

"Not like mine. My club. Worth every dollar." He leans over the table, glancing around to double-check no one is listening in. No one's listening. No one during the lunchtime rush cares what two middle-aged guys are talking about. "There's this back room. Holy shit. The women. To die for. Holy. Fuck. You've got to come with me. Thursday night."

"I don't think so." I pop a carrot into my mouth and let the crunch convey my low interest level in his chosen topic. I've nothing against a place that makes sexual encounters easy to obtain, but it's not my scene.

Harrison narrows his eyes into slits. He can push all he wants. I'm not changing my mind. I lift my wrap and bite.

A host of fast lunch options exist near the hospital, but That's A Wrap is the one we frequent the most. The cafeteria isn't horrible, but midday fresh air is a mental boost.

Harrison scratches his jaw, watching me. "That hottie tottie came back to town last weekend, didn't she?"

I shrug and take another bite.

"Damn. My man is off the market."

"It's not like that." I look him directly in the eye so he'll listen. "She needs a sperm donor. We're friends. I offered."

Harrison's mouth drops open into a dumbfounded gape. "Dude. Wait. Let me get this straight. The plan is for you to sleep with her, knock her up, and then what... go back to being just friends? Friends who fucked?"

I nod and swallow my water. It doesn't sound as reasonable when he says it, but that's due to the exaggerated emphasis he's putting on each word.

"For such an intelligent person, you can be a real dunce."

"This is what she wants." Besides, my family still sees her as Sam's. And I'm not an idiot. I'm violating serious bro' code, even if two decades have passed. She's not just a girl. She was his first love. But I'm not about to drop all that on Harrison while he's on a rant. It'll just make me look like a bigger fool. Or maybe the word is ass.

"Well, if you're just boning a friend as a favor, then you should totally come with me Thursday night. It's a leather and lace theme. Live out some fantasies. You're not in a committed relationship. She shouldn't mind."

I consider his argument. He's correct, Sunny shouldn't mind. But the fact is, last weekend I lived out my fantasies. I don't need a guest pass to Harrison's sex club.

"Dude. Think about what I am offering. It's rare I'll be able to bring a male guest. And there is no guilt. All these women want the exact same thing."

"We're not using protection." Harrison leans forward to hear me better, because out of respect for Sunny, I lowered my voice. "I'm not about to risk giving her something."

"Everyone at the club is tested monthly. And we use condoms." He crosses his arms, and I get the sense he's putting obstacles up solely to argue with me.

"Fantastic." I ball up my napkin and drop it on the tray. "Still not risking it."

"You don't comprehend what you're missing out on."

I shake my head and stand. "She's one of my best friends. Not doing it."

Harrison nods slowly. He either understands or he's decided it's not worth arguing over. "I guess you don't even want to hear about the orgy room?"

"No, really don't."

He looks at me like I smashed his Lego set into smithereens. "But I can meet you for a drink beforehand," I offer. It's the least I can do, and the offer seems to placate him.

"For the record, I'm against this. Trust me. Things like this don't end well."

"Things like what?" I taunt. Harrison is the last person I'd expect to give me trouble for a no-strings sexual arrangement.

"Relationships without a clear path forward. Crash and..." His lips pinch, he uncurls his hand like an explosion, and adds a "boom" sound effect.

I walk away, shaking my head at his nonsense. As if he'd know. And besides, we're not in that kind of a relationship. At the base of it all, Sunny and I have a friendship and clearly defined expectations. Hell, we even have a contract.

An hour later, after scrubbing in, I enter the OR. My standard mix, a selection of alternative rock from the early two thousands to now, plays on the iPod.

"No, something different. Do the Sunny mix."

Shelby, a nurse I work with frequently, scrolls through my Spotify mix until she finds my request. James Brown's familiar chords rip through the room, and wrinkles around every single person's eyes form. Behind the masks, you can't see the smiles, but the eye wrinkles… they always give them away.

"I feel good," James sings, and I bob my head in time to the beat as I check the monitor and converse with the anesthesiologist.

"Someone's in a good mood," Shelby says.

"Let's do this. Scalpel."

My focus falls to my patient, and, like always, my thoughts coalesce and muscle memory and focus intertwine. Two hours later, the knee replacement is complete.

My next surgery is a rotator cuff tear. Before scrubbing in, I shoot off a text to Sunny. She promised to text when she got back, but there's nothing on my phone. She left earlier this morning for Whispering Creek.

Me: All okay?

In the next OR, the nurse selects one of my frequently played soundtracks. A Chainsmoker song reminds me of dancing with Sunny on New Year's Eve. *This, I can work with.*

Less than an hour later, I scrub out and see Sunny still hasn't responded to my text. I speak briefly with the wife of my patient, check in on my knee replacement from earlier, then head back to my office.

What would the odds be that she was in a wreck on the ride home? Or if something else happened? What if she got home and checked on a cat in the barn or something? She could've been bitten by a snake. Or a rabid animal might have attacked her. She could be unconscious in the paddock, and no one would be nearby to help her.

Normally, I'd call my mom and have her swing by to check, but my folks are back at their place at the beach. I could call Oliver, but then he'd be clued in that she was here this past weekend. And odds are, she is absolutely fine. If I call him, she'll be pissed because Ollie will get suspicious and maybe in his own dumbass way kick start a swirl of rumors. He might even say something to Sam.

On my phone, I type in my parents' home address and check the route. There's one crash over the three-hour route. No information on it. Chances are it's not her. The timing wouldn't jive. If she got in a wreck this morning, the wreck would be cleared by now.

Fuck it. The problem with witnessing the results of statistically rare accidents all day is that statistics no longer provide comfort to me. I dial my mom. She answers on the fourth ring.

"Hi, there, sweetie. I was just on the phone with Ollie. He's having a great time in Costa Rica."

"He's in Costa Rica?"

"Yeah, with the girl from Jackson."

"Really?" Last May, he'd flown out there to see someone.

"Do you know her?" Mom asks.

"No." Oliver and I don't discuss our dating lives much. He texted back in May. There'd been some late season avalanche, and he'd been worried about her, but I didn't probe. But if he's in Costa Rica with her now, I'll need to try to remember to say something the next time I see him. Ask for a name, at least. I rub the back of my neck, biting down frustration. "Mom, I'm not calling to talk about Oliver." But the fact that he's out of town makes this request much easier. "Do you know anyone who could swing by the ranch and check on something?"

"What do you–"

"It's Sunny. She visited me in Houston this weekend. She had a singing gig Saturday night. Left this morning. She was supposed to call when she got back and hasn't."

"Oh, dear. Let me think. I'm sure we can get someone over there."

"Patty? Who's that?"

"It's Ian. He's worried about Sunny."

"Sunny?" The alarm in Dad's tone rings clear. Mom must put her hand over the phone because everything gets muffled.

"Your dad's on it. You know, he worries about her like she's his own. He's calling Frank now." I run my fingers through my hair. The setting sun casts a golden halo over the city, and I'm hit with the feeling I might have overreacted. Calling my mom, that's... "You know, you're just like your dad. Always worried about her."

"We grew up with her," I say, hoping to ward off any suspicion.

"That's true. And," she lets out a loud sigh, "you know, I think your dad still feels responsible for her mom."

What? "What do you mean by that?"

"Oh, wait. Hold on a moment." Mom disappears. There are muffled voices, so I can only assume Dad is updating Mom. Depending on where Frank is on the ranch, he could be really close to Sunny or far away. It's a sprawling ranch.

Sunny's mom died when she was a baby. Childbirth, but I don't think I ever heard more specifics than that. But now that I think about it, given what Sunny's trying to do, that could be important medical history. But why on Earth would Dad feel responsible for her mom's death?

"Honey, she's fine. Frank got hold of her."

"Mom, what did you mean by–" My phone beeps, and I check the incoming call. It's Sunny. "Mom, I'm gonna take this. I'll call you back later." I switch over and practically growl into the phone, "There you are."

"Sorry. So sorry! I got back and started doing laundry. I left my phone in the car. I just wasn't thinking."

"You need to add me to Find Your Friends. If I could trace you, I'd know you made it home okay."

"That's sweet. But, Ian, your mom? And Frank? Are you out of your mind?"

"Sunny." I stretch and flex the fingers of my free hand. "Do not."

"Frank," she squeals, like that's all the evidence she needs to put forth.

"Sunny, I told Mom you came into the city to sing. She didn't think anything of it. I promise. You were supposed to have gotten home seven hours ago. Seven. Hours."

She exhales, and I can practically see her caving. "I'm sorry. I'm not used to needing to report back to anyone."

"Yeah, well…" I let the words hang there. I'm flustered, tired, and need to go for a run. "I see the aftermath of the unexpected. When you leave Houston, you need to remember to let me know you're okay."

"Okay. Frank's waiting in the front yard. I promised him a brownie." Her chilly tone riles me up. *Unbelievable.* She's angry. At me.

"Fine." I end the call, and my grip around the phone tightens. This is one reason I don't do relationships. I don't have the time or the patience to deal with bullshit.

I've seen plenty of colleagues stressed after missing a dinner reservation, birthdays, anniversaries, or what have you. It happens all the time because we work in a field where our job is saving lives, and that takes priority over life's minutiae. I've had women pissed because I had to bail, or a week passed without us seeing each other. Then I feel guilty, and I call it. Why waste time on something that's just not going to work out? My schedule isn't going to change.

But this with Sunny, this isn't her mad at me for bailing on her or for my being unavailable. I tug on my running shoe and pull the lace so tight I risk bruising. No, this is completely irrational. On her part. She forgot to call me. I got worried. And then she got mad at me. *What the hell, Sunny?*

Chapter Nineteen

Sunny

Last Year in July

"You don't need to give me this," Frank says, but he's already got the package of brownies tucked up on his side.

"It's just me here. You're doing these hips a favor."

The skin just above Frank's salt-and-pepper beard flushes. He shifts his cowboy hat the way the men tend to do at the end of a long day, back and forth in quick jerks to scratch the itchy skin below the hat's band.

"Tell Mary I said hello."

"I will. She asks about you. When Patty called–"

"I know, I scared you." He's already said this many times. "Thanks for stopping by to check on me."

"Any time. You know, Mary and I are always here." I nod. "Patty said you were with Ian."

My muscles tense and lungs contract, and on reflex, I smile.

"How's he doing? I see Ollie all the time, never see Ian or Little Sam."

"Ian's doing good."

"That's good. Good to hear. Sounds like they all still look out for you. That's good, too."

With a smile plastered on, I give Frank a goodbye hug. From the front stoop, I watch as Frank climbs onto the tractor he rode over here. Apparently, he'd been nearby when he got the call from Patty.

Frank and Mary Barnes are close in age to Sam and Patty Duke. Frank had been friends with my dad, and they've been good to me over the years. Their kids are grown. One son lives in Arizona, and their daughter moved to Tennessee. There's no telling how this story will get spun, but on the bright side, it's unlikely it'll reach my group of friends.

I glance over to the empty pasture and imagine Polly's head hanging over the fence. She's not there, of course, but an emptiness strikes hard. My eyes mist, and I ache to bury my face in her musty neck and for her nuzzle to tickle my palm.

Oh, man, I need a drink.

But I do not drink alone. That's a lesson dear old Dad taught remarkably well. On a normal day, I'd meander up to the Dukes' house and find Oliver. But, since he's apparently out of town, I scroll through my favorites and press Noah's name.

"Look who it is. I was on my way to your place."

I hold my breath. If he says Ian called him, so help me... The purring of an engine and the low, distinct sound of wheels on gravel breaks through the tree hedge.

"Are you here now?"

"Sure am."

The hood of Noah's rusted green Bronco comes into view, and I end the call and slip the phone into my back pocket. I stand on the stoop, hands on my hips, and wait for him to climb out of his busted-up vehicle.

"How're you doing?" Noah's in jeans and the black boots he wears in the kitchen. He got into the restaurant business out of his love for cooking, but he's rarely a chef these days. His thick, light brown hair is pulled back into a low man bun, and his white t-shirt has stains all across it.

"Were you the chef today?"

"Helped out with prep. We were short-staffed at Thai Me Up, but it's all good now."

"I didn't think you were open on Mondays?"

"It's not a vanity business." Noah gives a teasing wink. "Hell, yeah, we're open on Monday. Seven days a week. But I swear, people up and quit all the damn time." His boot lands on the bottom step with a thud. "I need a drink." He gestures to the door that's behind me. "You gonna invite me in?"

"You don't need an invitation. You still staying with Oliver?"

"Nah. Got an apartment down near Main Street. But I have a key to the Dukes'. I can crash there if I need to."

"That kind of day, huh?" The screen door creaks loudly.

"Where do you keep your WD-40?"

"I think there's some in my dad's stuff under the carport, but don't worry about it. I like to hear when it opens."

The screen door slams behind him, and Noah follows me through the house. I open the fridge and peer inside.

"I've got beer, chardonnay, or there's vodka in the freezer."

"I'll take a beer."

I take a bottle out, snap off the lid, and hand it to him.

"You're drinking with me, right?"

Lord knows I want to. And chances are I'm not pregnant. I open the top cabinet and take out a wine glass, then fill it with the Chardonnay, sniffing it to see if it's still good. The aroma is a little strong, so I swirl it and focus my gaze on Noah.

"So, tell me about it."

"Nothing to really tell. Just another day raining bullshit." He chugs hard on his beer, and when he sets it down, the neck of the bottle fills with foam. "Where were you this weekend?"

Huh. So, Ian didn't call him.

"Houston. Did you come looking for me?"

He shrugs. "Oliver's out of town."

"Well, I wouldn't've been much good as a wingman."

"What do you mean by that?"

"From what I'm hearing, you like them young these days."

He grins and shakes his head, takes another long swallow, slams the beer down, and crosses his arms over his chest. "Don't believe everything you hear. You know how this town rolls."

He's right. I do. I take a dainty sip of the wine in my glass. It tastes fine, so I take another sip. "You know much about this girl Oliver's seeing?"

Noah's lower lip bulges out, and he looks thoughtful. "No. Neither does Liam. But he'll tell us if he wants us to know."

"Yeah, I guess that's true."

"What's this with Houston?"

I proceed to tell Noah all about my singing gig. He doesn't question it at all. Even tells me I can sing at one of his restaurants if I want. In the summer, he has live music at Sweet Magnolia, one of his Austin restaurants.

Noah's been a good friend for decades, and as he presses me about playing at his place, the truth tempts me. It's on the tip of my tongue to spill, to tell him what's going on. But the words get stuck. After all, the truth is a mouthful.

"Let's go sit outside," I say.

A swarm of lightning bugs beneath the old maple by the back pasture fence dots the darkness with intermittent golden bursts. The crickets and frogs kick in with a low hum that's synonymous with summer nights. A plane soars above us, the bright lights growing steadily closer as it descends for the approach to the regional airport. Some people like breathtaking views in their back yards, but me, I like this. Peace.

We sit outside talking about nothing and letting the evening slip by.

"Welp, girl, I better let you get to it. You got work in the morning, right?"

"I do." I look down at the two empty beer bottles beside Noah's chair. "You good to drive?"

"Yeah, but I'll probably just crash at the Dukes'. I need to put some food out for the barn cats."

"I'm sure Frank did that."

"Oliver says he's apt to forget. You good?"

"Yeah. Of course."

"I'm not asking whether that miniscule glass of wine is going to prohibit you from making it safely back to bed. You seem distant. Quiet. You okay?"

"Yeah. I'm fine." I give him a bright smile. "Just tired."

He accepts my statement, and I watch from the stoop until Noah's red lights disappear behind the tree line that separates our property from the packed dirt road that goes to the Dukes'. Nothing's wrong, but I was a little out of line tonight, or, at the very least, reactive. That's what my dad used to say when I'd get out of sorts. Sometimes, if Dad was in a strong place and felt like he could talk about her, he'd say I reminded him of Mom.

Ian Duke's name sits near the top of my favorites in my address book, and I stare at it and the time. It's too late to call him. He's an early to bed, early to rise kind of guy. I shoot off a text without wasting any time debating it.

Me: Sorry if I got a little touchy earlier. I screwed up. I should've called. I'm sorry I made you worry.

Three dots appear and disappear. *Is he awake?*

. . .

Ian: No worries.

———

The next three weeks pass without issue. It's wedding season, so I'm busier than normal. There's a saying that has more meaning now that I'm forty. The days pass slowly, but the months fly by. And it's with the where-has-the-time-gone dismay that I find myself staring at the desk calendar in my office. I pull out my phone and check my period app, just to be certain.

Holy smokes and grasses. I'm two days late.

It's probably nothing. But I immediately flick to the search browser.

"How pregnant do you need to be before a pregnancy test is accurate?"

The answer is in bold. Can be accurate on the day of a missed period, but more likely to be accurate if taken the day after a missed period.

I'm two days late. I'm in the accurate phase.

On the way home, I stop by the Rite Aid and buy a six-pack of pregnancy tests. The teenage guy ringing me up doesn't seem to register what it is I'm buying. He's got earbuds in and says all the appropriate things, like "do you have your loyalty number" and "thank you," but I suspect he's listening to something. Times have changed. Back when I was in high school, you couldn't buy a pregnancy test without every single person in town knowing by nightfall. But, I suppose, a guy that young really doesn't care what someone old enough to be his mom is buying.

Back in my house, I sit with the pregnancy tests. Excitement bubbles up beneath my skin in itchy patches. I can't believe it. I mean, this is just very unlikely.

I snap a photo of the unopened box and text it to Ian with the caption, "Will know shortly."

The plastic wrapper around the box proves difficult to open, and as I sit there scratching at it with my nails, my phone rings. Ian's name shows on the screen. I grin. It's an uncontrollable, giddy grin.

"I haven't taken it yet," I tell him the second I answer.

"Good. Don't." I hold the phone out a bit and look at it, then put it back up to my ear.

"What? Why?" It's too late to have second thoughts.

"Wait for me. I want to be there."

"Ian. That's sweet. But you are three hours away. I'll call you and tell you. Hang tight."

Chapter Twenty

Ian

Last August

I pace my bedroom. Waiting.

Fuck. What if she's pregnant?

It's what she wants. It's probably for the best. We had our one weekend. Things got weird between us after one weekend. If it went on and on...but damn, I wanted another weekend. I want tons of weekends.

And shit. I forgot to ask about Sunny's pregnancy history. I thought I'd have more time. And that thought has me glancing at the clock on my bedside table. It's too late to call my mom. Ask her exactly how Sunny's mom died. No one ever talks about it, but that would've been forty years ago, so why would they?

Shit. Shit. Shit.

The strap of my overnight bag hangs down from the shelf in

my closet, taunting me. I should just throw some clothes in and jump in the car.

What? Where did that idea come from? I have an early morning surgery. My pulse hums in my veins. My skin nearly vibrates, alert and energized. I should sleep, but there's no fucking way.

The phone lights in my hand. I hit accept so quickly it never vibrates.

"I'm pregnant."

Black dots mar my vision. I inhale. Breathe. "That's...wow."

"I guess you have super sperm."

"Yeah, I guess I do." The mattress sinks beneath my weight.

"Don't tell anyone. I mean, it's early."

"Yeah, yeah. It's early. Of course. And I wouldn't..." We agreed no one would know it's mine. Why would I tell anyone?

"Well, I guess...yeah. I can't believe it."

"Right. Well..." I rub my forehead, thinking things through. "Ahm, when will you go to the doctor?"

"I...I'll search it up."

"Do you...would you want to come to Houston? Or..." I can find her a doctor here, no problem, but with an OB, that's probably not the wisest course of action.

"Maybe. I don't know. Let me look into it."

"I'll look into it, too." I should've researched all of this shit already. What is wrong with me? "Ahm..." I hesitate, scrubbing my fingers through the hair on the back of my head. "When you...if I...maybe...ahm"

"Ian?" Her concerned tone snaps me out of whatever fog I'm in.

"I'd like to be there at the doctor's appointment. If it's possible. For you. Be there for you."

"That's really sweet."

I'm not trying to be sweet. I just... hell, it's late. I can't decipher my rattled thought processes. "I'll give you a call tomorrow. I'm in surgery all morning, but...later."

———

My surgeries pass without any complications. Last night, I considered getting on my laptop, but instead I popped some melatonin and forced myself to get some shuteye. Priorities.

But with the surgeries done, I can do some quick research. Or should I call her?

I'm not sure there's any protocol one has to follow in situations like this. But I do a quick search for information on when to see a doctor when you're pregnant. It's probably something I should remember from med school, but I don't. One quick Google search later, and I see we don't need to see a doctor until she's eight weeks gestation, and now she's, like, three weeks pregnant. Or, no, the way they count it would be from her last period, which would be approximately five weeks. So, we've got some time to research doctors. Hell, Sunny probably already has a gynecologist. She might want to stay with whoever she already sees.

My office door clicks shut, and I dial Sunny. It rings and rings. I set the phone to speaker and open my email on the hospital computer.

"Hey, you." Her tone is heavy with sadness, and all the energy buzzing inside me deflates, crashing down.

"Sunny?" She doesn't really have to say more. I know.

"I guess I jumped the gun."

"Got your period?"

"Yeah. I guess those tests aren't as reliable as they claim." Or she miscarried. It's highly probable she miscarried.

We sit there, on the phone, silent, for what feels like forever. There's a heavy weight bearing down on me, and I don't really know what to say. I wish I was with her so I could console her with a hug. She wanted this. "This weekend I'll come into town and–"

"Don't bother. I'm okay."

"But–"

"There are four weddings this weekend. If you're coming into town for me, don't."

"When are you coming back to Houston?"

"We'll see. It's wedding season. It's a busy season."

"Kind of like motorcycle weekend here?"

"Huh?"

The ER gets flooded on motorcycle weekends, but… "Yeah, just… You're not going to give up, are you? This is…"

"No. I'm just allowing myself an hour to feel sad. Then in the infamous words of Taylor Swift, I'll shake it off."

"I think it would be okay to be sad for more than an hour."

"Nope." Her tone is bright and perky. "One hour. That's it."

Chapter Twenty-One

Ian

Last September

The familiar symptoms of exhaustion envelop me as I open my refrigerator door.

"Did you eat?" I call out to Sunny.

It's been almost two months since she came to visit. Two months of infrequent texts and touching base. Two months of wedding season and completing applications for spinal fellowships and surgeries. Although it occurred to me we both might have been finding excuses. Harrison is actually the one who pointed it out. Or what he really said was something along the lines of, "If you want to spend time with someone, you find the time."

Harrison's insightful statement simply underscored the point that Sunny and I aren't in a relationship. We're friends, and the benefits component is strictly to serve a purpose. A purpose I suspect she's been scared to pursue after...well, the error. She was pregnant for all of twenty-four hours, so I hesitate to call it miscarriage. Although, if you believe the accuracy of the tests, that's what it was.

"I've eaten." Sunny enters the kitchen and grips the top of the refrigerator door, widening the gap so she can see in. "But I packed some food for you."

A few of the takeout containers I stacked on shelves are missing, and in their place are sealed plastic containers of food.

"Some things are in the freezer. But I know how much you like your mom's chicken and rice soup, so I made you a batch. And also, there's barbecue from Willy's. Oh, and I made some of the cucumber and tomato salad you like. It's all fresh from the garden. This year, I managed to keep the bugs out of the tomatoes."

Without thinking, I weave my fingers through her wet hair until the back of her head fits snugly in my palm and pull her to me, kissing her soundly on the lips. Her eyes widen and she doesn't push me away, but she doesn't open for me either.

Probably shouldn't have done that. Great. This isn't awkward at all.

I bend down and feign fascination with the contents of my fridge.

"There are two frozen casseroles in your freezer, but they'll take too long to thaw. Plus, there's a frozen chocolate cake."

"You froze a cake?"

"Well, I made it Monday, you know, my day off, and I wanted it to stay fresh. I was worried about how it would do in the cooler, but it did fine."

"Which one is the chicken and rice?"

Her hip bumps me on the side, and her arm curls around my back. Her touch sends tingles coursing along my spine. Her touch is over my shirt, but I want those fingers on my skin. The semi-wood I was sporting hardens. I call on all my self-control to refrain from grabbing her and sliding my hand down those loose pajama bottoms to squeeze her fine, delectable ass.

I back up to the kitchen counter, giving us both space. She

scoops out congealed soup into a bowl and places it in the microwave.

This evening at the hospital, I focused on the unexpected surgery. Sunny waited for me back here, at my apartment, while I spent extra time with the parents post-surgery, going over expected recovery times and the physical therapy their son would need and explaining that no, he probably wouldn't be able to play football for the rest of this season. And I drew upon all my patience when the father argued that it was his son's junior year of high school and really important he play. Obviously, none of those factors changed the medical diagnosis. The kid went over the handlebars mountain bike riding. Broke his collarbone and suffered a radius compound fracture. He could get a second opinion, but no doctor would recommend he get tackled for sport.

The moment I broke away, I prepared myself for Sunny, waiting back at my apartment. The second I saw her, I felt at peace. Like I'd been on a tight cord for months and hadn't realized it, and having her in my home set everything to rights. And I wanted her. A visceral need coursed through me like I've never felt before. There's fantasizing, and then there's need. And watching her move around my narrow kitchen stirs an unfamiliar level of warmth and desire.

Harrison has been after me to join him at his ridiculously expensive club. I've met him for drinks there more than once. But...I haven't done anything. I've blamed it on not wanting to bring any risk to Sunny, but as the weeks ticked by, I began to wonder if she'd ever come visit again.

I try to imagine her pregnant, with a protruding belly. And then a vision of her holding a baby surfaces. Her foster kid had been a toddler. Mom said he was as adorable as could be. She also said he was incredibly lucky to have Sunny in his life, as she was a natural mother. I can see it, just watching her move around my kitchen, hunting out my saltines, taking care of me.

If she were pregnant with my child, if that was my toddler

Mom called adorable, would I really be okay playing the distant uncle role? With no one knowing the kid is mine? Leaving Sunny to handle it all on her own?

If I receive a spinal fellowship, I'll have another year of training. I could be far away, across the country. Chances are I won't have a choice. I'll have no time to put in as a father. Hell, half the doctors I know who married in their twenties are now divorced or in their second marriages.

"Sit down." Sunny's warm, soft fingers nudge me in the direction of the bar stool. I blink, snapping myself out of my zone.

"Tough day?" she asks.

"Nah. Just a long one."

She pulls a hair band off her wrist, gathers her blonde strands, and ties her hair back, off her shoulders. My stomach rumbles, reminding me I need to eat.

"You know, when you were late tonight, I wondered if you might be re-thinking this decision." I glance up at her, dripping spoon midair over my lap. "And it would be okay. I would understand. I can easily find an anonymous donor. You don't have to do this."

She thinks I'm the one second-guessing this? She's the one who hasn't made time to visit in nearly two months.

The hot, buttery soup burns going down the back of my throat. A small amount remains in the bowl, and I slurp down all but a handful of white rice grains. When I set the bowl down, it clatters on the oversize plate she set down as some sort of placemat. I rest my elbows on the kitchen bar and look directly into those sky-blue irises.

"This is something I want to do. For you. I thought you might have changed your mind."

An all-too-telling flush climbs from her throat to her cheeks, and her gaze drops to her fingers. "I've been busy."

"You got scared." There's something about the way she's

picking at her nails that makes me remember we should look at her medical history.

She lets out a sigh then lifts her gaze. She sucks in that bottom lip and halfway smiles. It's an adorable combination that only Sunny does. "Maybe. And I think that's okay, all things considered. Just like it's okay if you change your mind. We can change our minds about this at any time, and it's perfectly acceptable."

"I'm not changing my mind." It's an honest statement, but I don't think I realized exactly how true it is until I say those words out loud. "If I can give you this, then I'll be doing something for a friend, and I'll get to spread my DNA so future generations can share in my greatness."

She mirrors the wide grin on my face, one I mean to be irreverent, and I reach out to touch her.

"Seriously, this is the best of all worlds for me. I can be around my kid, when my schedule allows, without disappointing him with my absence. He won't grow up with some chip on his shoulder or significant insecurity because his father spent too much time at work. I mean, you're planning on telling everyone that you had an anonymous sperm donor, right?"

She nods her confirmation. The plan hasn't changed. Those long lashes flutter, and I reach out to gently rub a smudged black mark on the corner of her eye then cup her cheek in my palm. An abundance of warmth for this woman flows from my chest. I'll do anything for her. Anything at all.

I stand and move closer, drawn to her. The scent of mint and lemon intermingle. All the exhaustion that had settled onto my muscles lifts. My lips find hers. What starts out as a chaste kiss evolves when she opens. Her hands roam my arms and shoulders, and she pushes off the stool. Her pelvis scrapes my groin, eliciting the best kinds of sensations and stoking the best kind of heat.

"Let's go to bed." I shift her in the right direction.

"Let me clean—"

"Tomorrow. I'll do it tomorrow."

I bend to pick her up, to carry her down the hall, but she backs away with the sexiest little grin. Her index finger wraps around my pinky finger and she tugs, not that she needs to, because I'm going wherever she goes. In my bedroom, we stand a foot apart, gazes locked. She removes her tank. I let my pajama pants fall to my ankles. Her thumbs loop under her waistband, and her loose bottoms fall to the floor.

We stand there, nude, bared to each other. Her palm presses to my sternum, and through touch, she shows me exactly where she wants me to lie. She kisses me as she moves her body over mine. Her nipples tease my chest, and her soft curves melt against me. With the seduction of a slow-motion film, she straddles me and rises, positioning my tip at her center, and slowly takes me. That tight heat grips me, and my balls tighten. Heaven. My hands grip her hips, just in case I need to slow her down, because she feels incredible, and it's important to me she finds her release before I do. She pinches her nipples while I stretch to knead her clit. Those full tits bounce as she rides me, up and down, and when her face morphs into one of ecstasy, I soon follow, pulsing into her and sending a wish into the night to please, never ever let me forget this moment.

Chapter Twenty-Two

Sandra

Last Christmas Eve

The lights on the Christmas tree flick on, thanks to the timer in the wall, as I stir the apple cider on the stove and drop in a couple of cinnamon sticks.

"Shelby and I were talking, and this is two years in a row we've missed Christmas with you."

"Well, Aunt Nora, you two could come here. I'd love to have you visit."

"We're going to have to come visit soon. But, for now, Shelby's mom isn't doing well, and it's just hard to get away."

"I understand. Maybe I can get away one of these weekends coming up. It's been a long time since I've seen you."

"Well, you coming to see us only works if the man in your life joins you." I can't help but smile, but I also roll my eyes at my crazy aunt. "Because, you know, I want to meet him."

"First, he's not the man in my life. Second, you've met him plenty of times."

"No, I met him as a kid. I want to meet the man." Shelby's muffled voice carries over the line and then grows more distant.

The spoon clanks against the tile countertop. One day, I will renovate this kitchen. But I've been slow to change things since inheriting my family home from my father. With just me in the house, there's been little need. My palm flattens over my belly, and I send out the thousandth wish into the ether.

"I want to meet the love of your life." Aunt Nora's voice brings me back.

I let out a huff loud enough she can hear me and argue, "He's not the love of my life."

"You don't love him?"

"Of course, I do. But you know there are different relationships in life, right? We mean a lot to each other. But neither of us is looking for that traditional setup."

"Katharine Hepburn famously lived next door to her lover for years, refusing to move in with him. Nontraditional doesn't mean he's not the love of your life."

I sit in the kitchen chair and pull my legs up under me, letting my gaze fall on the Christmas tree. "I don't know, Aunt Nora. I'd like to think my monthly hook-up isn't the best I'll ever have." The romantic in me wants more. And I'll never get more with Ian. Sure, I vent to him about the silly crapola that happens at the salons, and he's my person I call for, well, really anything these days. "Besides, I want a person I can share lazy Sundays with and cuddle with at night, and that'll never be Ian."

"Haven't I interrupted you on a lazy Sunday at his place?"

"Are you calling bullshit on me?" I grin. "I mean, yeah, you have, but those days are rare."

"Eh, well–"

"Aunt Nora, I don't need someone. I'm fine. I'm happy. But all I'm saying is I'm not quite ready to give up on the dream. At heart,

I'm a romantic. And I'd like to believe there's a great love out there, and I just haven't met him yet."

"Okay. But take it from an old lady. Don't let life pass you by while you're waiting for a bus that might be having engine troubles."

"Aunt Nora." The woman's truly unbelievable. And grumpy.

"Just saying." She huffs, but it's light and loving in the way she has. "You going over to the Dukes' for Christmas lunch tomorrow?"

"More like brunch." The Duke crew will arrive after lunch, and I want to be sure to get out of their way so they can have family time.

"What time is your man supposed to get there?"

"Would you quit calling him that?"

"Monthly hook-up doesn't work for me, dear. You could call him your gentleman friend. Mary from yoga likes that phrase."

"Aunt Nora." Before this call, my mood had been happy and buzzy, and yet here she is bringing me down into an eddy. "He's driving down today. He worked late last night and said he had some shopping to get done before he left Houston."

It's after nine. He definitely isn't in a rush to get here. As a matter of fact, it's so late now I won't be surprised if he drives straight to his parents'.

"And no news on the baby front?"

My eyelids close. There it is. The reason I can't speak to Aunt Nora as regularly these days. She. Always. Asks.

"No. I don't think it's going to happen." I probably need to tell Ian that, too. We've been trying for months now. I mean, yes, we missed October because work was too intense for me to get away. In early December I didn't think I'd get away, but he drove down, spent the night, and then was on his way back to Houston since I had to work. But no success.

"Well, hun, you can't give up. Sometimes it takes time. But this is what Shelby and I call your enjoyable Plan A. Maybe while you continue enjoying yourself, you could get the paperwork rolling on Plan B."

"Would that be IVF or adoption?"

"Either. But Shelby thinks it's time to talk to a fertility specialist and consider IVF. International adoption is also a possibility." Both options are inordinately expensive, but I won't moan about that, or she'll offer money she needs for retirement.

"You and Shelby talk about this a lot, don't you?"

"Of course, we do. We love you, and this is important to you."

"Yes, but it's…" Personal is what I want to blurt out. "I promise if I have any news, you'll be the first to know. But even then, the miscarriage rate for women my age is high." And sometimes you don't even get past the forty-eight-hour mark.

"And you live in that backward state. You'd better not tell anyone if you get pregnant. You don't want some nosy body questioning if as a single woman you had an abortion. I swear, I don't know how you live there."

She's not wrong. And given my career, I cakewalk with a horde of nosy bodies every single day. I can't imagine anyone would actually try to turn me in for an investigation, but you never know. Religion and self-righteousness can do funny things to a person. Not to mention a ten-thousand-dollar bonus.

Headlights flash in my driveway. Ian.

"You still there?" Aunt Nora asks.

"Yeah. I need to run."

"He's there, isn't he?" Somehow, her smile carries through the line.

"I love you, and I'll call tomorrow to wish you both a Merry Christmas."

"Video."

"Yes, video. Love you."

By the time I open the front door, Ian stands behind his car with an overnight bag over one shoulder and a shopping bag.

"You need to wrap presents?" I call out from the stoop.

"What do you take me for? Someone who buys unwrapped presents?" He mock shudders, and I smile but pull the shawl around me more tightly.

"Did you get dinner?"

"Yeah, I did. Sorry I'm so late. I needed to swing by the hospital to check on someone who is having some post-surgical complications."

"I thought you had off. Didn't you say today officially counts as vacation?"

"It's Christmas. Super light staff." His trunk closes, and a beep sounds.

"Did you get all your shopping done?"

"Yeah. Remind me to not wait to buy all the gifts on Christmas Eve next year."

"You didn't." I shake my head at him in disbelief. He has a large family.

"It used to not be a problem, but I didn't have somewhere I wanted to be before."

He saunters up the steps in jeans, brown dress shoes, and a light crewneck sweater. His tousled hair is a sexy mess. Several days' worth of growth along his jawline gives him the beginnings of a short beard. Ian Duke is one handsome man. My stomach flutters and pulse quickens. *He's here. Finally.*

As he approaches, I notice the skin below his golden-brown eyes seems slightly sunken and discolored.

"Are you tired?"

"Eh, I'm fine." He dips his head and brushes his lips across mine, then steps past me into my home.

"I have some lasagna I can heat for you. I also have a Christmas roll I made. But if we don't cut into it, I can bring it to your parents' in the morning."

"Why are we doing brunch? Everyone's going to get in after lunch. We should just go over for dinner."

"But then your parents would be alone in the morning."

"Trust me, I think Dad will be okay with that."

He sets the bag of presents down near my tree, reaches into it, and lifts out a bottle of wine, toes off his shoes, and pads in his socks into the kitchen.

"Want a glass of wine? This is a good bottle."

"Sure. Did you want the lasagna?" I cooked it in case he arrived earlier but ended up eating by myself.

"No, thanks. I ran through a McDonald's drive-through."

"McDonalds? You?"

He shrugs. "Christmas Eve. Pickings were slim. Besides, one thing of French fries won't kill me."

"I'm glad you realize that." His biceps bulge slightly as he strains to pull out the cork using my dad's archaic wine opener. "I have a better one of those."

"Nah, this is fine. I picked up some of your favorites from the French bakery. They're in the bag."

"My favorites?" I re-enter the den as he sets out two wine glasses.

"Macarons? You like them, right? It's the only dessert I ever see you buy."

"Well, they're kind of a pain to make. But, yes, I do like them."

He offers me my glass and sits in front of the Christmas tree.

"What're you doing?"

"Well, we're exchanging presents, right? That's what you do on Christmas Eve."

I stand in front of him, one arm over my midriff.

"It's late. Shouldn't you be getting home? Your mom is going to worry about you on the road."

"She thinks I'm driving over in the morning. We said we were spending Christmas Eve together." He looks at me like I've forgotten some important conversation.

"I know, but I just figured you're running so late, so you'd head on to your folks. It's Christmas."

"Yeah, it is. And that's why I'm here with you. Now, sit down so we can toast."

"What time is everyone arriving, again?" He said after lunch, but that's a broad swatch of time.

"You're asking me?" He holds up his glass for a toast, effectively ending that line of conversation. "Merry Christmas Eve."

Our glasses clink, but an unsettled feeling stirs in my belly.

"Have you heard from Oliver?"

Oliver spent the last few days with Kate in Vermont with her family. It turns out they actually met a year ago, when Sam's kids were sick and the Duke family Christmas got postponed. She moved to Texas about a month ago, and I've been getting to know her. She and I hit it off once I finally got to meet her in person. Oliver and Kate are flying to Connecticut, then flying down with Sam and his family in their private jet to Texas. Mrs. Duke filled me in on the plans, but she didn't share flight times.

"Here and there," Ian says, and I know that means he's texted sporadically with his brother.

"Have you met Kate yet?"

"When would I've met her?" He sips the wine and closes his eyes, letting the wine work its magic through what I imagine are tense, stiff, exhausted muscles. The man works himself to the bone.

"I don't know. She's going to be your sister-in-law." He hasn't been home since she moved down here, so I guess I am asking a silly question.

"They got engaged?" His face scrunches into one of complete disbelief.

"Not yet, but it's coming. Now that she's moved here, I can't imagine it will take long. Does he talk to you about her?" Oliver was slow to open up to me about Kate, but once he did, well, he talks about her all the time now.

"Not really. You've told me more about her than he has. You like her, right?"

"I do. She's down to earth. A much better fit than Camilla."

"Well, thank god for that." Oliver's ex-fiancée was a world class bitch, but I'd never say that out loud. "I think we all let out a big sigh of relief when that relationship hit the crapper."

I swirl my wine, considering his statement. I suppose all families tend to think that way about the exes. Yet, here I am, the ex.

"Anyway, enough about my brother. I want you to open some gifts."

"Gifts? As in multiple?" He grins, and I mentally kick myself. I purposefully went small so he wouldn't think I was seeing our arrangement as more than it is.

"Don't get too excited. I'm not the best shopper. But here you go." The shopping bag crinkles as he sifts through it, lifting out eight wrapped boxes.

"Ian. These are all for me?" If there is one thing I hate, it is under-giving, and I am so short on gifts. I have one present for Ian. One.

"Yes, ma'am." He lifts his eyebrows and smirks. "Get to opening."

"But... I only—"

"Hey, it's okay. I may have gotten carried away today. Don't worry, I know you don't need a man in your life, and if you wanted one, you wouldn't choose someone who is as unavailable as I am, but we're together for now... so, let me treat you right."

I force a smile I don't feel. He's correct about his limited availability. Once he enters those hospital doors, he seems to become another person. The people outside the hospital walls fall to lower priority status. He goes days without responding to texts. And now he's entering another specialty, spinal surgery. He's been accepted to a fellowship in Seattle.

The first box is wrapped in Tiffany blue paper with a white bow, but the shape of the box doesn't say jewelry, not that I would expect jewelry. I open the paper carefully, not wanting to tear the robin's egg blue wrapping.

"You. Take. Forever." He complains, and I slip a nail beneath the side of the gray cardboard box. "What were you like as a kid?"

I shrug, smiling. I once heard my dad joking with Ian's parents about how it took forever to wrap the presents and in less than five minutes the kids would tear through them all.

"Not much different from ya'll." A gleam of silver shines through the side of the box. Thin protective padding covers a silver frame, and I gasp.

"Where'd you find this?" The photo in the classic silver frame is one of Polly with a ribbon hanging over her neck and me beaming. She looks so much younger. Heck, we both do.

"Mom had it in one of her electronic photo files. I'd seen it before and knew she had it. Took me a while to find it, though. Mom's organization leaves something to be desired, and you're so young in it Google didn't do facial recognition at first."

I clasp it to my chest, then lean closer to plant a chaste, heartfelt kiss on his lips. Feelings of inadequacy sink down over me, because I did nothing thoughtful for him. I bought him clothes because I didn't want him to read into it or to think I saw us as more than we are.

"You liked the other photo, so I went with tried and true."

I stare down into the photo in my lap, remembering that Christmas Day so long ago when Dad—or back then, it was Santa —surprised me with Polly. There'd been a tack box sitting in the den along with a note card that read "Go To the Stable." That had been a simpler time. All I cared about was horses, and the boys down the road were nothing but friends and occasional nuisances.

Another present pushes into my periphery, this one in gold wrapping with a forest green bow. I let out a sigh.

"I didn't do enough for you."

"Open this. We can open the rest tomorrow."

The box in my hand is light, so light it might be empty. Dutifully, I open the present, curiosity driving me forward. The lines on the paper aren't as neatly pressed as the Tiffany box, and clumps of tape cover the sides.

"Did you wrap this yourself?"

His boyish grin speaks the truth. "It's a little obvious, huh?"

"No, you did a good job."

His eyebrows wiggle in mirthful agreement.

Beneath the wrapping paper is a white box, the kind you would buy in a store. Inside is an appointment card that reads "January 15 at 2:00 p.m."

"What is this?"

"I got us an appointment with the best fertility doctor in Houston. There's like a three month wait list. I didn't know if we'd actually need it, and we still might not, but we've got the appointment."

"You don't think it's going to work." My eyes tear up as emotions well up out of nowhere.

"Hey, hey." He pulls me onto his lap and wraps his arms around me, positioning my head against his comforting chest. "I only did this because I know how important it is to you. I don't want you to worry. He might tell you it's just going to take time." I nod, and he tips my chin up. "Tell you the truth, if it wasn't for you wanting this, I'd be happy if it took lots and lots of time."

His scent and heat surround me. My thighs clench together, and my pulse quickens. Those chocolate brown eyes intensify into molten pools. His kiss eradicates all thought. He shoves the presents aside and strips me on the floor in front of the twinkling Christmas tree. I'm not ovulating, but it is Christmas, and a flood of emotions get the better of me. I let myself go, giving everything I have to Ian, and he returns the gift.

Chapter Twenty-Three

Ian

Last Christmas

Christmas morning, I wake with my morning wood wedged up against Sunny's ass and one hand cupping her breast. She tried to send me home to my parents' last night after the Christmas tree episode. She also tried to tell me we didn't need to fool around, because it wasn't the right time in her ovulation cycle. Like I cared.

When I told her I'd be happy if it took a damn long time to impregnate her, I didn't lie. The only reason I made that damn appointment that got her all teary-eyed was because I know this is important to her. I'd like to think after she's pregnant we can continue seeing each other, but I doubt she'll be willing to come visit with a newborn in tow.

And she wouldn't want me to come visit her too often because she cares what the people in our hometown think and she wouldn't want anyone connecting dots. God forbid anyone learn her kid is mine. She's never said it, but my running theory is that she won't want folks to say she went after a second Duke brother. Folks in our hometown believe she never got over my brother. Hell, even my parents believe that, and she wouldn't want folks saying she pursued me since she couldn't have him.

If I could be around more, I'd fight for her. Try to prove to her and everyone else that I might be the youngest, but I'm better than second fiddle. But why fight? In the long term, it's better to keep the wagging tails out of our business. Let them all believe she found an anonymous sperm donor. They don't need to think about us in the same sentence.

Now, my family is a different matter. It's been ages since I kept secrets from Mom. And this morning I'll have to take care to avoid touching Sunny or acting like I've been seeing her regularly this past year.

Her lips curve into the slightest smile, the first sign she is waking. I press my lips to her shoulder and along the curve of her graceful neck. Since she is lying on her side, with little effort I find the sensitive erogenous zone beneath her earlobe and nibble.

Her body rolls slightly forward, and cool air circulates along my front. Before I can protest, she reaches behind her and grasps my erection.

"Eager this morning?" she teases.

"Always when I wake up next to you."

We've spent enough weekends together she knows it to be true. The pad of her thumb circles my tip. Then she raises her thigh and positions me right at her entrance. Following her direction, my hips push forward, into her tight warmth. Lying side by side, we discover our familiar rhythm, one that builds us both up. Her fingers cover her clit, and I swat them away.

"Let me."

It doesn't take long before she quivers her release and I roll her onto her back to chase mine and collapse over her. With my head burrowed in her hair, I whisper, "Merry Christmas."

Rolling onto my back, I take her with me, pulling her naked body up against my side. I lazily brush my fingers over her hip, down the curve of her stomach, and over her breast. I love this easy way we have with each other. We share an intimacy I haven't had with anyone else, maybe because I haven't invested the time. Maybe because she meant more to me before we ever touched.

"Thank you for my gifts," she says as she captures my hand and brings my fingers to her lips.

"There's more. You distracted me last night."

She softly kisses my open palm. If she continues to lie next to me like this, her soft curves nestled against me, I'll be ready for another round before we shower. She releases my hand, and I resume freely touching her.

"I really appreciate you getting me that appointment. It's hard to know who to go to. There are ads and stuff..."

"It might not be necessary, but I knew you were getting worried." I press my lips to the top of her head and pull her close.

"Well, it's not like we haven't been trying." Anguish laces her words.

"I have a proposition for you." I trace the lines of her rose-colored areola with my thumb.

"Proposition?" she prompts.

I swallow and lift my gaze to those hopeful blue irises. "Give me one week. You tell me when it's the right time, and let's go away. One stress-free week. Then, if that doesn't work, we'll take the next step. Whatever that is."

"You think I've been too stressed?" Her chin drops.

Shit. She's interpreting my offer as me believing she's to blame. Too many people blame themselves when they shouldn't. And of course, in the medical world, the inverse is also true, but the inverse doesn't apply here.

I tap my index finger on the tip of her nose. "Don't go reading into what I'm saying. But there is research that shows stress can have a negative impact on fertility. You run yourself ragged running two salons and maintaining your own clientele. Let's just get away. Vacation. When was the last time you went on vacation?" Those eyes appear mystified. "That's what I thought. Years, right?"

She collapses onto her back and lays an arm over her forehead. My gaze travels down her lithe, naked form sprawled on the bed. The sheets cross her pelvic bone, and I let my fingers travel the valleys over her smooth skin.

"I think that's a good idea." My fingers brush the sheet aside. "I've also read about acupuncture and reiki being beneficial. Suzanne swears she's four for four."

My fingers hesitate over her smooth, bare mound. "What?"

"Yes. If your chakras aren't aligned, it can cause issues with fertility. Here in the west, we don't pay enough attention to our chakras."

I raise my gaze from her delectable pussy to see if she is actually serious. She sits up and swings her legs off the bed, distancing herself from my roaming fingers.

"We need to get going. We can't be late for Christmas brunch."

"Are you really going to align your chakras?" I've been studying medicine for twelve years, and let's just say chakras don't make it into anatomy class. To me, that's about as sensible as taking horse dewormer for a virus. But I suppose if it has the same effect as a placebo pill, it could be as effective as my proposed vacation.

She shoves a drawer closed, and with garments in hand, waltzes naked to the bathroom. My gaze follows her slender, willowy form, hoping for an invitation.

"I'll be quick so you can get in." She's chirpy as she closes the door.

Damn. After locating my boxers, I meander into the kitchen to get the coffee started.

We finish exchanging presents, which is basically a bunch of clothes. Then I rush through a shower and she shoos me out the door, telling me we can't show up at the same time. When I climb in my car, hair damp and my overnight bag shoved in the trunk, an uncomfortable knot forms in the pit of my stomach.

The front door swings open as I pop open the trunk and lift out my overnight bag. I plan to stay at my folks' tonight, spend some time with Sam's family, then go back to Houston in the morning. Everyone else will head to Sam's place in Aspen, but I can't take the week off. Or, more precisely, if I'm taking a week off, I'd rather it not be in a crowded ski house with my parents, Sam's family, and Oliver and his new girlfriend. There was a time when I loved our Christmas ski trips, back when it was my parents, Sam, Oliver, and our brother from another mother, Jason. Times have changed.

"How was traffic this morning?" Mom asks from the stoop.

"Roads are pretty empty. Got here without any issue."

"I wish you would've come last night."

"Patty, he's a grown man. He probably prefers his own bed," Dad grumbles from within the house.

Once inside, he and I share a gruff man hug, complete with a pat on the back.

"How're things at the hospital?" Dad asks.

"Fine." I spend a fair amount of time at my private practice, but to Dad it's all the same.

Mom runs her hand over my cheek in the way she likes to do, then she pats her apron and heads to the kitchen with Dad and me following in her wake.

"Sandra should be here any minute," Mom says.

"Is that right?" I respond.

Mom gives me her all-knowing look, and that has me questioning my acting skills. She drops it, so it's probably all in my head. If Mom thought there was a bone to be found, she wouldn't stop digging.

Dad points to the Christmas tree set up outside on the back porch. "You can go put your presents under the tree out there. Sam and Ollie and all the rest of 'em will arrive in a few hours."

"Really? That quick?"

"Well, remember, they got a couple of hours jumpstart on us." That's right. Time change.

"Did you already talk to 'em?"

"No, your mom texted. Said we didn't want to slow them down this morning. We'd rather see 'em in person so we can hug their necks."

A knock at the door grabs Dad's attention. He says, "That'll be Sandra. Why don't you let her in? Bet it's been a long time since you've seen her, right?"

"Yep." My gaze falls to the well-worn wooden floor, and I head down the hall like a teenager caught in a lie. Maybe they already know? Or is it all in my head? A classic telltale heart issue. At thirty-four, I shouldn't have to lie.

When I swing the door open, Sunny bustles right past me. As I close the door, I hear her greet Mom and Dad with a loud Merry Christmas. I shuffle my socked feet down the hall to the back of the house with my hands shoved in my trouser pockets.

"There you are. I was wondering where you went off to," Mom says.

"Just let Sunny in."

"Oh. I didn't hear you two greet each other." Mom looks at me with that all-knowing look again. But then, she turns her back to me to mess around with the stove. Maybe it's all in my head. "Now, Ian, honey, can you set the table? We're going to have a down and dirty Christmas brunch this morning, because I want to have everything cleaned up so we can have a late lunch with the crew. They're gonna be hungry when they land, you know. Their clocks will be ahead of ours."

"By one hour," I say.

Dad peers at me over the rim of his paper. I read him loud and clear. *Do as your mother says.*

A spread for twelve covers the table, but the second it appears we've all reached our limit, Mom is up and gathering plates.

"Where's the fire?" I tease.

She waves at me like I'm being silly.

Dad says, "You gotta understand, son. She's got grandbabies coming. She's got a lot of stuff on her list to do to prepare."

"Oh, I was thinking they wouldn't arrive until later?" Sunny asks.

"Well, soon enough," Mom gushes. "But y'all sit back and watch football."

Sunny and I ignore her and help clear the plates and clean up. Then Mom gets serious and practically steers us both out of the kitchen, pointing to the back porch. "Y'all go sit by the Christmas tree and watch the TV with your dad."

"Oh, I think I'm going to head on," Sunny says.

"What?" Mom flattens her palms on her apron like she is wiping them clean. The thick glass on her frames makes her eyes seem larger than they actually are, and I don't miss how her gaze flits back and forth between Sunny and me. "Honey, you don't want to spend Christmas Day alone. And you just got here."

"Oh, I don't want to infringe on your family time." Sunny lifts her cooler and the empty bag she used to bring presents over. "And besides, I'm stopping by Liam's to see what his kids got, then Kara's, and then I'm having dinner with Noah."

What the hell?

"Well, okay, dear, but I don't want you rushing out. You know, you're family, too."

"This was so lovely. Thank you for having me over," Sunny says, gathering her things and getting out of the house so fast you'd think there was a medical emergency.

She isn't going over to see Kara. That's a bald-faced lie. Kara is in North Carolina with her family. Sunny told me she couldn't leave for Houston until New Year's Day because she is short staffed, and the closer it gets to New Year's, the busier they get.

I don't bother seeing Sunny to the door. Mom handles seeing her off. I join Dad outside on the sofa.

"Would you mind getting me some sweet tea?" he asks the second I sink into the cushion.

"Not at all." I head back into the kitchen. I can hear Mom's voice, trying over and over in her sweet way to convince Sunny to stay. Part of me wants to walk down the hall and tell Mom to give it up. If after twenty years, she still can't be in the same room with Sam, there isn't anything, or any person, that is going to change that.

Do I factor into this at all? Is she uncomfortable with the idea of being in the same room with Sam and me? Does that even make sense?

The uneasy feeling in my gut has grown into a full-on belly-ache. I pop some Tums. I'd like to crash on my bed and fall asleep. This feeling in my chest sucks. But it's Christmas. And if I close my bedroom door, Mom will worry. So, I shuffle into the den and feign interest in grown men tackling each other.

Chapter Twenty-Four

Ian

Mid-February

"I'm so glad you're getting away. You need this. You give so much
of yourself to your patients, but you have to hold some back, or
else one day you won't have anything left to give."

"I hear you, Mom." I emphasize her name to ensure she gets I
am partially mocking her. Under motherly concern on Wikipedia,
Patty Duke's photograph should be among the images included.
Her concern stems from my January schedule. I ended up filling in
for quite a few sick surgeons. Extremely long, stressful days bled
into weeks.

But as I sit in the back of a dated sedan with my dream girl
sitting two feet away in a white cotton skirt that hints at her lean,
shapely legs and a blue chambray halter top that cups her breasts
perfectly, life is too blue sky to seriously weigh a motherly
warning.

Sunny leans closer to the window as the island whizzes by outside her rolled down window. We left my apartment early in the morning, flew business class on one of the few direct flights from Houston to St. Martin, and then took a boat to Anguilla.

I would've waited to return Mom's call, but Sunny encouraged me to go ahead. Now and then, she glances over her shoulder with a soft smile as she listens to my end of the conversation.

"Are you staying in Sam's place?" Mom asks.

"No." Yes, Sam suggested this resort, and offered his villa, but I checked out the rental rate. When the hotel reservationist told me his villa rented for forty thousand a night, I asked for something more intimate and fitting for two.

"That's a shame. It's gorgeous. Did you see the pictures from when we went there two years ago? It's stunning. And it comes with a chef and staff."

"Sounds a bit much for just me, don't you think?"

"Are you really alone? Ian…" I might be in another country, but her don't-tell-a-lie tone crosses the distance with no issue.

"Mom, I just needed to get away. That's all." I wink at Sunny. "Let me go. I'm pulling up to the resort now. I'll call you when I get back."

"Well, have fun. Send pictures if you can."

"I'm planning on sleeping most of the week."

"Oh, that's a waste. At the very least, make it down to the beach or the pool. Maybe you'll meet someone."

"Right."

"You know, I heard Sandra is on vacation this week, too." I lean closer to the window on my side of the car and sneak a quick glance at Sunny to see if she can hear Mom. I don't want her freaking out that Patty Duke's sixth sense might be coming out to play.

"Is that right? Good time of year to get away, I guess." Sunny's attention remains fixated on the tropical landscape and the stucco and cinder block buildings with packed dirt front yards jammed up along the twisting road. "You and Dad have a good week. Love you, Mom."

The car turns into an elaborate white stucco entrance with gold lettering that reads "Four Seasons Anguilla."

I disconnect the call before she can say more.

"Does she really believe you came here for a week by yourself?" Sunny asks.

"Sure," I lie.

Things between Sunny and me have been distant since Christmas. She ended up getting a virus over New Year's and stayed home. But I stayed the course and booked this trip. It might be our last time together, and I'm determined to enjoy it. My primary objective for the next seven days is to ensure Sunny is utterly relaxed and well-fucked. If this doesn't work, the next steps on this pregnancy journey won't be nearly as much fun, but I'll still be there for her every step of the way.

We met with the fertility specialist on January 15, and with Sunny's blessing, I reviewed her medical history. Her mother died of heart complications. Sunny didn't know much about it, and I offered to get more information, but the doctor said that forty years ago medicine wasn't as advanced. To Sunny's knowledge, there are no medical records, and I'd expect she's right. Given the way things were back then, it's hard to imagine her father would've requested a copy of the hospital records. It's likely she had unknown heart issues, and the pregnancy strained her heart. Her mother died when she was twenty-four. Sunny is forty and displays no signs heart issues. The fertility specialist was optimistic about her chances of conceiving and wasn't worried at all about her mother's medical history.

Sunny taps her fingers on the car seat. Something is bothering her.

"What's wrong?"

"It's hard to believe a single man would come to the Four

Seasons in Anguilla." Sunny's skepticism is evident in what I can only describe as a frown.

"She's familiar with the trials and tribulations of being a surgeon. Good days and horrific ones. She was a nurse. She gets it. Everyone wants to think a doctor pops out of med school fully proficient, but that's not how it works. It's a lot of learning. A lot of trial and error. When I was beyond discouraged, she's the one who gave me gravity." Sandra rotates her lithe body and fixes those sky-blue irises on me. "So, would she doubt I'd go on vacation by myself? My first vacation, in, well, not including Christmas, ever as an adult? No. I think she's genuinely happy I'm getting away."

Of course, I'm lying to Sunny. But if I told her Patty Duke might suspect something is going on with us, that she might have even suspected something back at Christmas, it would be impossible for Sunny to relax. Mom would support us, I think, but I get that what we're doing is unconventional, and Sunny wouldn't feel comfortable with her knowing our arrangement.

Sunny's hand reaches for mine as the car pulls to a stop in front of an open-air resort entrance. A uniformed man in black linen shorts and a Four Seasons polo shirt opens Sunny's door at the same time another man opens mine.

"Welcome," the man says with a wide smile.

Our bags are whisked away, and my fingers intertwine with Sunny's as we step into a grand open-air lobby. A slight breeze blows. Deep green potted palms in black ceramic pots decorate the entrance. The lobby opens onto an expansive rectangular swath of plush green grass, and off in the far distance are rock formations and then turquoise blue as far as the eye can see.

I squeeze Sunny's hand and let my lips brush across her ear as I tell her, "Your eyes match the sea."

She waves me off like I'm being ridiculous, but she keeps her hand in mine. Together, we walk alongside a uniformed middle-aged man to our room. He asks us where we are from and if we're celebrating Valentine's Day. I send a mental thank you to the Four

Seasons employee who reached out and asked if I'd like to order anything or plan anything for the holiday. Valentine's Day hadn't been in my mental repertoire since high school when the student government sold paper valentines as a fundraiser. The person who accumulated the most paper hearts won something... maybe Cupid. I'm not sure exactly what the winner received, but I was the first Duke brother who didn't win the ridiculous contest his senior year of high school. I came in third. Fitting, actually.

Sunny takes the conversational lead, all the while absorbing the scenery with wide eyes. Her flat sandals smack against the stone walkway. Doja, the man guiding us to our room, lives on Anguilla but is from St. Maarten, and yes, he goes back home frequently.

Doja gives us a tour of the room, pointing out the small kitchenette in a room to the side with a selection of coffee options, an expansive den with white linen furniture, stone flooring, and floor-to-ceiling glass doors that open onto a wide covered balcony with an expansive view of turquoise ocean. A plush king size bed with white linens is centered on one wall in the bedroom. On the balcony, there's a soaking tub and a sitting area with two lounge chairs and a sofa.

Sunny follows Doja into the en suite bathroom, where they continue talking about Doja's kids.

I wait in the bedroom, my gaze centered on the balcony hot tub. Yes, Sam and I don't always see eye to eye, but he did me right when he recommended this location for a relaxing getaway.

After tipping the concierge, I toe off my shoes below a row of hooks, presumably for towels or robes. The suite has all the comforts of home with a breathtaking view. But the view outside doesn't compete with Sunny.

Outside on the balcony, her skirt flits around in the breeze, and the setting sun casts a golden halo against her blonde strands. I step up behind her and brush her hair to the side and place a kiss against her shoulder.

"This place is amazing," she says.

"Hhmmm." Goosebumps rise along her arms as I brush the pads of my fingers up and down.

"Where did you learn about this place?"

"Read about it somewhere." The lie rolls off my lips. It doesn't matter that Sam recommended it; I simply don't want to utter his name when in paradise.

"I've never been to a place like this."

"Want to walk around? Check the place out?" It isn't really what I want at all, but this week is all about her. "I booked you spa appointments for most of the days we're here."

"You didn't need to do that." She leans her delectable body against me, and my fingers explore the exposed riff of skin that's teased me all day.

"This week is all about relaxing you."

"You're being so good to me."

Her head presses down on my shoulder, her back to my front, and I fight the urge to pick her up and take her inside.

"I completed my rounds of reiki and acupuncture. I know it's kind of doing double duty, like one or the other should suffice, but I figured we're pulling out all the stops."

I support the acupuncture Sunny endured because peer-reviewed studies found an improvement in fertility using acupuncture. The reiki bit is too eastern for my western-minded perspective, but I don't think it will hurt. And I'm a big believer in the placebo effect, so if Sunny believes in it, I won't say anything that might impede those results.

Sunny's head lolls against my shoulder, her back still pressed to me. I breathe in the faint herbal scent of her shampoo and a touch of coconut.

"Is there something else you want to do?" I hope with all my might she says yes, because there is definitely something else I want to do.

She twists in my arms and walks me backward, directing me to paradise.

Chapter Twenty-Five

Sandra

His molten, golden-brown eyes singe. My body thrums with anticipation. Every time, it's like this with Ian. The distance, the length of time between seeing him, gives me a much-needed emotional breather. Space to get my head on right and remind myself he's doing this for me. We're nothing more than two friends enjoying the act of sex.

It's hard to keep my heart in line, though, because he's also giving me so much. Or at least trying to. This trip, this jaw-dropping resort, he's doing it all for me. This man's consideration alone could bring me to my knees. His warm lips suck on my neck, right where my blood pulses. He palms my breast over my dress, and the pad of this thumb brushes over the material, and I swear blood pumps to my eager nipple. I want skin on skin, the heat of his mouth, his tongue.

His crisp, clean scent and heat surround me, making my knees go weak. He backs me up to the bed, and my core clenches. My palms flatten against the hard, muscular planes of his chest. Familiar territory I have missed. I tug on his shirt, and my fingers dip below, onto his hot, bare skin. He groans and lifts his arms to pull the offending material over his head. My lips taste the skin along his clavicle as he palms my ass, bring me hard up against him.

With lightning-fast speed, need surges. I want him now, in me, stretching me, filling me. His mouth claims mine, possessive and demanding. The hot touch of his fingers on the bare skin of my thigh, then the curve of my butt, sets me off. I suck in air, breaking the kiss and fumbling with the button on his pants.

"Do you want me?" His chest rises and falls rapidly in time with his breathing. Those dark eyes question, but he's got to know the answer.

"You know I do."

"Show me." His tongue licks the seam of his glistening lips.

Mesmerized, I stand still as he disrobes me. His fingers brush up my thigh and over my sex, dipping inside, teasing.

"Damn, Sunny, it looks like you do want me. But I want to see. Crawl back up onto that bed. Show me. Show me exactly what you want me to do to you."

The overhead fan whips cool air over my skin. Skin alight with desire. So much need that I step right on out of my comfort zone and back up onto the bed, resting on the stacked pillows, gaze locked on his inferno.

I spread my thighs and drag my finger through my wet slit. His throat contorts as he swallows, watching my every movement.

"I want you here."

"And what do you want?" His pants drop to the ground, and his thick, hard erection protrudes. He grips the base and slowly strokes. "Do you want this? Or do you want my tongue?"

I suck my wet finger in my mouth, gaze locked on his cock. "Oh, I want your tongue. But first, I need you."

"Tell me."

The mattress dips as he climbs onto the bed, one knee at a time, his hand never missing a beat, stroking up and down.

He wants to push me out of my comfort zone. He wants dirty talk. And he's done so much for me, he's giving me so much, I can do this for him. My gaze settlers on the wetness on his velvety tip, and my throat tightens.

"I want to lick that precum. Swirl my tongue around your tip." My gaze flicks up to meet his, and all the while he strokes. "I want to fuck you with my mouth." I toy with my heavy, sensitive breasts. "But I don't want you to come. Because I want you to fuck me." I slip a finger inside, then brush the pad of my finger over my clit, timing it to his strokes. "Hard. Over me. From behind. I want to hear the sound of your skin slapping against me. And I want to ride you, over and over again."

"Fuck, Sunny." His voice cracks. The pace of his strokes picks up.

And, fuck, I want him so badly. "Please." It's a plea. Every atom in my body vibrates with need.

And then he's there, over me, pushing inside, stretching me.

"Fuck, you feel good." He breathes it out like it's a prayer.

I'm so worked up, I'm close within mere strokes. My toes curl. I lift my knees and wrap my legs around him. He hovers over me, and his hips grind into me, rubbing me just the way I like, and I whimper and squirm and make all the noises. I hold on tight as my body releases and he slows. His head drops to my shoulder.

"I've missed you." It's an admission. The kind we don't typically make to each other.

I pull his lips to mine and kiss him. He's still inside me, hard, but his movements are slow and purposeful. We move as one, finding a rhythm. Our singular path to nirvana.

He flips us, maneuvering me so I'm on top. And I take him, just the way I want him. Driving down on him, then leaning forward, letting my legs straighten beside him. He guides my hips. Our sweat smooths the friction. My breasts flatten against his hard chest. His pants fill my ears. And then my core clenches. A blinding orgasm rips through me. His head tilts back. And I feel him, pulsing deep inside me. His expression is one of divine ecstasy. Nirvana.

I cling to him as he continues pulsing, filling me. My head falls to his shoulder, and his arms wrap around my back, holding me in place.

Outside, the sky shines blue. The drapes are wide open. The Caribbean sea glistens in the distance, and yet I don't want to leave this bed.

Wetness warms my thighs, and with great reluctance, I shift. He slips out of me, but his hold on me tightens. With a groan, he pushes up off the mattress, adjusts several pillows, and positions us against them. Then he tugs at a light coverlet on the end of the bed and spreads it over our legs, up to our hips.

"You don't want to go explore?" I ask, curling against him.

"As I recall, we still have things you want to do."

I press my lips to his chest, then lie back down. The subtle pounding of his heart pulses against me.

"That was hot as hell," he says.

"One of your fantasies?" I ask as my fingers circle over his chest in small loops.

"Better," he says.

I playfully pinch his nipple, and he squirms. "Hey, what was that for?"

"Oh, I don't know. You. Exaggerating."

"Sunny, when it comes to you, I don't exaggerate."

He palms my ass over the coverlet, then shoves the material down so he's skin on skin. I close my eyes, letting his warmth soothe me.

"This ass. God. It's perfection."

I let out a girly giggle. He's being ridiculous. I'm not ashamed of my body. For my age, I think I'm doing pretty good. But it's hardly perfection. Especially my ass.

"You are full of it."

His palm slaps loudly against my skin, and I yelp.

"Don't beg for compliments."

"I'm not." I lift my head off his chest, grinning. "It's just, come on, now. I'm forty. Forty." I repeat it with emphasis. "There's nothing perfect on this body."

He flips me over so fast my teeth knock against each other.

"Hey," I protest.

His warm lips press against my throat. His thumb presses into my nipple as he cups my breast.

"Don't ever," he argues. "This body is everything I fantasized over for years. And more." He rises so he can look me in the eye. "Don't ever put it down. This body is perfect for me. Fits me like a glove. Tight and warm."

I snort. He's basically describing any vagina.

Raising on one arm, he lies on his side. His fingers trail a path from my breast, down to my belly.

"You don't understand, do you?" My teeth sink into my lower lip as his fingers travel lower.

He's the one who doesn't understand. Words like his are dangerous. To him, this is sex. But my heart has a tendency to ignore my brain, and oh, boy. He's pushing my heart into dangerous territory. Because I'm loving too much about him. His consideration. His kindness. For me, it went beyond physical months ago, and yet there's no future here. Not with him. But maybe, just possibly, within me.

His fingers dip between my legs.

"Fuck, Sunny. My cum is leaking out of you. Do you have any idea how sexy that is?"

"Is that one of your fantasies?"

His long lashes flutter, and he grins up at me as his fingers push inside.

"Oh, Sunny. After this week, you're never going to ask that question again."

My back arches and my knees rise as his fingers bend and curl and find all the good spots. "Why is that?" I pant.

"Because, sweetheart, you're going to live them."

Chapter Twenty-Six

Ian

Last Valentine's

Anguilla quickly becomes my favorite place on Earth. We spend our days alternating between a long, rectangular adults-only pool and a private beach area. Both offer waitservice and spectacular views. But by far, the best part of this holiday is the baby moon, meaning we have lots and lots of sex in our suite. When I told her she's perfect for me, I didn't lie. I'm not even sure what I love more about her. Those sunny, light blue eyes, her laugh, her giggle, her soft breasts that fill my palm, her responsive nipples, the little sounds she makes, or the way she feels around me, so tight, so perfect. No man could ask for a better vacation.

When she goes off to her spa appointments, I check in with the hospital and the practice. I also alternate between running through the resort property or weights in the hotel gym. Other than a few dinners out, we haven't left the resort. There's no need.

Tonight, we have reservations at one of the resort restaurants overlooking the ocean. Sunny plans on wearing the dress I gave her for Valentine's. I'm in shorts and a short-sleeve button down shirt, sipping water while kicked back in the lounge chair on our balcony, relaxing while Sunny gets ready.

When I hear heels clicking on stone, I stand, and, like she so often does, she leaves me breathless. Yes, that's a description straight out of a cheesy romance, but as a doctor, the cliche description fits. My ribcage tightens and lungs contract. Her presence forces me to breathe more deeply.

Her golden hair cascades down her shoulders in loose waves, and the blue dress I purchased because it so closely matches her eyes fits tightly around her breasts and falls loosely down to her calves. The gold heels I bought her glitter, and her sun-kissed skin glows.

"God, you're beautiful."

She glances down at her dress and touches it absentmindedly. "You have good taste."

"No. You could wear anything and you'd look stunning, but this...here, let me get a photo."

She rolls those blue eyes, silently rebuking me, but complies with a soft smile. I snap a photo on my phone, double-check it came out and slip it into my back pocket.

"Hungry?" Our reservations are in five minutes. The concierge helped me time our reservation so by the time dessert arrives, the sun will be setting over the ocean.

Fingers intertwined, we stroll through the resort, past the rectangular pool with a forever edge that visually blends into the turquoise waters, where we spent our day catered to by staff, to the open-air restaurant, SALT.

My muscles are putty. My thoughts clear. For once, I'm well-rested and thoroughly satiated. The hospital feels like it's a million miles away. After dinner, I'll take Sunny back to the room for another phenomenal fantasy-fulfilling night. Life is perfect.

As we approach the entrance, two kids run by us, shrieking with laughter. The girls look oddly familiar.

"Girls."

I freeze, staring ahead at the giggling girls, the younger one chasing the older one. Sunny glances over her shoulder, and her expression morphs into one of shock. *Fuck.*

In slow motion, I turn. Sunny discreetly pulls her hand from mine.

Olivia, my sister-in-law, smiles as she approaches. She's wearing a long, white dress that's identical to Sunny's except for the color, and that's when I realize Sam bought the dress from the resort shop.

But the similarities between the two women end with the dress. Whereas Sunny is a golden blonde with topaz blue eyes, Olivia has slick, long, dark hair and high cheekbones that lend a regal air.

Sam approaches, his facial expression stern. Sunny's sun-kissed skin has lost all its vibrant hue. My heartrate increases. I stare at my older brother, attempting to read him. Hunting for anger.

"Hi. Don't worry. You don't have to sit with us." Olivia's friendly intonations compete for my attention. "They sit the tables with kids a little farther back." She smiles graciously and extends her hand to Sunny. "Hi. I'm Olivia. You look so familiar. Have we met?"

Sunny stands frozen with a look of round-eyed astonishment. Olivia slowly withdraws her offered hand.

Sam's expression slowly transitions from menacing glower into a cordial smile. His hands rest on his hips, and he rocks back on his heels.

"Sandra," he says. Olivia looks between the three of us, then over her shoulder at her unleashed daughters.

Sam belts out a deep chuckle. His mouth drops open. The open-mouthed smile is a mix of astonishment and humor. One hand scrubs his hair back and forth, and then he pulls it together.

He loops one arm behind his wife's back and says, "Olivia, this is Sandra. I've mentioned her before."

To Olivia's credit, she doesn't miss a beat. She smiles widely, practically beaming. "Sandra, it's nice to finally meet you."

I study Sunny for signs she might be suffering from a panic attack. She hasn't moved since we spotted my brother. I'm not sure she's even blinked.

Sam, possibly recognizing her discomfort, says, "Sandra, I haven't seen you in years. God, how long has it been?"

She remains still, frozen. She's no longer holding my hand. I don't know when she pulled it out of mine, but the distance between us feels significant.

Sam looks to me. "I'm sorry, man. You're gonna laugh." He brushes his hand over the back of his head. "I thought you might be here with a guy. You've been so secretive. We only showed up here because I wanted to push the issue, as I thought you were afraid we'd give you a hard time and wanted you to know you didn't need to hide it." Sam's southern accent comes through, and I recognize the presence of the long-ago dropped accent as his endeavor to ease a tenuous predicament. My older brother is like me in that regard. He can hide the accent or play it up as the situation requires.

But I'm not sure how to handle the situation at hand. Or what to say to him. I thought—or, no, I hoped he'd never have to know.

"Ian, you've been so secretive." He's still talking. Chattering, really. As if he's the one who stepped out of line. "We all knew you were seeing someone. And, when Mom said you came here, and the villa wasn't rented," he shakes his head and grins like it's a big joke, "we didn't know how bad Texas might be these days. You know, in Connecticut, we're open-minded. It's been a long time since I lived down south. I wasn't sure. Olivia and I…we had theories. I'm sorry, man. I just wanted you to know—"

"It's not what it looks like," Sunny breaks in, her voice high-pitched and unnatural.

A sinking sensation pools with nausea, but somehow, I speak. "Sandra needed a break. We're here as friends."

Sandra wraps her arms around herself, and her gaze falls to the ground.

"Oh, well, in that case, come join us for dinner," Sam says. "Sandra, god, it's been what, almost twenty years since I've seen you?"

I search Sam's expression for any sign of anger or disappointment. I don't catch anything other than traces of embarrassment and guilt. Or maybe that's projection.

Sunny offers a weak smile. Those blue eyes are distant. Probably suffering from shock.

"Actually, we were just stopping here to ask about reservations for tomorrow night. I heard about a place on the island we're going to tonight. We have a car waiting for us." All of that is a lie, but I can make it true with a quick chat with the concierge.

Sam winces, and his expression could only be described as apologetic. Olivia seems amused by it all, but my family always amuses her. I give my nieces a hug and toss in the air, and endure awkward goodbyes with Olivia and Sam.

Shit. I don't think he's angry. But that had to have been strange for him. I owed him more than that. Surely, that's a rule somewhere. If you're going to break bro' code and date an ex, man-up.

Sunny remains silent on the walk to the concierge, then outside to a car and driver that had been conveniently waiting should a guest need a ride. In the back seat, she crosses one leg over the other and forces a tight smile.

"That was crazy," I say to break the ice. Her gaze remains fixed on the headrest in front of her. "I swear, I had no idea."

"There's no way he believed us."

"Is that the worst thing?" I have to ask the question. Why does it matter if Sam knows? It's out now. The world didn't end. I owe some apologies, but…

"What do you think your parents will say?" Sunny's timid voice trembles.

"I honestly don't think they'll care." Given Mom's comment about Sandra also being on vacation, I bet she already suspects. But sharing that insight with Sunny won't help. "If that's what's bothering you, I can ask Sam to not mention anything to Mom and Dad."

"I don't want to cause problems in your family." Those blue eyes glisten.

She's on the verge of tears. *Fuck me.*

"Your parents mean so much to me. I don't want to lose them."

"Hey, there," I unbuckle my seatbelt and slide closer to put an arm around her shoulder. "You're not going to lose them. Why would you think that?"

She sniffs. "They won't be happy about this."

"Sam won't say anything. And even if he did, they wouldn't care. They love you like you're one of their own."

At that moment, I'd say anything to keep her from crying, but I'm speaking the truth. She sits up straighter, and I pull my arm away. She doesn't want me to touch her.

As she stares out the window, her lower lip quivers, and reality hits me.

She's not afraid of my family learning. The quivering lip and the teary eyes are a byproduct of seeing Sam for the first time in twenty years. And she met his wife and saw his children. Sandra simply isn't over Sam. Oliver, my mom, and the entire town are correct. She isn't over my brother.

Chapter Twenty-Seven

Ian

February, Paradise Undone

My feet drop like lead as I enter the gym. Sandra pretended to be asleep this morning. For the first time since we began this whole adventure together, attempting to get her pregnant the all-natural way, we slept apart with several feet between us on the bed. Our conversation at dinner was beyond stilted. The waitperson picked up on the tension and couldn't get away from us fast enough. I didn't push it. Why would I? What was there to say?

I don't need to hear her tell me what I already perceive.

Our entire plan had been foolhardy. Selfish on my part because I wanted sex. But not selfish in that I wanted to fulfill Sunny's dreams. I wanted to be the man to give her what she wanted most in the world. And maybe, after almost nine months of trying, it's apparent I can't give her that. Regardless of all of Dr. Malpani's fertility tests, maybe the fact Sunny still isn't pregnant is the universe's way of slapping us both and telling us we are out of our minds with this preposterous plan we concocted.

Last night, a disturbing thought came to me, and now I can't get it out of my head. Every time she was with me, was she imagining my brother? Sam and I aren't twins, but you can see the family resemblance. She was my fantasy. Was I a substitute for hers?

Am I so conceited and cocky I never considered this possibility? I went into this pursuing a teen fantasy. And I never once thought she might pursue her own little fantasy? How much of a fool could one man be? It never once occurred to me that while I was fucking her, she was closing her eyes and pretending I was Sam. My older brother. The one who has always done everything better than me. Of course, she'd want him. Her first love. Her first everything.

I only thought about what I wanted. How I wanted her. Always had. She was the quote-unquote pin-up of my youth. The elusive woman I'd been too young to pursue and could only fawn over.

I should've left that woman in my past. Not invited her into my home in Houston and offered my contributions to her dreams. Dreams she dictated I would not be a part of after the contribution part ended. Once she conceived, she wanted no one to know. God forbid anyone know the youngest Duke son fathered her child. Ah, the mortification.

I swing the glass door of the gym open, ready to stalk back to the one punching bag hanging in the weight section of the two-room gym.

"Hey. Ian."

I scan the room until I locate Sam. Sweat drips from his brow. The treadmill under his feet slows, and his feet stagger as the machine liltingly crawls to a stop.

"Hey." I awkwardly rub the back of my neck. *Fuck*. So much for unleashing my fury on a punching bag. Sam will read into it. "I'm gonna go lift."

"I'll spot you."

I lift my shoulders in the slightest of shrugs and plow forward to the narrow doorway that leads into the room with all the weights and a few well-selected weight machines.

Sam catches up with me, and his hand clasps my shoulder. I shrug his hand away and regret it the second I do. He's not the guilty party. Sure, I'm pissed he showed up, but he's simply playing his big brother role. One he's always taken pretty seriously, and like everything else in his life, pretty much mastered. You can't hate a guy for that.

"So, you and Sandra?" He raises an eyebrow and gives me this grin I don't quite understand.

"It's not like that." The denial is automatic. If my brain had kicked in, I wouldn't lie to Sam. But I've been lying to everyone for almost a year. Each lie lays the groundwork for another lie. It's automatic. And it's not who I am. Or at least, it's not who I want to be.

"Hey." He holds one palm up, fingers spread out, that damn grin still on his face. "All I'm saying is, if it was like that, it's not a big deal."

I cross my arms over my chest and stare at his dusty running shoes.

"At one point, I thought Ollie and Sandra were together. Didn't bother me. I mean, I thought it might've been a little strange, but I don't think they were ever together, but... the point is, it didn't bother me. I mean, if it turns out she's dated all three of us, that's a little..."

My fists clench, and blinding fury comes out of nowhere, gripping my torso and raising my pulse rate.

"Hey. Chill. I don't know. I don't care. That's the point." Sam steps closer, his face way too close to mine given the irrational anger ripping through my veins. "Sandra and I were together a lifetime ago. I think the only people who haven't let go of that relationship is our family. And I need to make this clear. You're my brother. You'll always be my brother. No matter what. If you and Sandra make each other happy, I'm cool. All I want is for you to be happy. I'm happy. I love my life. Love my wife and kids. I want the same for you."

The black rubber floor has an indentation near the back of his foot, but otherwise the floor is in top condition.

"Ian, if anything's going on, there's no reason to hide it. Not from me." He claims a seat on the bench press, and I step up to the weight bar to spot him. Because he's my brother. I'll always spot him.

Sam is right, as always.

"You're really not pissed?" I can't help but ask the question.

"Not at all." He pushes up on the weight bar, and I stand behind him. "I mean, it wasn't what I was expecting. But, as long as she treats you right."

He lowers the bar. The iron clangs. Our brotherhood is intact. But damn if I don't feel like a total shit.

I've more or less catered to her viewpoints, letting her keep everything a secret because it was easier to agree than to fight her. But do I really think my parents will give a damn? No. Did I really think Sam would care? When he's happily married with kids and zero plans to return south? No. Not really.

It wasn't something I wanted to cop to, but it's not like their break-up is fresh.

What all this comes down to is Sandra. She's the one who hasn't let it go. She's the one who harbors feelings for Sam. The girl I fell for, the one I wanted to be the mother of my children, if I really spell it out, harbors feelings for my brother. My kick-ass, older brother who dropped out of college and created a billion-dollar company by the age of twenty-five. My oldest brother who has always been better at sports than me, better at riding horses, prom king, soccer captain, motherfucking Mr. Cupid, head of the robotics club, could climb higher in a fucking tree—I mean, of course she can't get over him. Who could?

I'd love to hate the guy, but I can't. He's my brother. At his core, a standup guy. He cared so much about me that when he suspected I was a closeted gay, he flew his whole family down here to support me and tell me he loved me.

It might seem backward to some, but there are some folks in Texas who have yet to open their minds, so his idea that I'd try to keep my sexuality hidden isn't so farfetched. Of course, Sam hasn't spent time in Houston. Or even the Austin of today. If he had, he'd realize I could be as open as I wanted. Being gay wouldn't negatively impact my career in the slightest. Not in my city, at least.

"You know, if I really thought you'd be angry, I wouldn't have done it. But I still felt bad. Like she was yours, and I…really didn't want you to know."

"She hasn't been mine for a long time, Ian."

He lifts the bar, straining, does his reps, and it clinks against the iron when he's done.

"I don't think she's over you." God, I hate admitting that to him. "I bet she still has that promise ring of yours."

"She might. I'm sure Olivia has things from her past. But that doesn't mean she hasn't let the past go. Sandra and I, we moved on a long time ago. That's what people do."

He might be right about other people, but there's no denying Sunny's reaction to seeing my brother.

After a thirty-minute workout, Sam and I grab a quick bite by the family pool. I throw my nieces in the water and let them ride around my back, which leads to shrieks of joy that turn heads and Sam and Olivia telling them to keep it down. Olivia invites us to join them at their private pool, and the girls beg me to go snorkeling with them.

I don't commit to any plans. All that anger fizzled out into something heavier. I don't quite have the words for it, but it isn't a positive emotion. Sadness could be the best descriptor. It's heavy and weighted. Maybe it's disappointment. Sam's arrival forces uncomfortable truths. And it's time to stop the lies.

Chapter Twenty-Eight

Sandra

The Valentine's Hangover

Seeing Sam rattled my brain. In reiki, they talk about how each chakra is a connection point for one's soul and body. Well, my chakras took a hell of a hit.

If someone had asked what I feared most, getting caught holding hands with Ian—by Sam, no less—would've been at the top of my list. Sam didn't seem to care. And I didn't think he would. It's just that now word will get out, and it will spread like an uncontainable wildfire. His parents will think I'm sick or twisted. All those pitying looks will return full force.

"Ma'am, would you like anything from the bar?" The dark-haired woman in her uniform of shorts and purple Four Seasons collared polo shirt breaks my chain of thoughts.

"No, thank you." She pointedly looks to the empty lounge chair beside mine. I'd had them spread out the towel on his lounge chair, because they do that here for each guest. It's the fanciest hotel I've ever stayed in my life. "He'll be down soon."

She doesn't care. I don't know why I'm compelled to tell her that. After Ian left for the gym, I hightailed it down to the adult pool. Yes, it's the one place I don't expect to see Sam and Olivia, but it's also the place we've frequented the most this week.

Olivia, god. I place a hand over my queasy stomach. Just thinking about that woman and her reaction yesterday does a number on me. Sure, Sam hadn't cared. But Olivia did. She'd clung to him like I was a vulture who might attack her husband. Her children were running around like uncontrolled maniacs, drawing frowns from almost all the adults in the area, especially those trying to have a fine dining experience in the ritzy restaurant nearby, and yet she stood right by him. There hadn't been any animosity in her expression, exactly, but it was more like I was a puzzle piece that didn't fit, and she wanted to flick me out of the box rather than make me fit. Does that even make sense?

Meeting her was exactly what I expected. Keeping things between Ian and me a secret was for the best. If his parents knew, Mrs. Duke would insist I join them for family gatherings, even if she didn't want me there, and I'd be in the way, making things awkward for the Dukes. An ex-girlfriend should disappear, she shouldn't remain around indefinitely. And she definitely shouldn't show back up on the arm of a brother. Olivia knows this, even if Sam and Ian are oblivious.

And, god, that's another thing. There's no way Sam believes we were in Anguilla, of all places, as friends. Maybe if we just end the whole charade, nothing will come of it. Sam might say something to Oliver. If he does, I'll deny it. Oliver will probably tell Noah and Liam. Liam will tell Jacinda. Noah likes to run his mouth, so he'll tell someone at one of his restaurants. Rumors will circulate, but if I don't leave town again for several months and Ian stays in Houston, there'll be no fan to the flames. Something else will happen, and everyone will eventually forget.

Jocelyn's baby arriving set off a rumor cyclone. Given enough time, someone else will cheat, and everyone will forget about the possibility of me and Ian. Of course, that's probably me being overly optimistic. After all, twenty years later, and I still get pats on the hand and sympathetic glances when Sam's name comes up in conversation. And now I'll be the one who lost out on two Duke brothers.

What will those expressions look like when the Ian rumor hits the mill? Will I get looks of disapproval? Jealousy? There are a lot of women who'd love to bang a Duke.

I close my eyes and attempt to focus my dismal thoughts on the ascending sun warming my skin. The warmth diminishes, and I open my eyes to check the horizon, and sure enough, a thicket of clouds blocks the sun.

"There you are." Ian joins me. He's in swim trunks, flip-flops, and a Patagonia t-shirt. He kicks his shoes off below the lounge chair and lies back on the chaise. Behind his sunglasses, I can't see what he's looking at, but I assume he's looking across the forever edge pool to the ocean beyond. "Sam and Olivia invited us to the beach today."

A heavy weight sinks onto my chest. Is my third chakra spasming? Or strapping my heart to my physical form?

"We don't have to go," he says.

Silence reigns for the next few hours. I pull a blanket over my legs and drift in and out of sleep. I wake from one such sleep to cool droplets along my arms. The sky has darkened.

I gather my things and put them in a tote. A waitperson approaches.

"You don't have to go. It never rains long in Anguilla." She adjusts the overhead umbrella, ensuring it covers both of our lounge chairs except for our feet. "You should be fine."

I offer her a grateful smile but fold the towel I used as a blanket and continue preparing to go. I don't want to be caught in the rain.

Ian wordlessly follows me back to the room. We are well beyond the pool and past the hotel gym when he speaks.

"Are you still in love with Sam?"

I stop and blink several times. My sunglasses cover my eyes. I don't need them under the dark skies, but I wear them anyway. And I squint at Ian, wondering how he could ask me that.

I've been sleeping with him for nine months, and he wants to know if I'm still in love with my high school boyfriend? I've already told him I'm not. And this is exactly the problem. You can tell people anything you want, but they're going to believe exactly what they want to believe. They might bat an eye in recognition of truth, but they'll easily disregard it if it doesn't conform to the worldview of choice.

I plow forward without offering an explanation. If Ian, of all people, can believe that, then I might as well give up. Everyone will always believe I'm in love with Sam. And that makes me and Ian reprehensible. An act of desperation.

I should've given up a long time ago. This whole exercise in attempting to enjoy ourselves and let's-relax-Sunny is a farce. I should've known better. I should've never come here.

"What're you angry about?" His voice rises to an attention-grabbing level.

A hotel room door opens down the hall, and the exiting couple takes one glance at us and heads the other direction. I don't blame them. The breezeway is open air, and I glare at a green skink crawling along the balcony railing.

Ian opens our hotel room door. "Inside," he snaps.

I bow my head and charge indoors. We had one more day in this hotel room, but I can't stay. Not when he, of all people, can't see my truth. Not when he, of all people, assumes what every other person we know assumes. I want to scream and throw things against the wall. But I settle for charging into our den, arms crossed, foot tapping a mile a minute.

He enters and runs a defeated hand through his hair. Without his sunglasses, I get a good look at his eyes. His skin tans easily, and he looks healthy, but his eyes are slightly bloodshot. Maybe he drank more than I realized last night.

"This was a mistake. A huge mistake."

I breathe out heavily in agreement. He is so right, but the truth still sucks.

"I'll see if we can get a spot out on the flight later on today."

"Won't that cost a fortune?"

"Probably just a change fee." He pulls his phone out of his shorts pocket and presses a number. "We're scheduled to leave on a Friday. The Thursday flight is probably less full." He walks past me, toward the balcony. "Yes, hi. I wanted to inquire if I can move my flight up."

He closes the door behind him, as if he can't stand to be in the same room with me. I enter the walk-in closet, because yes, this hotel suite has an actual walk-in closet, and begin packing, just in case.

"If we can get out of here in thirty minutes, we'll make it," Ian says, stepping past me to pull his suitcase off the top shelf. "The boat back to St. Maarten leaves in forty-five minutes. They'll hold it for us, but not for long."

Chapter Twenty-Nine

Ian

The Worst March of My Life

Metallica blares through the ER. The nurse lowers it, and I threaten her with a don't-you-dare glare.

"You know, Ian, we placed bets you were going through a breakup. But it's been over a month now. Did your music tastes change?" Rosemary taps away at the computer, doing her job, but I don't like how familiar she's become with me. Maybe that entire research study that shows working with the same OR team reduces surgical errors is bogus.

"Guess so."

"Wait. I need clarification." My nostrils flare. "For the pool. So we know who won." She says all this as if she's not testing my very last nerve. "Break up?"

"Fuck off." I never cuss within the hospital. I find it to be highly unprofessional. But there's a first time for everything.

Thankfully, the surgery before me is a hip replacement. I lose myself in the job as muscle memory guides my hands. The blaring music becomes background noise, and the surgery unfolds with a meditative benefit.

By the time I meet the family in the waiting room, my tension has eased along with some of the ache in my chest. It will all come back, but I bought myself a reprieve from an emotional hell.

Sandra exited the sedan after our return from the Anguilla flight and dragged her suitcase directly to her car. It was late when we returned home. She probably should've stayed at my place. It would've been safer. But she didn't ask, and I didn't offer.

We both admitted our little escapade was a mistake. Better to get away from each other. I haven't heard from her or seen her since that day in February.

I shower at the hospital, check in with my office, then head to meet Noah for dinner. He's in town to check out some space. A few of his restaurants are doing well, and he's considering expanding into the Houston market.

Noah is a couple of years older than me, but he's one of Oliver's good friends. He's one of the few people from Whispering Creek I keep in touch with.

He meets me with a fist bump. A tattoo on the inside of his wrist is rimmed in red.

"New ink?" I ask.

He grins. "Yep. Life's changing. Gotta mark it."

We approach the hostess stand together, but he does all the talking. For someone who's gone through some serious shit this past year, he seems pretty damn happy. I wasn't exactly expecting a chatterbox.

Noah's never said anything to me, but I heard all about his wife cheating on him from Oliver. Sounded like a nasty situation.

We take our seats, order beers, and he bumps his knee against mine. "Sorry, man."

We both immediately adjust so our legs aren't so close.

"So, did you hear the news?" he asks.

I shake my head and lift the menu. Since Anguilla, my conversational skills have taken a nosedive.

"Sandra's pregnant." His eyebrows rise as he rocks back in his chair. "Yep. Can't believe Ollie didn't tell you. No one knows who the baby daddy is."

I do some quick back-of-the-envelope math in my head. She has to be barely pregnant, and she already miscarried once. I can't imagine she'd tell anyone right now. This entire story smells of bullshit.

"She told you?" I clarify.

"Nah. According to Jocelyn, only a handful of people know."

"You and Jocelyn still talk?" That idea is confusing to me, but I'm still grappling with determining the validity of this rumor.

"We've made progress," Noah says nonchalantly. He lifts the menu and studies it, like that's the end of the conversation.

I don't want to know more about him and Jocelyn. If he's getting back together with his cheating wife, that's on him. Oliver didn't tell me much about Noah's bullshit because I didn't care. Apathy works wonders for developing sanity. But no, something's not right.

"This sounds like bullshit." Noah jerks back, evidently surprised by my tone. I don't give a damn. "Sunny isn't close to Jocelyn. Why would she tell her?"

"She didn't. Jocelyn heard it from Kara, or maybe Marissa… I don't know. One of them. Apparently, she tried to hide it, but she's been wickedly sick with morning sickness. Like she had to break down and admit it because she was canceling on clients and couldn't be at the salon in the morning." He relaxes and leans forward on the table.

Our waitperson delivers our beers, and he lifts his and sips. I leave mine on the table.

"At any rate, you're right." He shrugs. "Who knows if it's true? But word has it there was a pregnancy test in the trash. And then, you know, the sickness. That sickness is weird. I don't think Jocelyn was sick one day. But apparently it hits some women hard and not others. It's a good thing we don't get pregnant, right?" He grins and holds up his drink as if he wants to clink glasses.

She's fucking pregnant with my child, and she didn't even fucking tell me.

The waiter stops by and asks if we're ready to order.

"Can you bring me a bottle of Patron?"

Noah's eyebrows meet his receding hairline.

"Feel like doing some shots?"

He doesn't agree to shots, but he also doesn't disagree. The waiter sees a chance for a big fucking tip but possesses the moral integrity to ask if I drove.

"Nope. Walked. Live right over there," I say, pointing in the direction of my apartment building.

She smiles and goes to get us shot glasses and a bottle. I text my office. "Not feeling good. Can you find someone to cover for me tomorrow?"

It's the first time I ever pulled the sick card as a surgeon. But you can't spew germs over someone you're slicing and dicing. And no one wants you holding a scalpel in your hand while coughing uncontrollably.

I don't have a drip in my throat and haven't coughed in months. But I sure as fuck know I won't be performing surgery tomorrow.

One day blends into a week's absence from work. Noah left and went back to Whispering Creek. He'd said something about a new chick he's banging. Or maybe he's back with Jocelyn. I just don't care.

Oliver called me the day Noah returned home. He'd wanted to check in. Actually, my whole damn family has been calling nonstop. I don't know what the fuck Noah told them, but I can't handle the calls. Before Sunny, on good days, I didn't jump to return a call, so my lack of response shouldn't send any red flags. But eventually, I'll have to return their calls.

Andrea's fingers climb my thighs. The bourbon in my glass holds no appeal. After that first night with Noah, I must've hit my alcohol saturation limit. I've knocked back some bourbon since then, but not with the goal of getting plastered like that night with Noah.

Andrea wedges her body between my thighs, and she scratches along my jaw. The beard on my face itches, and her nails feel good, but my dick doesn't so much as twitch. With Harrison's encouragement, no doubt, Andrea is trying, but she isn't the woman I want.

That's why I've been in such a shitty mood since my return from Anguilla. The woman I want wants my brother. And now she's pregnant with my baby, but true to her word, she hasn't told me because she doesn't want me involved in the baby's life.

The truth sucks. It sucks so much I almost gave myself alcohol poisoning and took a week off from the hospital. And Harrison, wingman extraordinaire, paid some extravagant guest fee to bring me to his sex club because, in his mind, all I need is a good fuck. Only then will I be right as rain.

"Baby, you look so sad. What can I do for you?"

Lola slides another glass my way. I knock it back in one long swallow. I wipe my lips with the cocktail napkin Lola thoughtfully set out. Pressure on my wrist and a heavy floral scent reminds me Andrea is still there, and she awaits an answer.

"Can you help me forget?" I ask.

"And what, exactly, are we forgetting?"

Her breath warms my ear, and those fingers stroke my thigh.

"The sun." Her breast presses against my bicep.

I drop my head and have the strangest desire to lean against Andrea and ask her to just hold me. How the fuck did I get here? How did I get to this place?

"The sun?" she questions. I probably don't make sense. It's a long story. One Andrea probably doesn't want to hear.

"Or maybe the rain."

Harrison steps up behind Andrea and caresses her hip. He seeks my gaze and lifts an eyebrow. "Care to share? Or you prefer solo?"

Yes, we shared once before. A lifetime ago.

I stand, sending both Andrea and Harrison stumbling backward.

"I've got to get out of here." My life is fucked, and I sure as fuck don't have answers, but I'm not drunk enough to mistake a mindless fuck as the solution.

Chapter Thirty

Sandra

March, This Spring

The adorable, squirrelly puppy twists in my lap, its fluffball tail wagging back and forth. Tiny, razor-sharp teeth chew my finger raw. The pain intensifies, and I reluctantly stand to save my fingers. The puppy attempts to climb my leg.

"She is the most adorable thing I've ever seen."

Mrs. Duke beams at my words. "It's been years since we had a dog on the ranch. It's time. And now... we're going to have a wedding."

She scoops up the puppy and puts her in the small crate, prompting the puppy to whine, and in a loving voice that doesn't sound a bit like scolding, she says, "Hush, now. It's time for you to go back to your mommy for a little bit."

Oliver has planned an elaborate proposal for Kate, and this

puppy is the linchpin. Mrs. Duke picked up the puppy to take her to our local vet as a favor to Oliver. She'll return to her birth mom until the big day. Mrs. Duke called me over to come meet the adorable, yet-to-be-named pup.

This coming weekend, I get to play a role in Oliver's grand plan. I'll pick the puppy up and bring her back to the ranch house. Under Oliver's strict instructions, there can be no balloons or signs of congratulations. For his vision to be complete, when Kate walks into the ranch house, it has to feel like any other day. Although Mrs. Duke's already ordered a cake, and Mr. Duke purchased the best champagne he could find. It's currently hidden in the garage refrigerator, and Mrs. Duke has been stressing for a week over the menu for the celebratory family dinner that night.

Oliver's plan is for Kate to enter the house and for the puppy to come bounding down the hallway to meet her with a note, a bow, and ring attached to her red collar. That's the plan. I think Oliver is placing a lot of trust in an untrained puppy, but one thing he has going for him is that Kate will probably chase the puppy if it doesn't come to her... so one way or another, the proposal note should end up in her hands.

Mrs. Duke opens the crate to give the baby a chew toy, and the heart-rending crying ceases. With that resolved, Mrs. Duke turns her motherly concern my way.

"How are you doing, sweetie? I heard you're not feeling well."

"Oh, I'm fine." The response is automatic. I breathe in deeply to quell the ever-present nausea. I tell everyone I'm fine. She tilts her head to one side, and I get the sense that she sees right through my *fine*.

She always has. She's a really good mother, and I just hope she remains in my life. But, for now, fine is the best plan. There's still a very good chance I'll miscarry, given my age and odds and all that, and so there's no sense in upsetting the apple cart or getting everyone in a tizzy. Not yet.

My eyes sting, and I glance away because she's too perceptive. I go to lift the small kennel so Mrs. Duke doesn't have to, and her hand covers mine.

"I've got it, honey." She glances to my extremely flat stomach, and that nausea kicks up a notch.

Damn this town. Nothing remains private. But, for now, denial is my game plan. If something happens, folks can chalk it up to vicious rumors.

"Well, I'm gonna get out of here, then." I head to the door, unnaturally fast because I need fresh air.

The black weighted bands on my wrist do a good job of alleviating my nausea, but they aren't foolproof. I haven't been able to eat much, but I'm told that after the first trimester, if I'm still pregnant, the nausea should subside.

The nausea first struck on the drive back from Houston after we returned from Anguilla. I thought it was my body reacting to ending everything with Ian. But now, looking at the calendar, I swear I think the nausea started the second Ian's sperm fertilized my egg. Which is probably scientifically inaccurate, but that's certainly what seems to be true. Two weeks later, my period didn't come when scheduled, and I bought a pregnancy test.

My doctor doesn't want to see me until I'm approximately eight to ten weeks along, so I've got a way to go before I even see a doctor. It'll be months before I show. And yet rumors are already flying.

Some women don't have any symptoms. When I was pregnant before, for that couple of days before I miscarried, I didn't have a single symptom. Maybe the sore boobs and the nausea are good signs? That's my hope.

The gravel under my tires crunches as I drive away from the Duke ranch house. Through the rearview mirror, I see Mrs. Duke waving and I stick my arm out the rolled-down window and wave back.

Dang it. She knows. And bless her heart, she'll stand by me. She won't care that I'm a single mother out of wedlock. But will she stand by me when she learns it's Ian's?

On one hand, I think she'll stand by me more fiercely. She's a fierce momma bear, and her grandbabies are her cubs too. But then doubt nags at me. How appalled will she be that I've been with two of her sons? What on Earth will she think of me? And the worst thing is, for a while, people suspected I'd been with Oliver. I was never with Oliver, and those rumors are patently untrue, but it won't change what people believe. People are going to say I've been with all three sons. They're going to say I'm obsessed with the Dukes and desperate to have one of their babies, so desperate I somehow played Ian and purposefully became pregnant. And then, when he and I aren't together, the rumors will grow teeth. They'll say I became pregnant to trap him, but it didn't work, and now I'm a single mom. Folks will probably be torn between feeling sorry for me and feeling sorry for Sam and Patty Duke. I can hear it in a gentile southern accent. *They took her under their wings, and look what she did to them. To that family.*

Vicious rumors. It's like all the crap in the tabloids. You know a lot of it is gross exaggeration and gimmicky headlines, but there's a shred of truth. Why are the worst human traits and the most personal mistakes entertainment?

My car pulls into the driveway of my home within minutes of leaving the Duke ranch, because that's how close I live to them. The empty paddock greets me. There's still a stack of hay near the shade hutch that I need to go clean up one day, maybe haul it to the Duke ranch for their horses or cows. But that day is not today.

I head inside, straight to the bathroom, and hurl. The orange juice I got down earlier in the day comes up with a bitter taste. I brush my teeth, wash my face, and head into the kitchen to find the herbal tea that's supposed to be good at settling nausea.

I settle onto the sofa. Normally, in the morning, I'd drink

coffee, but I lost my taste for coffee a week ago, so I curl up and close my eyes.

The phone rings, and nausea combined with a sense of dread stirs.

I check the phone, and my throat tightens. Ian. I'm not ready for this. My body feels too weak to face him, but I force myself to answer.

"Ian. Hey," I answer softly, fully aware of how we ended things.

"Have something you need to tell me?"

I close my eyes. *Dang it all.*

"I can't believe you didn't tell me. Did you think I wouldn't find out?"

"Ian, it's not–"

"I don't want to hear it." He's cold. Angry. I get it. But things were so awful when I left, and it doesn't feel definite yet. It's so early.

"I want to be a part of the baby's life."

I don't know what exactly I was expecting from this phone call, but this isn't it. I sit up straighter on the sofa, one hand protectively over my stomach. "That's not what we agreed to, Ian." My eyes flit to my tote bag that holds my laptop and somewhere the electronic version of the contract. The unsigned contract.

"If you want to fight me, you need to lawyer up. Because I'm fairly certain, given I never signed your contract, the courts will support my paternity rights. And we didn't follow the standard donor channels, so I'm guessing you're not really going to want to go to court on this."

Court? I don't have the money. Or the heart. Tears well up and spill over. But this doesn't have to be a bad thing. This is Ian. He's a friend. He wouldn't take my baby away from me. Would he?

"What, exactly, do you want, Ian? What are you asking for?" He said he doesn't want to be a father. This doesn't make sense.

"Joint custody." My hand rises from my belly to my heart, and I clutch at the fabric.

"Have you told your family?" Did he already tell Mrs. Duke? Earlier today, did she know it's his?

"That is the thing you'd be most worried about, isn't it?"

Chapter Thirty-One

Sandra

Oliver and Kate's Engagement Weekend

As I approach the Duke ranch house, my lips quiver and my blasted eyes well up. I breathe in deeply, sniffing hard, attempting to keep all that down. Since Ian's phone call, I've been more emotional than a bachelorette contestant. I haven't been able to bring myself to tell Aunt Nora. I'm too ashamed. I didn't get the contract signed. And now he's insisting we tell everyone. And I don't know if he's thought about it, but I can't help but wonder, does he envision taking my baby away half the time? Like a divorced couple?

I'd known this was a bad idea. But I did it anyway. Only now I'm confused as all get-out. I offered him exactly what he wanted. Sex. Lots of it for many, many weekends. No strings fun times with zero responsibilities or expectations, and now he's angry? And he wants responsibilities?

I haven't contacted a lawyer. I have zero plans to fight Ian on parental rights. If he wants to be involved in the baby's life, of course he can be. But I don't know how he'll have time. He always said he wouldn't have time. He's switched on me, which is exactly why I should've had that contract signed.

Normally, I'd go to Oliver about something like this. Or Noah. But I can't go to either of them. I won't put them in the middle between me and Ian.

So, in a weak moment, on the bathroom floor at the salon, I did something that's unlike me. I opened up to Kara. She'd suspected because of the morning nausea. But she gave me something I didn't expect. A friend. More than a friend. A warrior. In a flash, Ian became persona non grata. Enemy of the state. An asshole of epic proportions. A man not worthy of me or my time. Do I agree with her? Not necessarily. I'm so confused. But damn if it doesn't feel good to have someone leap to my side. And somehow I know that if she's around when someone says something nasty, she'll pull out a defensive shield to protect me, and her sword if needed.

Nausea swirls in my belly, more than normal, as does an unprecedented degree of trepidation. I'd like to think Ian wouldn't spill our secrets to his family without us agreeing on what we will say, but I just don't know. The Ian on the phone the other day poured vitriol. So much anger. He wasn't the Ian I know and love. He sounded hurt, but we followed the plan. And then Sam showed up, and I'm not even sure what happened, other than our arrangement felt wrong. Like one very bad idea.

Mrs. Duke answers the door with an enormous smile. She lifts the puppy crate from my hand and glances sideways across my stomach to the shiny present tucked against my side.

"The engagement gift might be premature, but..." I shrug. Etiquette for being a part of the onlooking crowd of a marriage proposal is murky.

"Ollie keeps calling the pup his magic lasso." Mrs. Duke hustles down the hall to the back of the house, and from behind her, I roll my eyes. As if someone should lasso a woman.

The fine hairs on my arms lift. Sensing him, I scan the hallway and the living area, searching.

He's here.

Through the sliding glass door, Ian's dark gaze burns. Blasted tears rise from nowhere.

Fuck. I really just cannot. Bile rises in the back of my throat.

Mrs. Duke hustles right on out, by-stepping her son. She busies herself getting the puppy set up on the back porch. Ian steps through the glass door and shuts it behind him. They don't always keep the door shut, but the pollen has been bad this spring. Either that, or he wants to get our talk done with right now.

He doesn't need a lawyer. I should start with that, but instead I say, "I didn't realize you'd be here." My gaze falls to the table, and a tear spills over.

As promised, there are no balloons or anything to clue Kate in that this is a special day. Oliver wanted it that way, so he'd get the maximum bang out of his surprise. I set my present on the kitchen table and inhale deeply to quell the slight dizziness and to dry up some of those inconvenient tears.

"As I understand it, this is a family event. Last time I checked, I'm a member of the Duke family."

I nod, absorbing his harsh words while staring at the scratches in the varnish on the wood floor.

"I wouldn't have come here if I'd known you'd be here." I step away from him, down the hall. He doesn't want to see me, and this is his home. I should've known—

"So, that's your plan? Avoid me like you've avoided Sam for the last twenty years?"

Bile pushes higher in the back of my throat, and I charge down the hall to the front door, hoping I can make it outside. I gulp in fresh air as the front door slams behind me. With my hands on my hips, I exhale and inhale rapidly, letting the warm spring air calm me. Pesky tears overflow, and I blink, fighting them back. My palms wipe my cheeks. The lightheadedness returns, and I sit down on the step, bending over my knees. Once I've got things under control, I'll leave. I can text Mrs. Duke and tell her I'm not feeling well. She'll understand. After all, the entire town fucking understands.

The front door opens behind me. I don't need to turn around to know that it's Ian who stepped through. He takes a seat on the step beside me, leaving a good two feet between us. He rests his forearms on his thighs. I risk a glance his way. He's staring forward. It's a brooding, battle-ready stare. His ruffled hair and short beard look good on him. As does his moody persona. Crap. He must hate me.

"I've talked to a lawyer. I have rights."

I close my eyes and wipe the tender skin below my eye, hoping if my mascara's running, I'll catch it.

"That isn't the agreement." Kara's words fill my head. But it's more than words. Her support lends me strength. "We had a verbal agreement." And he's a rat bastard to do this. Kara's words. But I need to understand. That's what a mature person would seek first. Understanding. "What, exactly, do you want?" A crushing resignation falls over me. Maybe we can get this conversation over before Kate and Oliver arrive. Although I'm not sure I can stand to be around them all this afternoon. "Have you told your parents?"

There's no way he'll move back here. I've thought about this, but I doubt he has. It's hard to envision what a shared custody arrangement would look like with us living three hours apart and his work schedule what it is. It's even crazier to be worried about it when I'm still high risk.

"No, Sandra." He leans over his knees, gaze fixed on the distance, cheeks muscles flexed. "I haven't told my parents. I'm an adult in my thirties. They aren't my first priority. But that's really all you care about, isn't it? What everyone thinks about Sunny Sandra Turner."

The sound of a distant combustion engine and wheels crunching gravel travels from the direction of the trees. Oliver's red four-wheeler appears. He's smiling wide, and Kate's arms are wrapped around his middle.

Ian charges toward his car without saying another word. Which is crazy, because he hasn't told me anything. I don't know what he wants. Or why he's angry. Or why he's being such a rat bastard.

I jump off the stairs. I will not ruin Oliver and Kate's big day by breaking down and crying in front of them. Or by vomiting and grossing them out. I express my apologies and reach my car as Ian's back tires spin gravel. *Rat. Bastard.*

Tears blur my vision as I slowly make it down the gravel road I know so well. I roll down the windows and let the fresh air circulate. My heart aches, and my brain is awash in confusion. I don't understand how it all went so wrong.

This was the plan. This was our agreement. And yes, I ended things a little early in Anguilla, but only because I realized how screwed up this situation is. Obviously, I ended things a little too late.

When I turn into my drive, Ian sits on my front stoop. He's in the exact position he was in back at his parents' house. He parked to the side, leaving room for me to pull up under the carport.

I stop in my driveway, behind his car, blocking him in, turn off the ignition, get out, and slam the car door shut. My hands are freezing, and I ball them up and tuck them under my arms.

"Probably best we have the conversation here." He didn't need to drive away like he did, but I'll concede this is smarter. "We shouldn't risk ruining Kate and Oliver's day."

He narrows his eyes and interlaces his fingers. "That's one reason for driving away. We need to have this conversation. I guess you could say this is my version of a life M&M. Do you remember what that stands for?" I stand before him and stupidly nod. Or I try to. He doesn't seem to register my response. "Morbidity and

Mortality. I need to know a few things, so I don't repeat this mistake. Did we ever stand a chance, or were we DOA?"

"Dead on arrival?"

"Is there anything I could've done differently to arrive at a different outcome? Or were you always gonna be hung up on—"

"Don't you dare say it." I point an index finger at him as self-righteous anger surges. Thank you, Kara. "You know I'm over Sam. You, of all people, have to know. This is not about that."

"Really, Sunny? I was there." He stands now and paces the ground. "I saw how you reacted to him. Don't lie to me."

"I. Was. Shocked." He lifts his gaze, and it's then that I register the hurt. A little of the surging anger melts. "And the ridiculousness of us being together became clear as day. The truth plastered in front of me. Olivia wasn't comfortable around me. And what were we doing?" I hold my hands out, pleading. He has to see this.

"Olivia was fine around you. If you saw anything, that was in your head. Your perception." Frustration seeps from him, which is absolutely ridiculous. Besides, this isn't about us. It's about my baby.

"You said you don't want a wife or a child. That's what you said, Ian. What is this? Why the about-face?"

His head bows. He clasps his hands, and his thumbs circle each other.

"I want you." He's speaking to the ground. I can barely make out his words.

"Ian. We did too much based on what we wanted. We should've never risked problems with your family for a secretive arrangement. When I saw Sam, I just saw our arrangement for the mistake it was, and I…" I'm at a loss for words.

"The only reason we were secretive is because that's what you wanted." His tone is cold and professional. "So, is that the error? Where I screwed up? If I told you I wanted a chance — dating you for real without an end date — with every single person in the fucking world knowing, would anything have turned out differently?" His head shakes back and forth in short, determined shakes. "'Cause I don't think it would have. Let's play this through."

With a jerk, he stands and paces the ground. It's easy to imagine him in a white lab coat, standing in the front of an auditorium, discussing the errors that led to mortality.

"Let's say I told you I wanted to, well, bring you home for Thanksgiving. Tell our family that you and I were dating. I think that would've made you panic. And you would've ended things then. Probably would've gotten the same reaction had I told you at Christmas." He kicks a piece of gravel and watches it sail into a thicket of grass. "Do you remember how panicked you were at the idea of my parents finding out that I stayed at your house Christmas Eve? You're forty years old, and my thirty-fifth birthday was last month, but you acted like we were teenagers. No, I don't think there was a time I could have told you without having the exact reaction we had in Anguilla. Where you shut everything down. Us down."

My stomach sinks. The nausea dissipates, but guilt replaces it, marred by confusion.

"You see, Sunny, I am completely and totally in love with you." My hand smashes my heart. It pounds beneath my palm. "When I was a teenager, it probably didn't qualify as real love. But every single woman I have been with, I have compared to you. And she has always come up short. For me, it's always been you." He walks along, his head bobbing as he reviews the facts and considers them. "I know I'm in love with you, because since you walked out of my life, I have felt like someone ripped out my vital organs. And physiologically, bear in mind, that sensation is nonsensical. And, normally, I would've been at your door. Begging. I would've looked into job opportunities in Austin. But I called time of death on us, because you, Sunny, are in love with my brother, and if after eighteen years, you aren't over him, you never will be."

Dizziness returns, a lightheaded, uncontrolled sensation, and I back up to my car, resting against it, letting everything he said wash over me. "You're in love with me?"

He exhales, and it almost sounds like a laugh. "That's what Lola says. When I told her our story and how I felt, she said that's what falling in love feels like." He exhales and wanders back to the steps.

"Who is Lola?"

"Someone." He sits on the steps and scrubs his face with his palms. "This sucks. Rationally, I know the pain will go away. The ache. But what I also know is that you're going to have to deal with the rumors. And we can tell people whatever you want. I can't force you to be in a relationship with me, but I want a relationship with my son."

Tears burn my eyes, and I sniffle.

"That's not what we agreed to, and I apologize for that. But I can't imagine not being a part of my son's life."

"It might not be a boy." It's not really a particularly important point, but it's what falls out of my mouth.

"Our child." He sounds resigned.

I flatten my palm over my forehead and clutch my middle with my arm. As the dizziness subsides, I come back to the one thing. "You love me?"

His gaze remains on the ground as he paces. "Obviously."

"Maybe you should've started with that."

"Like it would've made a difference." He returns to the steps and sits, elbows resting above his knees, rumpled head of hair in his hands.

I chew on the corner of my lip, waiting for a good response to fall into my brain. It's difficult with him sitting on the steps looking like a broken man. "I believe if you shared your feelings before Anguilla, it could've led to a different outcome." He lifts his head, and I stare straight into those chocolate brown eyes I've missed so much. "Because I'm completely and totally in love with you, Ian. I just didn't tell you because I didn't think that's what you wanted. That wasn't part of our arrangement. And…I really don't want to be an uncomfortable presence within your family." His family is all the family I really have, other than Aunt Nora, who lives practically across the country.

Call it pregnancy hormones, but those pesky tears well up and stream down my cheeks. My lower lip trembles, and I wrap my arms around myself, waiting.

He stands and approaches slowly, hands in his pockets, thoughtful as always. "You love me like a friend, someone you've known your whole life? Or you're in love with me?"

"In." I sniffle and wipe my nose with the back of my hand. "I'm in love with you."

Brown leather shoes cover the gravel next to my sandals. His body heat warms my cool skin. He caresses my cheek and brushes his lips over my forehead. His index finger rubs beneath my chin, and he applies gentle pressure, encouraging me to lift my gaze.

"Sunny, I'm in love with you, too."

"But…" A watershed of tears coats my cheeks. "You're moving. You don't want a…" The word *wife* gets stuck on my tongue because he doesn't even want a girlfriend.

"I want you."

"But your family." It comes out as a whine.

"My family loves you."

"But–"

"Sam doesn't have an issue with us. Neither does Olivia."

I shake my head, thinking back to Olivia.

"Sunny, she didn't know who you were at first. Whatever you thought you saw…she and Sam don't have an issue with us." His lips brush my forehead. "And even if they did, I wouldn't care. But they don't. I talked to Sam."

"But…" Two Duke brothers. Some will say all three. God, I can't even say that out loud.

"I don't care what anyone else thinks." It's like he can read my mind. "No one else out there can possibly understand. They haven't been us. They weren't there. If they're friends, they'll support us. If they don't support us, they don't matter."

"Yeah?" I ask for confirmation. His words ring of truth. And a common sense that's sometimes easier to accept with your brain than your heart.

"Hey, look at me." He nudges my chin up. "Yeah."

His lips softly brush over mine. A warmth emanates from deep within, and I hold him close. Our chests press against each other, and my head rests on his shoulder. We're so close, his heartbeat reverberates through my ribcage, and a healing sensation curls through my core. This is what my fractured soul needed.

I sniff and rub my dripping nose against his shirt, and he chuckles. With the pads of his thumbs, he gently dries my tears.

"God, I love you, Sunny."

I look at him, really look at him. This man I do love, have loved, but I put on blinders and tried to set us into a temporary box. And why? Because of fear. Senseless, useless fear.

His lips brush over mine, and my soul shudders with relief. This is where I belong. Right here, with this man. I press my lips to his neck, to the spot where I can feel his pulse, along his jaw, to his lips. When we kiss, it's like a homecoming.

When he breaks the kiss, he holds my head in his hands and stares down at me as if I'm the most precious thing in the world to him. And I wonder, has it always been like this, and I just didn't see it? Maybe. Maybe I've been a fool.

"God, I've missed you." His forehead presses to mine. "I've been in hell."

"I thought you might want to take the baby away." My voice cracks.

"Never." His gaze pours over me. "You're going to be a wonderful mother. I just want to be a part of our child's life, too."

Realization dawns. He's not being realistic. "Baby, I'm still high risk. We don't—"

"You. What I want most is you."

Tears well up and my nose gets stuffy and my throat tightens. All I can do is nod. I want him, too. Whatever that looks like. And I have some ideas about where we can start. "Want to go inside?"

"I do." He kisses the tip of my nose and tightens his hold around me. "But why don't we start this by telling my family? As I understand it, you put a lot of work into my brother's engagement proposal that's going on right now... so why don't we go join them? You're nervous about how my family is going to react. Let me prove to you that's not something you need to worry about."

I search for the fear I'd expect those words to bring. But there's none there. If this is what he wants to do, I can do it. Even if his parents get upset, or think horrible things of me, we'll work through it. If Ian wants to be together, really be together, we can do this.

Ian and I re-enter his parents' home with our hands linked. Mr. Duke rounds the kitchen and does a double take at our hands, but just gestures out back and says, "I'll be at the grill. Sunny, you want cheese on your hamburger, or no?"

Given I can keep so little down, I tell him no cheese. The way I'm feeling, I might need to just nibble on the bun.

"Dad, can you come into the back yard with us for just a minute?" Ian's question delivers the first twinge of fear. But his squeeze of my hand eradicates it.

We step outside onto the grass, and everyone looks at us. Ian's still holding my hand. Kate's on the ground with the puppy and a sparkling ring on her finger.

"Congratulations," I say.

"Thank you," she beams.

Oliver has the widest grin I've ever seen. He fell slowly for Kate, but he fell hard. Seeing the two of them so happy makes it feel completely normal when Ian steps behind me and pulls me against him, one hand on a hip and one arm wrapped possessively around my middle.

"Guys, I don't want to take away from your day. But we have an admission. Sunny and I are together. We have been for most of this past year."

I don't miss the knowing smile Kate tosses in Oliver's direction. *How would Kate know? Who told her?*

Mrs. Duke beams and clasps her hands together. "That is wonderful news."

Kate slaps her palm against Oliver's thigh and says, "I told you."

Mr. Duke chuckles. "Son, you better get used to hearing that."

And that's it. We go about preparing for an early al fresco dinner. It's like a normal day in the Duke house, except I admire Kate's ring and she gives me a hug. Mrs. Duke hugs me multiple times, just quick ones where she pulls me to her side. And Oliver mentions casually during dinner while glancing at his vibrating phone that Sam and Olivia send their congratulations. "To all of us," Oliver adds, with a wink to me.

Apparently, Kate shared online that she's engaged, and Mrs. Duke did, too, and both Oliver's and Kate's phones have been blowing up. Oliver's been texting, and I guess he texted Sam.

I'm overwhelmed with relief, but it's also a little embarrassing. I expected drama. Disapproval or anger. Yet no one seems to care. It's almost like they all knew. Well, except for Oliver, and he's so caught up in his own day of happiness he doesn't care at all.

In the kitchen, Ian caresses my shoulder. "You barely ate. Are you doing okay?"

"Yeah." I give him a reassuring smile. "The nausea's been bad."

Mrs. Duke steps through the door as Ian's fingers brush over the black bands on my wrist. He's a doctor, but it's not like gynecology is his specialty. Still, from his thoughtful glance, I suspect he's pieced together the natural remedy I've chosen.

Mrs. Duke bustles into the kitchen and smoothly maneuvers me away from the sink.

"Now, you two," she says as she turns the water on and holds a finger below the stream, "I know it's too early to be sharing, and things change, but there's a rumor going around, and I just have to know. Is there a grandbaby in the works?"

Ian's arm wraps around my shoulder, and he pulls me into his side. He doesn't say a thing, but with Mrs. Duke, you really don't have to say much. She claps her hands like she did outside and reaches for my arm, giving it a quick squeeze.

"Don't worry. I won't say a word." She turns off the faucet, steps away from the sink, and pulls me into her arms. "Sandra, I love you so much. Your father would be so proud and thrilled."

And all the tears fall.

Chapter Thirty-Two

Ian

The Weekend of Oliver and Kate's Engagement

"Ian, can you bring me the platter?" Dad calls through the open window.

Given Mom and Sandra seem to be having a moment, I gladly step away, leaving the two of them to it.

I deliver the platter to Dad, and he coughs into his hand.

"You okay, Dad?"

"You betcha. So, is it true? Sandra's pregnant?"

"It is," I tell him, rocking back on my heels, feeling absurdly proud, which doesn't make a lot of sense, but after the hell I've been through over the last month, I'm soaring. Nothing can bring me down.

"You gonna marry her." Dad doesn't really say it like a question, but I treat it like one. He's a traditional guy, and he loves Sunny like a daughter.

"Yes, sir." Of course, that's if she'll have me. She may have lingering doubts, but I don't. For as long as I can remember, I've wanted her to be mine.

He flips a couple of burgers and steps back.

"And you know about her Mom, right? You be careful with her."

Wait, what?

"I love that girl like she's one of my own." Dad raises his glasses, and his eyes are glassy from emotion. He closes them and pinches the bridge of his nose, squeezing like he's holding back tears. He resets his glasses, sniffs, and seemingly pulls it together. I place a hand on his shoulder, watching the burgers sizzle.

"Dad, if you're worrying about Sandra's heart, she's been to one of the best doctors in Texas. She got the all-clear. She's got a healthy heart. There are no medical concerns."

Dad sucks in his bottom lip, and his eyes squint. It's his thoughtful expression. "You don't know, do you?"

"Know what?" An uncomfortable sensation churns in the pit of my stomach.

"Son, Sandra's mom committed suicide. Postpartum depression when she was barely two weeks old. Now, your mom tells me they know a lot more about it than they did forty years ago, but you gotta watch her. Her mom got left at home a lot with her dad working, and..." Dad's words trail as he flips the burgers one by one.

The oxygen seeps from my lungs far too quickly. But, no... "That's not right, Dad. She died from heart issues."

"Her father may have told her that, but...that's not what happened. Nearly killed him. If he'd gotten home thirty minutes earlier." Dad's face exhibits so much pain, and I remember Mom saying Dad blamed himself. He must've kept her dad working long that day.

"Dad. You can't blame yourself for someone's suicide." He nods and checks on a burger. "How did I not know this?"

Dad shrugs. "You weren't even born. No one talks about it."

He loads the platter with patties, and I think about all the rumors about her dad. They all said he'd never gotten over her mom, but no one ever said what happened. At least, no one my age did.

During dinner, conversation buzzes around us. I've lost my appetite, but only Sunny seems to notice. She places her hand on my thigh and gives me concerned glances. I try my best to focus on the positive, but there's a part of me that wants nothing more than to research postpartum depression and the likelihood that it's genetic. Of course, Dad is correct. Medicine has come a long way in forty years. As has our awareness of postpartum depression.

After dinner, I take the first opportunity to whisk Mom back to the laundry room.

"Is everything okay?" she asks.

"Why didn't you tell me?"

Her eyes widen in confusion.

"About Sunny's mom?"

"Well, honey, I...we're going to be there for her. Don't you worry." She places her hand on my shoulder. "Your dad and I, wherever y'all are, we'll be there. She knows you work long hours, and...don't you worry. We're gonna watch her like hawks." She pats me, but all I can think is that I do work long hours. Sometimes in the middle of the night, I'm called away.

"And no one ever thought to tell Sunny?"

She purses her lips. "Johnny didn't want her to know. And then, so much time passed."

"She told the doctor her mom died of heart problems."

"Johnny took a risk not telling her. With this town, I'm surprised someone didn't tell her at some point. But it was so hush-hush. It was like this thing no one could say out loud. I guess most of all Johnny."

"You know, Mom, I don't think anyone our age knew. I don't think even Sam knew."

"Probably not. It would be a hard thing to tell kids. But now all this time has passed, there's no need for you to tell her."

"Mom." My parental tone startles me, and I have to inhale and put a hand on the counter for stability. Until recently, I would've said above all else, I am a doctor. Now, the truth is, above all else, I'm Sunny's partner, and hopefully one day soon, a father. But as a doctor, I understand the importance of an accurate medical history.

I place a hand on my mom's shoulder, and with all the love I feel for her, say, "Sunny has to know the truth. It's not a slight on her, but the truth is going to help safeguard her."

Mom purses her lips and slowly nods. "But don't tell her today," she implores. "It's a special day."

"It is. Let's get back out there and celebrate." I move to the door, but Mom hesitates.

"When do you think you'll tell her?"

"Before the next doctor's appointment. But not this weekend." No, there are other things I need to do this weekend.

Chapter Thirty-Three

Sandra

Tuesday after the most magical weekend

When I glimpse myself in the glass reflection of the salon on Tuesday morning, I almost don't recognize the carefree, happy, bouncing woman. I'm seeing clients, so I'm wearing black scrubs, but my skin literally glows under the morning sun. I used hot rollers in my hair, something I haven't done in months, and the curls that have yet to settle bounce with each step. And my smile. I didn't even realize I was smiling, but I think I haven't stopped since kissing Ian goodbye this morning.

We had the best weekend. And he consulted with a friend and had some prescription nausea medicine called in for me. That alone led to me feeling worlds better. His friend warned it doesn't work for every woman, but thank the gods, it worked for me. I've been able to keep food down. Which is good, because I needed the energy for our weekend.

He left, promising to come back this weekend. And we don't have an answer for how we're going to align our lives, but we're going to figure it out. As I flip on the lights, golden light infiltrates every recess. I scroll through my phone, searching for my feel-good, happy mix. It's one Ian created for me earlier this year, and it's titled *Sunny*.

Playlists are his thing. Apparently, he's one of those surgeons who loves to have music playing in the background of the OR. Which is quite the coincidence, since I always have music playing in the salon. Admittedly, in my treatment room, I'm more of a spa-nature girl, but out here, this morning, I'm in the mood for a happy beat. The first song on the soundtrack breaks the silence. One of the best bands of all time, The Beatles, strike the first chords of *Here Comes the Sun*. Ian's ringtone. It's going to be a fantastic day.

The bell over the door rings, and I sing out, "Morning!"

Kara frowns over her to-go coffee cup. "I take it someone's feeling better."

She trudges over to her station, and her keys clank when she plops them onto the counter. She opens the cabinet and stuffs her pocketbook inside, and I hum along to the song as I turn the computer on at the register.

"No morning sickness?" Her gaze flits to my wrists, and yes, they still sport black bands.

"Feeling great." I beam at her.

She sips her coffee, eyes narrowed, gaze traveling up and down me.

Repulsive coffee odor clouds my nostrils. "Do you mind, maybe, drinking that a little farther back?"

Her face immediately relaxes. "I thought you must've miscarried. So, did the nausea just go away?"

"Ian consulted a friend, and he called in a prescription. I feel like a new person."

"You look it. I'm glad you're feeling better." She follows me back to my treatment room and leans against the doorframe, watching as I prep for my first client.

"Ian?" she asks cautiously. "Did you guys work things out?"

I fist my hands and bounce a little on my heels. "We did. We're together. Well, I mean, we're going to try."

I let out a squeal, and she grabs my hands, and we jump up and down like someone asked me to prom. Her coffee spills, and the sight of that brown liquid on my hand has us parting mighty quick. So strange. Before I was pregnant, I couldn't get a day started without coffee.

"So, he's not a rat bastard?" she asks as she bends on the ground to wipe up her spill.

"No, he's not. I think we just…well, we didn't do a good job of communicating. Talking to each other, you know? But he said he loves me." She looks up at me and I let out another girly squeal.

"And that's why he wants to be a part of the baby's life." I nod. "He should've just started with that."

"I know, right?" I could tell her that I'm probably just as guilty because of how I acted and all my bullshit, but I like having someone in my corner, so I leave all that out.

"How was your weekend?"

"Fine. Uneventful." She leans against the doorway again, keeping her coffee far away from me and my desk and my highly sensitive nose.

"I heard Oliver Duke got engaged."

"He did!" This is feel-good gossip, so I eagerly tell her all about the puppy and Kate's excitement. She'd already heard about the puppy proposal—which, of course she did, because that's life in a small town, baby. Plus, he put it on Facebook. So, there's that.

"And you like this Kate?"

"I really do. She's fantastic for Oliver."

"I should be angry at you." She narrows her eyes, but there's enough of a smile that I know she's teasing.

"Why?"

"Because I would've loved to go out with him. And now he's off the market. I suppose all the Dukes are off the market."

"Well, for now." I give her a smile, because I'm basically walking on air. But, at my age, I've had more than one relationship high, only to crash with time. And there's a part of me, a part I'm attempting to ignore, that reminds me pre-pregnancy he didn't want a relationship. He wants one now, and we're going to try.

The salon bell dings, announcing the arrival of Mia and Alicia. The others are off today. I should go ahead and tell them. Everyone already suspects I'm pregnant. I should just tell them I'm pregnant, and it's Ian's, and we're dating. Just rip it off like a Band-Aid, the same way Ian did with his family. His family didn't care. They weren't offended. And they're Ian's family. Surely my salon family will rally behind me. And, at the end of the day, who cares what people who don't really know me say?

There's more to a person than a family name, a profession, and a street address. It's two decades since I've been in high school. A lot of the residents in this area know the surface details, but they don't know me. The ins and outs, my reasons, my fractures and scars, my growth, or my goals. What we perceive about others is all in our head. That doesn't make it true.

But, still, people harbor all kinds of perceptions. I'll keep my pregnancy on the down low until it's safe. After all, this is Texas. If I do have a miscarriage, I don't want some person coming after me, thinking they can punish me and simultaneously earn ten thousand from the state of Texas.

"Hey, guys, come look at this. There's a parade," Mia shouts.

I follow Kara through the salon. A float pulled by a tractor passes by in front of the salon entrance. We're on Main Street, and this is where we do parades, but it's Tuesday morning a little after ten a.m. in March.

Kara, Mia, Alicia, and I pile outside onto the sidewalk. I shield my eyes from the bright morning sun. A police car leads the parade, lights on, sirens off. The song *My Universe* from Coldplay blares through speakers.

A green tractor pulling a flatbed slowly makes its way down Main Street. All along both sides of the street, folks gather on the sidewalk, watching curiously. As the tractor draws closer, I recognize the driver. It's Noah. A group of people on the flatbed he's pulling are waving flags. I recognize a lot of the faces. They're his restaurant employees, and paper cut-out hearts are stuck to their clothes.

The convertible behind Noah's float is driven by Liam. His kids are hanging out on the back seat, throwing out candy on the sidewalk, basically littering. Liam's wife is in the passenger seat, and she holds a giant white posterboard with the words "Say Yes" emblazoned in red.

And everything stops when I look past them and see Oliver driving the second tractor. He's pulling another flatbed. They set speakers up on all the corners, and Ian stands in the middle of the flatbed with a microphone in hand.

The music ends, and the rest of the world falls away.

"Dear Whispering Creek, I've got an announcement. And lest you fear, this is streaming live on Instagram. My future sister-in-law is right over there videoing for prosperity, and she's gonna tweet it and TikTok it too. I think she said something about Reels."

Kate waves. She's farther down the sidewalk and holding her phone sideways, presumably videoing. She's grinning wide. My heart is at risk of pounding out of my chest.

"I want every single one of you to know something. I love this woman. All of you call her Sandra. But I call her Sunny. Always have. I have loved her since I was fourteen. But don't go starting any rumors… she left my virtue intact. She was someone I loved from afar. And yes, she dated my older brother, Sam." He pauses and rolls his hand dramatically. "Twenty years ago. All of you remember that. I know you do. But they figured out early on they weren't a great fit. I went to med school and residency and built a life in Houston. Without my sun. But against all odds, I came back into her orbit. And I don't want to ever return to the dark. Now, I know this town loves to gossip, so I'm going to give you all something to talk about for years to come."

His Gibson hangs around his neck. He strums a few chords, and my eyes fill. The world blurs as the lyrics to *I'm Yours* by Jason Mraz vibrate through me. It's a little slower than intended, but at the same time, it's the best acoustic rendition I've ever heard. With the last refrain, he bows to scattered applause, jumps off the flatbed, and approaches, a sexy smile behind the microphone. "I'm going to let every single one of you watch me get down on one knee and ask the love of my life to marry me."

My hand clasps my mouth. My cheeks are soaked. The nausea medicine must do nothing for pregnancy hormones.

"Breathe, baby." Around us, people laugh. But I don't. I'm in awe as he goes down on one knee and asks into a microphone, "Sunny, will you marry me? Will you spend the rest of your life with me, as my wife?"

I'm nodding, and I think I must say yes, but the microphone shrieks when he drops it to the ground. He picks me up and spins me around, shouting through the applause, "She said yes."

Epilogue

Ian

The October My Universe Flourished

As a medical resident, I learned a lot. That's what residents do. We learn.

After a few grueling years of learning under trial by fire, and observing and partaking in both successes and failures, I developed a philosophy regarding medicine. Medicine, you see, can be taken as more than it is, and viewed as less extraordinary than it can be.

Sunny expanded that philosophy for me. Those truths also apply to love.

I expect that raising a child will be a lot like surgery, and I will learn skill and confidence through experience. You could say that about anything, really. Tennis, cooking, gardening. Your pick. But the difference here is that surgery and parenting are practiced on human beings.

The tiny human lying before me, legs bent and held up in the air, squirms. Her eyelids are half-closed, and her paper-thin nails curl outwards in an unnatural direction. There's a mop of black hair on her head that my wife says will change color, and her eyes are currently a mystical, deep-water blue, but those may change too. I will love my baby girl with all my heart through every change.

Shelby stands at my side. She insisted I learn by doing. That's the way we do things in the hospital. Her dark thumb contrasts with the extremely pale, splotched skin of my baby girl, and it slips with ease, far too much ease, beneath the diaper.

"I think you need to try that again, Dr. Duke. When you lift her, that diapers going to fall right off."

"Well, I didn't want it to be too tight." I don't know why I'm arguing with Shelby. She's familiar from seeing her over the years in the cafeteria and around the hospital, but my work doesn't bring me onto the maternity ward.

We're in Houston because I know the doctors here and that was important to me since I want the absolute best medical care for my family. Knowing the doctors gave me more control, just in case.

We purchased a home in Austin near the hospital, and I'll start working there next month. My private practice expanded with an office in Austin. I'll still come back to Houston regularly, so I kept my apartment here. And we still have Sunny's family home in Whispering Creek, right down the road from the Duke ranch.

My amazing wife watches Shelby and me from the hospital bed, clearly entertained. Her blonde, sweat-dried hair is tied back with a multi-colored flowery strip of cloth. She's not wearing any make-up, and her blonde eyebrows blend into her smooth forehead, letting those blue eyes shine above her flushed, rosy cheeks.

We ran into some complications during delivery, and she had to have an emergency c-section. I'm not one to cry, and I'm not one to pray to a god I don't believe in, but I did both. There's nothing quite like being a surgeon and having to watch your universe disappear behind the OR doors.

There was no medical reason to believe Sunny would suffer from complications from her c-section. But statistics and reasoning disappear in the face of a threat to life.

My phone vibrates. I ignore it and re-do the diaper with the highest degree of concentration.

"Are you sure this diaper fits?"

My daughter weighs five pounds, six ounces.

"There you go," Shelby says. Her hand guides my fingers, ensuring it's snug before I press the white tab down. This time, there's no gap for her thumb to glide under.

I take out my phone and see my parents, Oliver, and Kate have arrived. They're parking in the hospital garage, so we still have some time before they show up. Sam, Olivia, and their daughters will fly down tomorrow. Olivia came down for Sunny's baby shower, and from what I can tell, Olivia, Kate, and Sunny are all becoming close friends.

Harrison grumbled about losing his wingman, but he stepped up to the plate and teamed up with Ollie and Sam to throw me an unforgettable bachelor party. He's not thrilled I left Houston, but things are changing for him. I haven't had much time to talk to him about it, but from what I gather, he might be moving out-of-state for a woman. Maybe. He plans to visit us in Austin after things calm down, his words. I don't expect things to slow down with a little one in the mix, but I do expect him to visit.

My phone vibrates again, and I tap out a quick response to Noah. Shortly after our engagement, Sunny started playing for Noah occasionally at Sweet Magnolia. She got to know a lot of the staff, and he's got a big group that wants to say hello. I respond, telling him that she's doing well, but to bring the crew by once we're home. I'm not sure when Sunny will resume her acoustic nights on stage, but one day, she will. Kara will do her best to make it happen, since she's one of her biggest fans.

"You going to finish with this baby, Dr. Duke?"

Chastised, I drop the phone into my slacks. My daughter lies on the changing table in front of me. "Sorry."

Shelby pointedly stares me down and says, "It's okay. Now swaddle her. It's cold in here."

I curse myself for having been too busy to attend the parenting classes with Sunny. But, in my defense, between expanding our practice, starting my spinal fellowship, and locating and buying a home in Austin, I've been busy.

But as I struggle to fold the cloth around my little girl, I realize I might have mis-prioritized a few things.

Shelby pats my forearm. "You're getting the hang of it. You're going to be a good dad." Her words make my eyes burn. "Now, are you doing okay, Mrs. Duke? Do you need anything?"

Sunny smiles and lolls her head back and forth.

"You probably need sleep," I tell her. She just smiles the smile that lights my world. And a wave of gratitude and relief she's still here with me washes through me. I love this little bundle in my arms more than I ever thought possible, but god, if I'd had to do it all on my own, without Sunny with me, I'd lose it.

Through the years growing up, people said all kinds of things about Sunny's dad. But I've never had more respect for him than I do in this moment. He struggled over the years, sure, and I believe some of the rumors about his drinking were true. But he kept it together enough to raise a phenomenal daughter, without the wife he loved by his side. Tears threaten, and I grit my teeth and sway the baby in my arms, letting the action soothe those grim thoughts.

True to my word, I did tell Sunny about her mom. But her reaction wasn't exactly what I thought it would be. She said that all those pitying looks she'd assumed were for her dad drinking made a lot more sense. She was sad for a few days, and she let herself feel that emotion. But it was something that happened over forty years earlier. And she had books that talked about postpartum depression, and she understood enough about it to know her father hadn't lied when he said her mother died from pregnancy complications.

Shelby pulls the hospital room door closed behind her, and I sit down on the chair beside the bed. Sunny pats the bed and shifts her legs, creating room for me. For us. The mattress sinks under my weight, and I cradle our baby in my arms, holding her so she can see her mother.

"Did you decide on a name?"

"I think Penelope Anne, after your mom."

My mother's name is Patricia. We want to honor my mother, but we also wanted a more modern name, and so we picked Penelope as a similar name starting with P in her honor.

"She's going to love it." It just so happens that Anne is both Sandra's mom's middle name and my mother's middle name. I blink back emotion as a wealth of love overflows. Between my daughter and my wife, I have everything I could ever ask for in life.

Unfortunately, my daughter isn't yet awash with the same level of gratitude and love. A squawk-like sound startles me and evolves into a wail. "I think someone's hungry."

She's already eaten once, but they have advised us to let her eat as often as she wants on her first day. She's brand new.

Sunny sits up, and I help situate the pillows behind her back. She takes our baby from me and adjusts her top. The top has buttons that allow her to open it so she can breastfeed.

"I'm so glad she took to breastfeeding," Sunny says.

I watch, mesmerized as my daughter clasps her mother's nipple.

"I heard all those horror stories."

That's something else Sunny endured without me. She met with all these other pregnant women and read all the books.

I reach out and caress my wife's cheek and with care lean over her to press my lips to her forehead. "Don't you ever leave me." I'm not sure where that comes from, but my voice is gravelly, and there's a rawness to my chest that would make you think I was the one under the scalpel mere hours ago.

She glances up at me, and her face immediately contorts. "What's wrong?"

I inch closer to her and glance at the closed wooden door. We don't have long before the outside world comes through.

"Being a doctor's wife isn't going to be easy." Guilt descends for all the times in the future I won't be there. I can't easily walk out of a surgery. Doctors' marriages dissolve all the time. "I'm going to do my best," I promise.

"Where is this coming from?" She reaches for me and touches my arm.

"I just..." I can't tell her what it was like. And yet all this emotion is still there. The fear. Realizing what I might've lost. "It's always been you, Sunny. You just... if I'm screwing up, tell me. I want to be everything for you."

She smiles down at our daughter as she adjusts Penelope, and with a world of love flowing through those sky-blue irises, she reassures me. "You can't be everything. But you are enough. You love to say it was always me. But, Ian, it wasn't always me, and it wasn't always you. When the timing was right, we became us." She gazes upon our baby, lost in reverie, until she remembers I'm here and our fingers intertwine. She's mine, always.

From the Author...aka Izzy

If you enjoyed the story, I hope you'll take a moment to leave a review. Five-star reviews truly do sell books, bringing me closer to the day when I might be able to do this full time. So I'm deeply grateful for them.

In case you are curious…
Technically, Always Sunny is not a part of a series. But, you can read about the Duke brothers, and Ian's friend Harrison in these standalone romance novels.

Trust Me (Sam and Olivia) - Suspenseful, billionaire romance.
How to Survive a Holiday Fling (Oliver and Kate) - Age gap, small town vacation romance.
The Romantics (Harrison and Zuri) - Second chance, later-in-life romance

Also by Isabel Jolie

Arrow Tactical Security Series

Better to See You (Wolf and Alexandria)

Sure of One (Jack and Ava)

Cloak of Red (Sophia and Fisher) - Releasing August, 2023

The Twisted Vines Series

Crushed (Erik and Vivi)

Breathe (Kairi and David)

Savor (Trevor and Stella)

Haven Island Series

Rogue Wave (Tate and Luna)

Adrift (Gabe and Poppy)

First Light (Logan and Cali)

The West Side Series

When the Stars Align (Jackson and Anna)

Trust Me (Sam Duke and Olivia)

Walk the Dog (Delilah and Mason)

Lost on the Way (Jason and Maggie)

Chasing Frost (Chase and Sadie)

Misplaced Mistletoe (Ashton aka Dr. Bobby and Nora)

Standalone Romances

How to Survive a Holiday Fling (Oliver Duke and Kate)

The Romantics (Harrison and Zuri) Releasing Winter 2023

Notes & Gratitude

In researching Always Sunny, I read several books, most notably *Complications* by Atul Gawande and *Hot Lights, Cold Steel* by Michael J. Collins.

It's amazing to me what the medical profession goes through from the moment they decide as a student to strive for a career in medicine. The medical profession as an entity holds my eternal gratitude and respect.

As always, heart-felt thanks and appreciation goes out to my ARC readers. I'm always so grateful to you for investing the time to read my book. It's those initial reviews that have so much impact on the life of the book. Thank you so much.

I did have several beta readers who helped shape Always Sunny, and I'm grateful for your feedback. I especially need to thank my cousins, Leslie and Sara, for beta reading *Always Sunny* when I realized somewhat last minute I needed a medical accuracy read-through (and then they gave me so much more!).

And of course, thanks go to my editor, Lori Whitwam, who makes every book better, and my proofreader, Karen Cimms for all her special care and attention.

Most especially, **thank you**, dear reader, for reading. Thank you, thank you, thank you!

About the Author

Isabel Jolie, aka Izzy, lives on a lake, loves dogs of all stripes, and if she's not working, she can be found reading, often with a glass of wine. In prior lives, Izzy worked in marketing and advertising, in a variety of industries, such as financial services, entertainment, and technology. In this life, she loves daydreaming and writing contemporary romances with real, flawed characters and inner strength.

Sign-up for Izzy's newsletter to keep up-to-date on new releases, promotions and giveaways. (**Pro-tip** - She offers a free book on her home page…just scroll down after arriving at her site.)